FreeForm

Saga of the Dandelion Expansion, Volume 1

Orrin Jason Bradford

Published by Porpoise Publishing, 2012.

Also by Orrin Jason Bradford

Watch for more at www.wbradfordswift.com.

FreeForm

Orrin Jason Bradford

A top-secret investigation on a secluded mountaintop and a mystery that will rock the world

In 1993, a remote North Carolina mountaintop was the site of an event destined to change the course of mankind and Earth itself, discovered and investigated by Pat Vogt, a junior member of the Bureau of Investigation of Unidentified Flying Objects. A slight woman with a hard streak of determination that would put larger men to shame, Pat insisted on being dropped into the remote wilderness area, a feat her pilot thought was insane, but for Pat, it's all in a day's work. It brought her face to face with Earth's first verifiable UFO and set into motion a series of events that not only threatened her life but destroyed her career.

Ten years later, Pat, now a private investigator, returned to the nearby town of Waynesboro to try to put the nightmarish events that happened on that mountaintop to rest. Waynesboro was larger now, but the mountains are the same and the mystery surrounding them just as puzzling. A chance encounter led her to Dr. Allan Pritchard, the town's small animal vet with secrets of his own.

FreeForm is the first book in the FreeForm series and the start of the Saga of the Dandelion Expansion that includes the action-packed Kindred series.

Part One

Something Wicked This Way Comes.

Mountain Mystery
Saturday, March 5, 1993

The helicopter swooped low over the crest of the mountain, and Pat Vogt held her breath and her stomach.

"Ease up, James," she said as soon as she could take another breath. "If we catch a downdraft off one of these mountains, we're likely to be wearing those trees." James, an ex-Gulf War 'copter pilot, often flew as though he was being pursued by some unidentified enemy aircraft. Pat suspected he occasionally experienced flashbacks of those grueling war years.

"In fact, take it up a couple hundred feet, and let's take another pass from a different perspective." James nodded affirmatively and gave her a sly wink, which Pat ignored. She drew a lot of winks from her male co-workers and once in a while a pinch on the ass from some brave fool... but only one.

Her five-foot, two-inch frame of muscular curves had stopped plenty of men in their tracks, but no one hung around Pat long without discovering she was a woman with whom you did not fool around. Oh sure, a little kidding around was okay; it was to be expected, and Pat was far from being a prude. She knew she was attractive, maybe even sexy. Pat had spent many long hours in the gym and karate dojo in the pursuit of a healthy frame, but it wasn't for her shape she worked so hard. It was the desire for excellence in everything she took on in her life, especially her career.

"We're getting low on fuel, sweet thing," James shouted to her over the whirl of the blades. "We'll have to take it in for refueling."

"One more pass," Pat replied. "I thought I saw a glint of something just over the ridge. It could be a metallic surface reflecting the sun."

"These babies don't stay afloat very long when the blades stop rotating," James answered. Pat turned and stared at him for a long few seconds.

"One more pass," she mouthed slowly.

"Whatever you say. You're the boss."

The helicopter eased over the ridge. Pat placed the set of binoculars to her eyes. She studied the rough terrain below, looking for the scar in the thick growth of trees she'd noticed on the previous pass. It had looked like some-one had selectively cut a thin line through the dense growth. A fast-moving object striking the surface at an acute angle as the report had suggested could have caused such damage. Yet with heavy snowfall, it could quickly go unno-ticed.

She lowered the glasses for a moment. There — just to the left, a long thin line angled obliquely across the crest. She raised the glasses back to her eyes and traced the scar, shouting to James as she did.

"Turn east about fifteen degrees and come in a little slower. I think I see something." She felt James make the adjustment quickly.

As she studied the defect in the landscape, her gaze stopped at the end furthest from the crest. As they passed over the area, a flash, like from a flash-bulb, momentarily blinded them; or was it the reflection of the noonday sun? But from what?

"See that thin break in the trees we just passed over? I want you to put down there."

"No way, babes," James replied. "Not with this wind and us sucking on fumes. One little hesitation and we'll be eating those trees."

"I thought you were the great Gulf War 'copter pilot with ice water flow-ing through his veins."

"I'm just not interested in picnicking in these woods for several days while a search party tries to find us. Not even with a gorgeous dame like yourself."

"Okay, fine. Set me down with the crane. Note the spot on the map and head back for fuel. Bring the others back in the other 'copter while this one is being refueled."

"Are you crazy? I can't lower you..." James stopped short as he noticed Pat already strapping the rigging around her slender frame.

"Lower me as close to the ground as you can, then I'll cut myself free. Don't worry, I'll take full responsibility."

"Our orders were to return to base and report anything we found to the rest of the search team. Not to investigate on our own," James shouted.

"I'm in charge here, James," Pat shouted back. "Your orders were to follow my directions. We haven't found anything to report. I'm simply going down to take a closer look. If there is anything down there, you'll be back with the team. I'll just be hanging around waiting. Don't worry, I'll be fine." Pat patted arm. "Now lower me down."

"What in the world could possibly be down there worth risking your neck?"

"Oh, nothing. Just the most likely candidate for a bonafide UFO in the last several years. I intend to be the first person to set eyes on it." She set the glasses under her seat and picked up her camera, slinging it around her neck by its strap.

She left the passenger seat and scurried to the rear of the chopper. She clipped the crane rope to her rigging and waited for James to give her the go-ahead.

As James made a final pass over the site (a second pass beyond what the fuel gauge indicated was possible), James signaled for her to ease out of the door. As they approached the narrow gully in the trees, Pat wondered if she'd made a wise judgment call. Who was this James character, anyway? Hell, she'd only met him a few hours ago. How good of a pilot was he? Hell, she couldn't even remember his last name; she'd known him for such a short time. How did she know if he had really flown in the Gulf War? For all she knew, he could be as new at flying copters as she was at investigating UFO reports. She wasn't comforted by the thought as she glanced down at the Longleaf Pines reaching their long fingers to tickle the bottoms of her feet.

Pat hung from the undercarriage of the copter as James continued to lower her with the crane, as well as dropping the helicopter closer to the trees. A gust of wind started Pat turning slowly on the end of the thin fiberglass cord.

He better know what he's doing, Pat told herself as she tried to slow the spin, growing more uncomfortable with her situation by the moment.

Just as she was sure James was about to plop her into the thick growth of trees, dashing her body against the pines, the thin break appeared, and she was deftly lowered into it. Heavy tree limbs whizzed by on both sides. She felt like she could reach out with either hand and grasp a handful of needles. Despite a reduction in the wind gusts, she continued to spin out of control. She thought on one pass that she could see the gleaming metallic object at the end of the thin canyon formed by the trees, but she couldn't be sure.

She estimated that she was still a good thirty feet in the air when she felt the shudder of the helicopter through the line. *Oh, shit, James is running out of fuel,* Pat thought as she glared up at the copter's underbelly. *Lower me quicker, you fool.* But she continued to hang there as though suspended in the web of a monstrous spider, waiting for the spider to return home for his evening meal.

She had to do something and quick. She couldn't count on James. She realized you couldn't rely on anyone when the chips were down — only yourself. She continued to hang there for several seconds trying to decide what to do.

She stared below her at the rough terrain of the mountainside, she estimated there was still a good twenty-five feet to the ground. The copter shuddered a second time. Enough is enough. She'd take control of the situation herself. She punched the safety release on her chest and felt the familiar rush of free fall.

She'd spent a summer between her sophomore and junior years of college skydiving her heart out. In a three-month time span, she'd made over fifty jumps, most of them free falls. The training paid off now as she landed on the irregular surface of the mountainside. As the ground came up fast, she held her feet and knees firmly together. She did not try to stay on her feet but rolled to one side, her hands and arms clasped tightly across her chest.

She rolled down the mountainside, picking up speed as she fell until her left shoulder struck a large rock embedded in the ground. She came to an abrupt and painful stop. She lay there for several seconds wincing in pain. Then she staggered to her feet to give James the okay sign, but the helicopter had already sputtered over the crest, dragging the line behind it.

Pat dusted herself off with her right hand and felt a sharp pain shoot through her left shoulder. She gently moved her left arm to be sure it wasn't dislocated and was rewarded with another shock of pain which threatened to black her out. *Maybe not dislocated,* she thought, *but sure as hell not one hundred percent, either.*

Pat stared in the direction where the helicopter had disappeared. *I sure as hell hope he makes it back to camp,* she thought. He's my ticket out of here. Having had the thought, she now placed it out of her mind. There was nothing else she could do about it right now, so why worry? It was time to go looking for a UFO.

Before setting off in the direction where she anticipated finding the UFO, she made a thorough inspection of her camera. *A bit scuffed and dirty,* she thought, wiping it off with her handkerchief. *But still serviceable,* she concluded as she snapped a picture, relieved to hear the familiar click-click of the shutter.

She picked her way across the rough terrain, occasionally stopping to enjoy the rugged scenic beauty of the mountain. She took a deep breath of fresh air and let it out slowly. What a great job. No sitting behind a desk all day for her. Being a part of the new team assigned to explore the highly secretive "Waynesboro NC UFO Case" was still a little hard for her to believe. She had finally found a position that fit all of the interests she'd inherited from her parents. Her interest in investigative work was passed down from her father's thirty-year career as a police detective in Atlanta. She had undoubtedly inherited her love of science and speculation from her mom's career as a science fiction novelist. It was quite an accomplishment to be the newest member of B.I.U.F.O. (the Bureau of Investigation of Unidentified Flying Objects) and to be assigned to a field case, particularly one as juicy as the Waynesboro case.

She'd been with B.I.U.F.O. only three months and she knew her being on the case had irritated some senior investigators back in Washington. Well, as her dad had always said, "Fuck 'em, if they can't take a joke."

She'd earned the opportunity, and it wasn't by sleeping with some high-level politician, as she knew several of the other investigators suspected. She had worked her butt off for this chance, and if everyone would stay out of her way, she'd make sure the hard work paid off.

The early spring thaw and rain had been a good omen, although the wet ground now made walking a slippery mess. Since the initial reports from the Strategic Air Command over three months ago of a high-speed UFO originating from outside the earth's atmosphere, no one had had any luck locating where it might have gone. North Carolina had suffered one of its worst winters ever, with a heavy burden of snowfall that surpassed all previous records. It had been two days after the radar sighting before anyone could investigate the report. By that time, a good eight inches of snow had fallen in the region.

If the UFO had struck the earth, it had been buried under a heavy blanket of white.

B.I.U.F.O. had spent several days of reconnaissance and several thousand dollars of taxpayer money with no results, so they had called off the search until the spring thaw. The thaw had come early, and in the interim Pat had joined the investigative team. She was about to make all that hard work worthwhile.

As Pat neared the end of the thin clearing, it became more apparent how the UFO had avoided detection. Evidently, the object had come in low and hard, burrowing its way into the side of the mountain, leaving behind a thin gully that was quickly covered by the snow. Since then the sides of the ravine had partially collapsed, leaving only the upper few feet of the dull gray dome exposed.

Pat ignored the patches of the last remnants of snow, strolling straight through the slush to reach the alien object. *I may be the first human to ever see an alien spaceship,* she thought. But she didn't believe it. More likely she had just joined the club of a select group of other humans who had witnessed similar objects, although she suspected very few people had been as close to one as she was at this moment. Most UFO sightings were of strange objects streaking across the sky. There were much fewer reports of people visiting crafts that had landed.

As she reached the metal dome poking out of the side of the mountain like a giant cold sore, she strolled around it looking for a way in.

There's no question, it's man-made—oops, alien-made. Then she stopped. Could it be man-made? What if this wasn't an alien vessel but one from some foreign country or even a top-secret American project? Now that she was down on the surface standing next to the craft, her bold move to explore the ship on her own didn't look like such a wise decision.

I could have asked James to loan me his revolver. The Colt .45 he wore strapped to his waist wasn't Pat's favorite weapon, but it sure would be comforting to have in case the inhabitants of the ship proved less than cordial. She stopped long enough to be sure the knife, a present from her dad, was still securely strapped to her left leg. Small comfort if she met a foreigner with an automatic rifle or an alien with a death ray, but better than nothing.

She turned her eyes casually to the trees around her but could see or hear nothing except the usual sounds of the forest, the chirping of the first spring birds mingled with the rustling of the trees. She started walking around the metallic dome again, searching for a way into its interior. She strolled around the complete circumference, finally arriving on the other side of the deep channel. She peered over the edge of the channel. She thought she could just make out a slight irregularity at the base where the ship's exterior disappeared into the side of the mountain.

She scooted down the steep side of the gully, struggling to maintain her balance on the slippery mud, but within a few yards found herself sliding on her backside out of control. Within moments, the wet mud had soaked through her jeans. As she reached the bottom of the chasm, she threw her right arm out against the ship and caught herself, sending another lightning bolt of pain coursing down her left side. She found the ship's surface surprisingly warm. Could it be from the sun's radiation or did the heat come from within?

She regained her footing and squinted her eyes, trying to pierce the dark shadows created by the sides of the channel. What was that, in the dark hole next to the ship's surface? An irregularity or dried mud packed against the smooth side?

She stumbled over to the short tunnel, finding it difficult to balance on the rocky, muddy surface. It was mud caked on the side—and an irregularity. As her eyes adjusted to the dark, she could make out a raised circular pattern. She dug into the pocket of her jeans and pulled out the small flashlight, another present from her father. She twisted the head to turn it on and shone the light beam into the dark recess.

"Yes!" The word slipped from her lips with a hiss that sounded eerie as it bounced off the metallic surface. An entrance, it had to be.

Did she dare enter the ship before help arrived? It was an insane thought. Her orders from Oliver had been particular. *Do not investigate any findings on your own. Wait for backup from the rest of the team.* She should climb out of this dark muddy ditch, back to the sunny surface where she belonged, and wait for James to bring Oliver and the rest of the search team. She had had enough heroics for one day. Already, she would receive top recognition for finding the alien vessel, if that's what it turned out to be. Please, dear God, let it be alien. She would get credit for the discovery, whatever it was. Yes, it would be best to wait.

She shrugged her shoulders in one of her favorite gestures and winced at the pain on the left side. "Daddy always said I didn't know what was best for me." She slid into the dark tunnel.

Confrontation

The bear groaned softly as it stretched its long body, almost touching the two sides of its lair. It rolled onto its back and wiggled, trying to reach the itchy spot in the middle. As it turned, it bumped against the frozen carcass, mostly bones, lying next to it. *Is it time,* he wondered? *Is the metamorphosis complete?*

The grizzly lumbered onto its feet, kicking the carcass to the side. It stood frozen to the spot for several minutes, its nose in the air, its eyes closed. Something was amiss. He'd been awakened by something—something besides hunger. The metamorphosis was not quite finished. Almost, it would do, but...something was wrong.

After a couple more minutes, the bear lowered itself onto all fours and strolled outside. Once again, it stood on all fours and waited. The ship. Something is wrong with the ship. He must get back. His link with the ship, although weakened in this form, clearly indicated an intruder. Perhaps only a curious animal sniffing around the perimeter. But maybe not.

His adaptation to the new planet was all but complete. The little that remained would have to wait. He was safe now. His body had made the necessary re-calibrations. The foreign environment was now his. He now owned this planet as his own.

He stood there for a moment longer, debating whether to transform back into the hunter-survivor form of his people. No, the bear would be better. It was less likely to draw attention from other inhabitants of the planet. At least until he found other forms to add to his repertoire.

He returned to his lair. Stepping over the carcass of its former occupant, he crouched down so he could reach the back of the cave. In the dim light that filtered from the mouth of the cave, he could just make out the two objects upon which his entire mission rested—the cocoon and the crystal.

Amazing, we are indeed an amazing race, he thought. For as long as he had been settling planets, he never lost his appreciation for these two pieces of technology. Hard to imagine that in the small sphere of the cocoon, far smaller than the size of the bear's head, could be housed ten thousand souls of his people. Equally amazing was the crystal, so small that it could easily be worn around his neck as an adornment, yet it held the entire technology of his people. His people were the most advanced civilizations of the galaxy, at least as far as they'd been able to determine in the five hundred plus years they'd been exploring it.

But the question is, do I leave these two precious objects behind or take them with me back to the ship? There's something wrong with the ship. Every fiber of his body blared the warning. He could not afford to let either of these objects become lost. No, better to leave them here where they'd be safe and return to them when he was satisfied everything was okay with the ship.

Having decided his course of action, he backed out of the narrow part of the lair to where he could once again stand up. He started to take a final meal from the frozen carcass but decided against it. He wanted fresh food. Perhaps on his trip back to the ship, he would be lucky and find some.

THE SOUND OF A SPUTTERING helicopter pulled Oliver's attention away from the stack of reports lying in front of him.

It's coming in low, he told himself, glancing in the direction of the sound. *Too low and on fumes.* He jerked his large frame out of the director's chair and lumbered out of the tent in time to see the whirlybird's landing sled scrape the top off of several trees. It wobbled in midair like a huge eagle that had been shot, then amazingly stayed in the air long enough to make a bumpy landing at the edge of the clearing. As he ran towards the 'copter, Oliver noticed only the pilot was inside. *Where the hell is Pat?* He wondered. A familiar burning sensation in the pit of his stomach had already begun. Something told him he wasn't going to like what he heard from James.

A few minutes later, the burning from the "dormant" ulcer flared into a full force bonfire, and he reached for the economy size bottle of antacids in an attempt to extinguish the familiar blaze.

"YOU DID WHAT?" HE SHOUTED. "Why in the world would you do such a foolish thing?"

"Damn it, Oliver, she insisted. I don't need to remind you how persuasive Pat can be. Besides, she was calling the shots. That's what you told us when we started the search."

Oliver groaned. "Well, as soon as the second helicopter is back and yours is refueled, we'll go see if we can find our roving dare-devil. You made sure she was all right before you left, didn't you?"

James nodded. "She's fine. I have to say, she's got guts. I'm not sure how smart she is, but she sure has guts."

Oliver started walking back to his tent then stopped and turned back to James. "What did it look like? Could you make anything out?"

"DAMNATION!" PAT YELLED for the third time in the last thirty minutes as her fingers slid off the lip of the door. She winced at the now familiar pain in her shoulder. In the forty-five minutes she had been wedged in against the ship, she had managed to break three fingernails and scrape just about all of her knuckles—and move the door by perhaps half an inch. The most frustrating thing, the door had moved. Within the first couple of minutes, it had moved. She was certain.

Which means it's not locked, just stuck, Pat concluded. *And if it's not locked, then I'm going to get inside, one way or another. If only I had the full use of both of my arms,* she thought. *And if just...* "the queen had balls she would be king," she heard her father's familiar voice ringing in her ears.

I'm getting in, she told herself again. *There is no way in hell I'm getting this close without finding some way into the damn thing.* What if she ran the blade of her knife along the crack again? Maybe that would dislodge something. *I'll try it again.* "Third time's the charm," her father added. *Buzz off,* Pat retorted.

THE ALIEN SPOTTED A stag in the woods just above him. *Does it smell me?* The alien wondered. *No, I'm upwind. A gorgeous beast. Much more attractive than this clumsy body. And fresh meat,* he thought. *But what about the ship? I should get back to the ship. The intruder is still there, although outside.* He hesitated. *I'll be fast. Fresh meat and a new form to add to my collection.* It made sense to take a few minutes. But not in his present form. The bear was too slow, too cumbersome. The hunter-survivor was not. Without moving, he called his natural body forth. He felt the familiar surge of energy and the welcome sensation of coming home to the body he was most comfortable in. *Welcome home, Sluneg. Nice to be in my own body again,* he thought. Such a fine form. There was just nothing in the galaxy that could compare. No other structure was as efficient —the perfect killing machine.

As he completed the transformation, he glanced down at himself. The customary black coloration would not do in this situation. Too visible. He gazed around at the browns and greens of the forest and called them forth out of himself. Not as attractive, but more functional. *Now, let's go have some fun.*

He crept forward on padded feet, being sure to keep the three-inch stiletto-like nails retracted. *Just a little closer,* he thought, *before I let it know I'm here, just a little closer.*

Now, the alien thought as he reached out and purposefully stepped on a thin branch on the path. Crack.

The stag had returned to grazing on the lush new grass of the meadow. At the sound of the breaking branch, it raised its head again, a clump of grass hanging out of its mouth. It looked around, the skin on its neck twitching nervously. It sniffed the air. Still nothing.

It's alert, the alien thought. *A worthy trophy to add to my collection.* He thought of his ship again. *Okay, mustn't dawdle. Get on with it.* He stepped out into the clearing just as the stag began to lower its head for another nibble of grass. The two animals stared at each other, both frozen in an instant in time. The stag was the first to break. It reared on its hindquarters, turning to its left.

Even as the alien leaped after the stag, it marveled at the beauty of the beast. The deer fled across the pasture, picking up speed with every stride. The hunter survivor matched it step by step for the first fifty yards, still studying its beauty. As the two of them neared the edge of the forest, the alien picked up its pace, quickly closing the gap between the two of them.

Ten yards from the forest, the alien left the ground in a leap that covered the final five yards. As he sailed through the air, his front legs fully extended, he protracted the twelve razor-sharp claws, each of them already spinning on their axis at full speed. He hit the right flank of the stag-like a freight train, knocking the rear legs of the animal out from under itself. Each claw spun their way deep into the stag's flank, easily piercing skin, fat, and muscle.

As the two animals fell into the woods, the alien withdrew the claws of one paw, holding on with the other, leaving behind six holes, each an inch across and three inches deep, blood gushing from each one. He jabbed the nails in again, farther up the flank, and again, reaching for the stag's backbone. The panicked stag flung its head back in an attempt to free itself. The alien ducked under the rack of antlers. As the stag turned its head to take another swing, its antlers caught in the low-lying branches of a nearby tree.

You're all mine, now, the alien thought as he walked his way up the stag's back, leaving behind a set of deadly fingerprints.

PAT WEDGED THE KNIFE in the narrow crack again and twisted, holding her breath as she did so. Each time, she risked breaking the thin blade, leaving it stuck in the crack as an additional obstacle. But so far the tempered steel had stood up to the punishment. And the method worked. Slowly, painfully slow, Pat pried the door open.

Just a little more, she told herself. *Hold on just a couple more times*, she instructed the knife, *and maybe I'll be able to get enough of a hold on the door to wrench it open with my one working arm.*

She paused for a moment to wipe the stream of sweat from around her eyes. By this time, her entire body was drenched in her perspiration. Her short dark hair lay matted against her scalp. *And I'm beginning to smell like a men's locker room*, she observed. *Come, take me now, James.* She kidded with herself. *What, you aren't interested? Why, you fickle bastard. Just like a man.*

She wedged the edge of the knife in again and twisted, holding her breath once more. *Holding my breath, that's the key. If I don't hold my breath, I'll get cocky, and the knife will sense it. It'll think I'm taking it for granted and 'snap,' it will be all over.*

As she continued to work, she began to speculate about what she would find on the other side. Poisonous gas? A ten-foot cockroach waiting hungrily for its next meal? Maybe a ship filled with gold and diamonds. *If I were an alien, I'd be sure to bring along plenty of booty for the natives.* If aliens had been studying them for the past fifty or more years, as many experts claimed, wouldn't they know how much earthlings valued gold and diamonds?

One particular question kept haunting her though. Was the ship occupied? Was there something waiting inside for her, ten-foot cockroach or other? Who was to say this was a manned or alien-occupied vessel? All indications pointed to the contrary. The landing had been a far cry from smooth. If there were aliens on board, would they still be alive and what had they been doing for the last three months? Certainly not waiting for Pat Vogt to arrive to rescue them.

"All in good time." She mumbled out loud then smiled. Another one of her father's favorite lines, used whenever an overly inquisitive little girl would ask too many questions. "All in good time, Patti. All your questions will be answered—all in good time." Pat hoped he had been right.

Pat adjusted the beam of the flashlight to take in the next section of the door. The flashlight was stuck in the mud wall a few feet from the door, and it was a simple matter to move the beam where she needed it.

She stuck the knife in the crack again and levered it back. She felt the usual resistance; then suddenly the knife slipped. She scraped another knuckle, and the knife fell onto the ground. She picked the knife up from the mud and wiped it on her pants. She started to insert the knife back in the crack when she noticed the blunt end.

Damn! She thought as she placed the knife more directly in the beam of light. About a quarter inch of the tip had broken off. *I wasn't holding my breath,* she chided herself. She inspected the knife closer and decided she had been fortunate. It was still serviceable, and when she got back to town, she could probably get someone at the hardware store to grind the end to another point without damaging the rest of the knife. *Hold your breath*, she reminded herself as she went back to work.

The next time she wedged the knife in the crack, she felt the door move a little more than before. The next time she was sure. *It's coming. The damn thing is finally giving me a break.* But she continued to hold her breath. No point in getting cocky.

Ten minutes later, she carefully placed the knife back in its case strapped to her leg and wiped her face again with the soaked sleeve of her right arm. *Okay. This was it. Time to pop this son-of-a-bitch open.*

Wedging herself firmly between the ship and the back of the mud cave, she took a firm grasp of the ledge at the top of the door. One, two, three—heave. At first, nothing happened, except for her face turning red and the pain in her left shoulder reminding her to take it a little easier. But she didn't relax, only strained even harder. Still nothing.

"Come on, you bastard. Give me a fucking break!" She shouted at the top of her lungs.

The door moved. A half inch, then another half inch.

"All right. There you go," Pat shouted again. "Now we're cooking." She readjusted her hand-hold down a quarter turn and pulled again. The door moved easier this time.

She reached a hundred and eighty degrees across to the other side. It was more challenging to get a firm grip, but she found the door had loosened sufficiently to be able to pull it another three-quarters of an inch out. She bent to the top and repeated the process again. Although she could not see them because of the mud, she'd calculated the door was hinged at the bottom.

"Any moment now!" She said out loud to give herself encouragement. Suddenly the dark tunnel was far too quiet. The other side? What would be on the other side?

She stopped. *Let's not be foolish,* she told herself. The thought of poisonous gas returned. How would she be able to tell? Not all toxic gases had an odor. Take natural gas. Odorless. The smell came from an additive. She pondered the question, finally deciding there was no way she could be sure. The best she could do would be to sample it, slowly, carefully. If she felt the least bit light-headed, she'd get the hell out of the tunnel and wait for the team.

Sometimes, life is risky. Her father used to remind her often. This was one of those times. She grasped the top of the door again and pulled. This time it came easily, and Pat stepped to her right to give the door room to open. And held her breath.

No sound, she noticed, no hiss. Nothing to indicate a change in pressure. Didn't mean the gases were the same, but it did make her feel a little better. She sniffed the air. Was that a sweet smell? Had it been there before? It was hard to tell. Mostly, all she could smell was herself. Oh well, here goes.

She took another whiff, a little stronger this time. And waited. Smells the same as it did. Right? Feel fine so far. Right? Yes, she concluded as she pulled the flashlight from its spot in the mud wall and shined the light into the ship. Slow and easy. Just take it slow and easy. She took a short breath, then holding it again, she stuck her head through the crack and looked around.

"Holy, mother-of-pearl!" She said in a hushed voice as though she was entering an ancient cathedral. It felt that way. She half expected to find herself looking into a small air-lock with the real inside of the ship on the other side of yet another door. So she wasn't prepared for what she saw.

It looked like the central section of the ship. The room stretched at least fifteen feet into the center and was nearly that wide. Pat estimated the distance between the ceiling and the floor to be eight, maybe nine feet. So much for a ten-foot-tall cockroach, she thought as she stepped over the rim of the door and entered the ship. *Oh, Roachy is probably no more than seven feet.* She smiled at her own joke.

As she did so, she felt the first wave of dizziness. Toxic gas! Her mind screamed at her. Get out—get out! Fighting the panic, she stopped in mid-stride and suddenly realized she'd been holding her breath for at least a minute and a half. She slowly let it out and took a careful breath and immediately felt better. The air was stale but harmless.

As her foot hit the decking of the ship, Pat heard a low-grade hum followed seconds later by a blast of light from overhead. She ducked for a moment as though she'd suddenly been attacked by a flurry of bats, but there was nothing there. She stepped back, and as she did so, the lights flickered off.

Not bad, she thought. *I wonder how you turn them off when you're ready to let the cat out and go to bed.* She re-entered the ship, and the light immediately cut on again, so she switched her flashlight off.

The room was austere with only a few unfamiliar objects along the far wall. A storage room? Pat wondered. It was possible that this was not the main entrance. Likely, in fact. If the ship had come in right side up, the main hatch was probably buried fifteen or twenty feet. More than likely, this was an auxiliary way in and out of the ship, close to the top of the ship in case of unexpected crash landings.

Besides the door to the outside, there were two other doors which led to other parts of the ship, one almost directly across from the exit door and a second one on the wall to the left.

"Which shall it be?" Pat asked herself out loud and was startled by the sound of her own voice. *It's too damn quiet in here*, she thought and began to whistle a tuneless melody.

She walked over to the door directly across from the exit. What if the doors were locked, waiting for the unique thumbprint of the ship's owner? Please, Lord, let it be open, she prayed as she approached the door. Much to her amazement and joy, when she was a couple of feet from the door, it noise-lessly slid open.

"All right," she exclaimed. *Now we're cooking.*

Pat strolled through the ship. Each room seemed more amazing than the one before. As she left one room, the light automatically cut off in it and on in the next one. *Like having an individual ray of sunlight following you around*, she thought, her mood lifting with every minute.

She didn't understand anything she saw, but it was definitely high tech. Much more advanced than anything she'd ever seen, even in the hundreds of sci-fi movies her mom had taken her to.

And definitely alien. No way, could any of it have been made by or for hu-mans. The equipment lacked the usual symmetry she'd come to expect of hu-man design. There were almost no right angles or rectangular objects. Every-thing was more free-flowing, almost amorphous. The shape appeared to de-pend on the need or function, without any preconceived expectation that it had to look a particular way. Pat found her mouth gaping open for the third time and clamped it shut. She snapped a couple of pictures in each room, be-ing careful to ration her only roll of film.

It was in the fourth room where she found the two empty cylinders. They spanned from the floor to the ceiling and Pat estimated they were about three feet in diameter. As she studied them, cold, creepy fingers began to dance along her spine. Empty now, but she felt sure there had been something inside. She didn't know why she felt so strongly about it, but there was no question in her mind. What had been inside? More importantly, where were they now?

She suddenly jerked her head around, looking in every corner. In a millisecond, her mind flashed through a half dozen of the most gruesome aliens of her movie-going days. But despite squinting her eyes and looking into every deep recess, none of the aliens materialized.

Pat sighed with relief, but the breath caught in her throat as she heard a faint metallic clink behind her. A second later, the lights overhead blinked out. The sound had been so soft. Had she imagined it? Her heart rate doubled for the second time in the last few minutes. Her palms dampened with sweat and she feared she'd drop the flashlight she still held in her hand. It was suddenly very slick. Quickly, she switched it on.

Time to leave...calm down, it's nothing. The ship is empty. No, not empty. The only thing empty was the two cylinders in front of her. Leave. Leave quickly. Her mind raced. Meanwhile, her body knotted from the rush of adrenalin. She took a deep breath and let it out slowly. Be calm. No matter what, getting all worked up would only make things worse. If there was something in the ship with her, she didn't know if it was dangerous. It was possible, despite all the stories to the contrary, that aliens could be friendly.

The second sound, louder and much closer behind her dashed the notion of friendly aliens from her mind. Friendly or not, she was not equipped to meet them on their grounds. To them, she was an intruder. How would she react coming home and finding someone in her home?

She was alone without any idea how far away help was. She was unarmed and vulnerable—as vulnerable as she could ever remember feeling. It was time to visit the cold reality of the light of day. Now.

Hunter-survivor

The alien stood in the entrance, looking at the small object that had fallen from the console. He didn't like what he had found on his return to the ship. He had, in fact, left a well-deserved meal, when his sensors notified him that the outer security of his ship had been breached. Whatever had been on his ship had not been a harmless creature of the woods. Somehow, it had managed to find its way into the ship and was here this very minute.

Had his presence been discovered by the primary species of the planet? Shortly after his arrival, he had on a couple of occasions observed from afar a small village of bipeds. These strange, bipedal creatures appeared to own this world and were probably the cause of the poor condition it was in. Could one of the bipeds have stumbled upon his ship? Could his luck be so rotten? Having been on several other settlement missions, he knew the answer to the question was a resounding yes. The unexpected twists and turns were what he lived for, and at the same time, he had noticed of late, he sometimes found himself wishing for one smooth, trouble-free mission. Clearly, this was not to be the one.

He considered his options. If his ship had been discovered by a biped, his entire mission must be considered in jeopardy. If the biped had in some way communicated with others of its kind, they might be on their way at this very moment. Which meant, he didn't have much time to rectify the problem. This called for bold, immediate action.

The ship would have to be destroyed. He could not afford to have his enemy study it. There was nothing in the ship that could not be replicated given enough time and resources. All the plans for the necessary equipment to recover his people from the cocoon were housed in the memory crystal, both of which were hidden back in the cave. Destroying the ship would be a definite setback but not one from which he could not recover. His was a patient race.

He stared at the small object that had fallen from the console. He picked up the detonation unit where it had fallen. Clumsy of him perhaps, but it could still serve his purpose. The noise would almost certainly bring the intruder running to the entrance and give him the opportunity to revenge the invasion of his privacy. He'd then leave the ship in the ready mode. He'd wait for others of the intruder's race. If they came, he'd destroy the ship by remote. If not, he'd return and defuse the system. Either way, the intruder would pay for stumbling on the ship. Most important of all, his secret would be intact.

A sound from deeper inside the ship drew his attention away from the warning lights of the detonation unit. His first direct contact with his enemy was about to occur. He shivered with anticipation. Perhaps he'd be surprised. Maybe the intruder would put up a better fight than his previous encounters. He always enjoyed a good match. Should he cut off the lights? No, not yet. What did he have to worry about? Let the biped get a good look at him. It would be fun to see its reaction.

He was disappointed when the intruder entered the room. As he had suspected, it was one of the bipeds, which meant his mission was definitely in jeopardy. It was also a female of the species which meant he wouldn't even have the pleasure of a good fight. Seeing one up close like this, it became evident to him that this species was much more fragile than he had first imagined. *Hardly worth playing with,* he thought as he strolled forward, still holding the detonation unit. Best to end it quickly in case others were on their way.

As he narrowed the distance between them, the biped backed out of the room and deeper into the ship. *It's apparently terrified of me,* Sluneg thought. *No wonder. No doubt it's never seen the likes of me. At least it appears smart enough to realize it's about to die. Well, maybe I'll have a little fun with it before I snuff out its life.*

PAT RETRACED HER STEPS as quietly as possible, forcing herself not to run. Three doorways still separated her from the outside when she came face to face with the alien. For just a heartbeat or two, she stood frozen in the bright light of the room, staring in disbelief.

Before her eyes had fully adjusted to the light, Pat backed out of the room, adding a new image to her impressive collection of alien memories. This one was far more horrible than all the made up ones if for no other reason than this one was real, and standing before her blocking her exit from the ship. As the door closed behind her, Pat switched the flashlight to her left hand and pulled the hunting knife from its sheath with her right hand. She kept the flashlight on but pressed it against her leg to hide the light. If she was to get out of this mess alive, a surprise was her only hope.

The biped had retreated to one of the storage units of the ship. The clutter of supplies and equipment would make the hunt a little more challenging. He would play with it a little while. Let it think it had a chance to escape before killing it. *Not long*, he promised himself. There was too much work ahead to indulge too long. Before opening the door, he signaled to the ship to keep the lights off. As he entered the storage room, he paused for just a moment to let his eyes adjust to the darker room. He scanned the room with his multiple senses and found the creature hiding behind one of the backup computers.

He wondered how such a helpless species had become so dominant on the planet. Many of the other animals he had come in contact with seemed a more likely candidate. He ran his razor sharp claws along one wall, adding a deep-throated growl for effect. He had seen larger animals break their cover, fleeing in fear from the combination of sounds. This one did not. *Interesting*, he thought. *Could it be paralyzed to the spot? Whimpering in the corner in terror?*

Probably so, he thought as he stepped around the console to take a look. As he did, he was suddenly blinded by a brilliant flash of light, and in the next instance felt the searing pain of cold metal penetrate between the protective plates of his chest.

He screamed in pain and anger, stumbling back in confusion. It took him an instant to realize he'd been wounded. Not a severe wound, only painful and disturbing. The biped had drawn first blood.

What was this? The human must be insane with terror. It was coming after him again. Through the glare of the unexpected light, he saw the gleam of metal as it slashed through the air. He raised his left arm to fend the human off and felt a second explosion of pain as the weapon sliced through the sinewy muscles of his forearm. Again, not severe but aggravating to think the sick little beast was actually trying to kill him. He roared with anger and was surprised to hear an edge of fear in his voice.

He leaped away from the attack onto a storage container several feet above the biped. The sudden quick movement and distance of the leap seemed to catch it by surprise. The beam of light shining from the end of one of its appendages did not follow the path of the jump. Instead, it scanned the room in front. He took the opportunity to examine his wounds. Already, the clotting mechanism of his blood had started to seal off the wounds. Neither injury was serious. More blows to his pride than anything. Perhaps it was time to stop playing with the human. He had serious work to accomplish. Time to kill this aggravating animal and be done with it. His next approach would be more careful, more deadly.

He slipped behind the storage container just before the search beam found his hiding place. He would slide up behind it and finish it off quickly. But when he came around the container, the animal was nowhere to be seen. The search beam which he had counted on to locate the intruder had been snuffed out. He stopped his own breathing for a moment and listened carefully for its breathing. Nothing.

Had it died from fright? Not likely. Given what he had recently learned of his enemy, he had a new respect for it. Fear did not seem to control this species as it did most of the others on the planet, which might, in part, explain its dominance.

Then he heard the biped. It could not hold its breath as long. The sound had come from the other side of a stack of food cylinders. The long cylinders were seldom needed on an expedition but were included on the ship in case of emergency landings on inhospitable planets. The heavy cylinders were tied together by a thick elastic band.

He crept to the other side of the stack and listened again. A second breath confirmed the beast was still hiding on the other side. Protracting one long nail from its sheath, he slid it under the strap, sawing easily through the plastic. As the final strands were cut, he pushed the cylinders towards his enemy and then leaped away to safety. The biped, caught by surprise, was buried under the cylinders.

He waited for the last cylinder to come to rest and then strolled over to the still form. As he did so, it moved, groaning softly. The light source it had used earlier to blind him lay, still on, a few feet away. Not a bad little fighter, he thought as he stopped several yards away from it and studied its small frame. Smarter than he had expected. As he watched, it turned over on its back and stared at him. It shook its head as though trying to clear its vision. The eyes opened wider as it realized its fate.

Time to end it, he thought as he took a step closer. A distant sound from outside the ship stopped him. He cocked his head, listening carefully. He could not identify the sound, but it grew louder as he listened. Something was approaching at a fast rate of speed. Other of its kind? Had the small, resourceful animal lying before him somehow called for help? His eyes darted around the room looking for any way it could have accomplished this.

His eyes came to rest on the slender figure lying on the floor. As he stared into the biped's eyes, he was shocked by what he saw. No fear—only hate. Then it also turned towards the distant sound. A thin smile formed on its lips and a torrent of short staccato sounds shot from its mouth. He regretted he had not taken the time to simulate his enemy's language. If the biped recognized the sound, it could be persuaded to tell him what it was. It would be best simply to kill and be done. Get away from the ship and watch for signs of new visitors.

Having decided his course of action, he started towards the biped again, determined to make the killing swift yet as painful as possible. After all, it had ruined his plans for an easy takeover. It deserved to suffer a little. He was only a few yards from it when he noticed the quick flick of the human's right arm. He watched in sudden surprise as a gleaming metallic object flew through the air, implanting itself deeply in his neck.

A new and much more intense shock of pain soared through his entire body. His defense mechanism instantly alerted him to the serious nature of the injury he had just received. The scream of anguish that escaped from his lips was strangely guttural. His windpipe had been severed, and part of the cry had escaped from the wound.

He fell backward in pain. As he hit the floor, the sound from outside grew in his ears. Must escape. Must get away from the ship. Must survive — survive — survive. The instincts of the hunter-survivor took over his bodily functions. He reached up to claw the sharp piece of metal from his neck, but then stopped. If he removed the object, it would leave a larger hole for his defenses to close. Better to leave it in place for now and let his body seal around it.

As he struggled to stand, he felt a sudden jolt of energy as the hormonal mechanism of survival strengthened his body with new reserves. He found himself standing, his legs were shaky but able to direct him towards the door. He stumbled against the entrance, his head slapping painfully against the metallic corner. His mental processes threatened to shut down from the blow, but a new jolt of hormone released from a gland beneath his brain cleared his head sufficiently to allow him to stumble towards the exit.

As the hormones coursed through his system, he was able to think beyond just the instinctual drive to survive. Should he go back and kill the intruder? No, it was incapacitated enough. It would not be able to escape before he destroyed the ship. The loud whirring sound from outside demanded his attention. He should transform out of his hunter-survivor form and protect his identity. Almost certainly the noise was from others of the dominant race. It was important he not be seen like this. But could he transform or had the wounds weakened him too much? He had to try, but to what form? The bear was too slow. The form of the biped would draw too much attention from other of that kind. The deer form was the answer. Quick and strong, but more importantly, it would be natural for a deer to run away from the noise outside. It would draw little attention.

As he exited the ship, his body began the alteration, slowly at first and then with more speed. He was operating almost entirely on hormonal energy at this point, and he'd pay dearly for it in the long run. It would take weeks for him to recoup, but that was not important right now. All that was important was to survive — at any cost.

Deer Run

As the blades of the helicopter slowed, Oliver opened his eyes and took a breath. He hated flying, but most of all he hated flying in helicopters. As far as he could tell, they weren't made to fly. They defied all the natural laws. But this had been the worst flight ever. As they had approached the thin separation in the thick foliage of the mountain forest, he couldn't believe there was any way for the two copters to slip safely between the two lines of trees. Space was simply too tight. As he had closed his eyes and gripped his knees with white-knuckled hands, he imagined one of the helicopter's rotors clipping a tree branch, forcing the copter into the path of the other one. The two copters falling to earth in a massive fireball seemed to be more of a premonition of what was about to happen than his vivid imagination.

Although not a religious man by nature, Oliver gave a prayer of thanks as he opened the door and climbed out. By some miracle, they were still alive. He tried not to think about the return flight out of the wooded canyon. Maybe he'd stay until a road was built. It probably wouldn't take more than six months.

Leaning over to avoid the slowly turning rotors, Oliver glanced around at the surroundings. About fifty to seventy-five yards ahead the metallic hump they'd seen from the air lay mostly submerged in the side of the mountain.

"Damn! Can you believe it?" He said to no one in particular. He almost straightened up to get a better look then realized he was still under the rotors. He scurried away from the copter, cursing at it quietly under his breath.

Oliver jogged a safe distance from the helicopter, then stopped to study the mysterious object again. He stood there for a moment, appreciating his first sighting of a legitimate UFO when he noticed a large stag suddenly appeared from nowhere. *Had it come from the ship? No, that didn't make sense. It probably had been there all along,* Oliver thought. *I just didn't notice it until it starting running.* Such a majestic form of nature was in sharp contrast to the alien form behind it. The deer continued to gallop down the deep chasm favoring one leg, apparently frightened by the noisy intrusion of his sanctuary. As it neared the two helicopters, it made a sudden and ungraceful detour up the left side of the chasm. As it turned, Oliver noticed the bright red blood stain on its neck and caught the glint of sunlight on metal. Had something been sticking from its neck? He couldn't be sure.

Oliver squinted his eyes closed for a second then reopened them to be sure of what he saw, but by the time he looked again the deer was at the crest of the channel and had turned away from him.

"Did you see that?" He asked as James came up from behind him.

"Yeah, a deer — a real beauty. They're common in these mountains," James answered.

"Did you notice anything unusual about it?" Oliver asked as they jogged towards the other men exiting from the second copter.

"No, can't say I did, but I didn't get a very good look. Mostly just saw its backside."

They joined the other two men from the second copter. As the four of them strolled towards the UFO, Oliver quickly determined he had been the only one to get a good look at the deer. No one else had noticed anything unusual about it. Oliver began to wonder what he'd seen himself.

They were still fifty yards from the ship when they saw Pat sprinting through the gully following almost the exact path of the deer. *She's limping some too*, Oliver thought *and favoring her left side. What's going on here?* He wondered. As she drew nearer, she shouted at the top of her lungs between gasps for air.

"Get outta here. It's going to blow! Get out!"

All four men stopped short in their tracks as Pat's warning reached them.

"What did she say?" James asked, the color draining from his face, suggesting he had really understood.

Oliver made a quick decision. "No time—just do what she says. Back to the copters—now!"

Without hesitation, the other three men followed their boss's order and hightailed it back to their respective copters. Oliver hung back a little and waited for Pat to catch up. As the two of them ran towards the copters, he couldn't help but ask.

"What's going on here? Did you get pictures?" Oliver noticed the bruises and scrapes on her face and neck. A fresh trickle of blood stained her right temple, and deep creases of pain lined her face.

"No time . . . " Pat gasped, then came to an abrupt stop. Her right hand flew to her neck, a look of anguish deepening the lines of her face.

"Oh, God, my camera. It's still in the ship." She started to turn back towards the ship, but Oliver grabbed her arm.

"No time," he repeated her own words as he dragged her towards the helicopters. They reached the copter and climbed in, gazing out the window to study the alien object. It had taken on a strange glow, resembling hot flowing lava.

"We've got to get away from it." Pat voice was little more than a whimper.

She needn't have worried. James had already started the rotors.

As the two copters lifted from the ground almost simultaneously, the second copter drifted towards them then, with a sudden jerk, veered in the opposite direction towards the brightly glowing sphere. The pilot fought for control while at the same time climbing for altitude. Meanwhile, James struggled to keep his own copter from crashing into the trees on either side. The crosswinds of the mountain made it difficult for both pilots to judge which direction to turn their sticks.

James finally managed to get enough altitude to get above the searing wind. The second helicopter was not so fortunate. The wind caught the copter under its belly, pushing it down the chasm towards the alien vessel.

"Pull back—pull back, Jerry!" James yelled. Oliver reached over and grabbed James' shoulder.

"Steady there, James. Jerry knows what he's doing." It suddenly dawned on him why James was so concerned. The two pilots had come to work at B.I.U.F.O. at the same time, having flown together in Iraq. James was watching one of his best friends fight for his life.

After a struggle which seemed to take hours but actually lasted only a few seconds, Jerry finally mastered the controls, and the helicopter stabilized about twenty yards above the glowing sphere. He had just started his upward descent when the alien ship reached critical mass. The resulting fireball enveloped the helicopter like the flames of a campfire consumes the unsuspecting moth.

Oliver watched his pilot closely as James pressed his face hard against the window, staring for several moments at the spectacle below. Finally, James leaned back in his seat and through tear stained eyes, turned and looked at Oliver and Pat.

"He was a better pilot than me," he said simply. "He didn't deserve to die."

THE ALIEN FINALLY STOPPED his flight up the mountain, leaning heavily against a tree to rest and watch the scene below. As he relaxed his body, it returned to the hunter-survivor form so it could continue to heal itself. He turned in time to see the ship that had carried him across light-years of space explode in a glorious fireball. He was surprised and delighted when the explosion engulfed one of the biped's machines, but he knew it was only the first of several encounters that would no doubt result in bipeds dying. At the same time, he had a new respect for this species. They only looked fragile. They might actually prove to be a worthy adversary, he thought, as he resumed his trek up the mountain and back to the cave that would now have to serve as his primary home, at least for a while longer.

Cover Up
Friday, April 1

Pat gazed out the office window to the postcard view of the Washington Monument. The Cherry blossoms were at their peak, and hundreds of tourists were busily strolling the gardens around the monument, taking thousands of pictures. The blossoms are early, Pat thought. Just like the winter thaw down in North Carolina. A month ago, the thaw had looked to be a blessing from heaven, but now, with what had happened since then, it appeared more of a curse from hell.

Three men sat across the table behind Pat listening to the tape of her story that had been made less than 24 hours after the disaster on the mountain. Oliver sat at one end of the table, separate from the council.

Separate from me as well, Pat noted. Despite telling herself differently, she was nervous about the meeting. 'Government bureaucracy can be a strange and dangerous animal,' her father had always told her. In the past couple of weeks, she'd witnessed it for herself.

She had begun to suspect something was up the day after the explosion of the UFO. She and Oliver had been flown to Washington D.C. for their debriefing where they'd been held in tight security; "protected" from the press, they'd been told. So it had been entirely by accident when she stumbled upon a copy of the morning paper. It had been left by someone in the room where she and Oliver were waiting before the debriefing. On the front page was the headline:

**MILITARY AIRCRAFT CRASHES IN
NORTH CAROLINA MOUNTAINS**

As she read on, she realized the story was a cover-up for what had really happened near Waynesboro. Her fears began to mount when she showed the paper to the official conducting the debriefing. He was obviously embarrassed and upset that the article had so carelessly been left in the room.

In the last month, she'd been interviewed only by government officials, given no access to legal counsel, although until recently she hadn't thought she'd need it, and kept completely isolated from the outside world. She'd only been allowed to send her parents a brief, censored telegram informing them she was fine and that she had been assigned to a vital mission which would have her out of touch for a while. Sending the telegram was preferred over email or phone because they could control what the final outcome of the telegram would be. Looking back, it had been the telegram that had warned her she was in a *lot* of trouble.

As the tape came to an end, one of the men across the table shut off the recorder. Pat took another moment to look out the window and wished she could be an innocent tourist enjoying the nation's capital and the cherry blossoms, and then she returned to her seat. The three men stared at her for several seconds as though each of them was waiting for the other to begin. Finally, the man who had turned off the tape, cleared his throat, smiled blandly and said, "Ms. Vogt, I'm William Hartford and this ..." nodding to his left, " ... is Mr. Stephen McAllister, and this ..." nodding to his right, "... is Dr. Henry O'Donnell. Of course, you know Mr. Sykes," he said as he nodded toward Oliver.

The formality of the names made Pat more nervous. *What is this, a trial, or what?* She decided to find out. Resting her arms on the table, she leaned across it and smiled demurely at the three men.

"Well, Bill, Steve and Henry, is this a trial or what?"

The three men looked at each other as though uncertain how to answer the question. Finally, Bill said, "No, Ms. Vogt, this is not a trial. We simply want to ask you a few more questions."

"That's good, Bill," Pat replied, continuing to ignore his attempts at formality. "Because if it were a trial, I would have to insist on having my attorney here." She turned and winked at Oliver and was surprised when he didn't so much as return a smile. The two of them had always been on good terms. What was going on here?

"Ms. Vogt, as Mr. Hartford said, we only want to ask you a few questions." Dr. O'Donnell now took the lead. "You must understand. What happened on that mountain is of major importance to national security. We just want to be clear about exactly what did happen."

"I've told you what happened. It's all on the tape we just listened to. What more do you want to know? By the way, who are you guys? Really. I don't mean your names. I want to know what agency you belong. And what is this meeting? If it's not a trial, what exactly is it?"

Hartford looked first to O'Donnell, then to McAllister before answering. "I'm with the Defense Department, Ms. Vogt. Dr. O'Donnell is with NASA, and Mr. McAllister is with the CIA. This meeting is, well, a meeting to determine your future with B.I.U.F.O. and to determine what, if any, actions are to be taken following the incident on the mountain."

"What? The three of you are supposed to determine 'my future with B.I.U.F.O.,' but you aren't even with B.I.U.F.O. Doesn't that seem a little strange?" Pat turned towards Oliver. "Oliver, what exactly is going on here? I feel like I'm under attack. I didn't do anything wrong up there. Oliver, tell them I didn't do anything wrong." Pat pleaded with her former boss. Oliver did not answer but simply looked down at the notepad in front of him.

Finally, without looking up, he said, "Just tell them what they want to know, Pat. They're conducting this investigation at the request of the White House. If you don't cooperate, it'll only make things worse for you."

Pat groaned softly under her breath. *The White House. Oh shit, I've had it now. They think I blew the damn UFO up. They don't believe a word I said.* She felt herself tearing up from frustration. The stress of the last month that had been all bottled inside her threatened to escape all at once. No! She'd not cry in front of these bastards. She'd never give them the satisfaction. She straightened her back and glared at the three men across the table.

"I refuse to say anything else until I have legal counsel. Now, if you gentlemen will excuse me..."

"Ms. Vogt, that won't be necessary," McAllister spoke up for the first time. "You have made your position perfectly clear." He glanced at O'Donnell and Hartford. "Now, we'll make ours clear as well."

"You acted out of poor judgment on your last mission. What's more, you disobeyed a direct command from your superior, Mr. Sykes. You were a young rookie at B.I.U.F.O., on your first assignment. You acted rashly and without forethought. In so doing, you greatly jeopardized the mission and placed the rest of your team in grave danger. Two men lost their lives on your account."

"We will never know exactly what happened inside the structure that was dug into the mountain nor will we ever know what the structure really was. You saw to that. You claim there was an alien inside and that it destroyed its own ship. But no one else saw anything remotely like what you described. The only thing reported leaving the ship was you and a deer." McAllister paused for a moment and leafed through a folder of papers in front of him. When he looked up, his jaw was firmly set, and his eyes stared intensely into Pat's eyes.

"We're sweeping this one under the rug, Ms. Vogt, and you will cooperate. If you don't, you will be arrested as a spy and charged with espionage. We can make a case, a solid case, that you were operating for a foreign interest and your purpose was to find and destroy a top-secret military craft which had gone down on U.S. soil.

"The story we expect you would prefer to support is this. You have been under a lot of pressure lately. It took everything you had to get accepted into B.I.U.F.O. You then lost two team members on your first mission through a bad call on your part. It was more than you could handle. You've accepted B.I.U.F.O.'s offer to undergo extensive psychotherapy as well as accepting their suspension. Six months from now you will voluntarily resign from the bureau. You will never mention anything about the Waynesboro assignment. If anyone asks, you will simply say it was a difficult time of your life, and you'd rather not discuss it. Is that understood?"

Pat sat in her seat, her back still straight, icy fingers running down her spine. They'd set her up to take the fall. Whatever it was that had been on the mountain, B.I.U.F.O. was not prepared to share it with the rest of the world. But what about the alien? Had it died in the explosion? What if it hadn't? It could still be out there somewhere.

"Ms. Vogt." Hartford's voice interrupted her thoughts. "Do you understand what Mr. McAllister said?"

Pat nodded slowly. "I understand."

She glanced over to Oliver, but he would not meet her gaze. He knows something that he isn't saying. He saw something, and he's afraid to say what. Somehow, she had to find out. What happened on the mountain might be swept under the rug for the rest of the world, but she would never forget it. She had walked through an alien spaceship, had almost been killed by its occupant. More importantly, it might still be alive. She'd cooperate, but for only one reason. If the alien were still alive, it would be up to her to find it. Something she could not do if she were behind bars.

A vivid picture of the alien standing over her flashed in her mind. It had meant to kill her but had misjudged her. She'd gotten a good look at it and despite being dazed by the blows from those cylinders; she would be able to recognize it again. How could such an ugly beast hope to hide? Even if it was mistaken for a panther which it only vaguely resembled, how many reports of panther attacks did you hear about in this part of the world? It would turn up, and when it did, she would be around to be sure it received the proper welcome it deserved.

She tossed her head back in a carefree manner. "I understand perfectly, gentlemen, and you can count on me to cooperate fully. You've made it very clear. Is there anything else you need of me?"

"No, I think that will be all, Ms. Vogt," Hartford said as he glanced at his two companions for the last time. "We appreciate your cooperation."

Pat stood up to leave. As she turned towards the door, her eyes fell once more on Oliver who continued to study the pad of paper in front of him. *You know something, Oliver dear, and I'm going to find out what role you played in this. You owe me that much.*

"Are you coming, Oliver?" She asked innocently. Oliver shook his head and without looking up said, "No, I have a couple of things to go over with Bill, uh, Mr. Hartford. I'll see you in the next day or so." *You bet your sweet ass you will*, Pat thought as she left the room. *You bet your sweet ass.*

THE COFFEE HOUSE WAS in the basement level of a run-down apartment house. Although Pat had walked by it dozens of times before, it had never been the kind of place she'd consider frequenting—until now. Now it was the perfect place, reasonably close to her home, but more importantly, it was dark and secluded. Oliver had made a good choice.

She hesitated at the top of the stairs. She wanted to look around her, to be sure no one had followed her but it would only make her seem that much more suspicious. With all her willpower she resisted the temptation. She'd been careful, and her father had taught her well how to keep from being followed. She was sure the van that had been parked outside her apartment was still there. She'd left her television running and a tape recording of extraneous sounds she had made a couple days ago. She had at least an hour before anyone listening in on the bug would suspect the was empty.

As nonchalantly as possible she strolled down the short flight of stairs as though she was going to her favorite neighborhood coffee house. Inside, she paused in the foyer, waiting for her eyes to adjust to the sudden darkness. The only word she could think of to describe Benny's Coffee House was dingy. No, two words —dark and gloomy. And perfect for the meeting with Oliver. She walked through the beaded curtain and into the main room. A middle-aged lady looked up from her *Reader's Digest* and smiled through heavily made-up lips.

Before Pat had a chance to describe Oliver to the lady, she pointed over to the far corner booth. Oliver sat there with a cup of coffee in front of him and a thick cloud of smoke partially obscuring his face. He's taken up smoking again, Pat observed as she walked over to the table. After six months of proudly accusing everyone else of not having the willpower to stop, he'd picked it up again. I'm not the only one under a lot of pressure these days.

"Thanks for agreeing to meet with me," Pat said as she slipped into the booth across from Oliver. "No problem," Oliver replied simply. "I can't stay long. My secretary is covering for me, but ..." He didn't bother to finish the sentence.

"I understand. Let me get right to the questions then. What did you see on that mountain?"

Oliver looked down at his coffee and back to Pat. "Nothing, really. It was all in the report. We didn't have much time. I saw a large metallic object dug into the mountainside. It was difficult to determine its shape, but I'd guess it was spherical or oblong. When we first approached the site, it was resting quietly, but by the time we landed, it had begun to glow." The words sounded well rehearsed as though memorized straight from the report.

The hostess came over to the table to take Pat's order. Pat looked at the thick brew in Oliver's cup and decided to pass on Benny's special coffee. The hostess nodded and left without saying a word.

"What else? Was there anything else? Think hard. I know you saw some-thing you're afraid to say. Damn it! Oliver, I'm taking the rap on this one. Okay, I'm willing, but you've got to help me. I've got to know what you saw."

Oliver hesitated. He studied his cup, twirling the dark liquid as though he might find the answer in the bottom of the cup. After almost a minute, he shook his head and without looking up, said, "It's all in the report. I don't know what you're looking for from me, but I can't help you." He picked up his coffee cup and took a sip, then sat back in the booth as though he was fin-ished with the interview. Then he suddenly sat forward again.

"I like you, Pat. I really do. I liked you the moment you walked into my office for our first interview. So, I'm going to tell you something. It probably won't make any difference, but you need to hear it from someone."

"You're not a team player. Oh, you're a great individual player. You've got a lot going for you, but you're not a team player. And in this world, if you're not willing to go with what's good for the team, well...you get cut."

Pat nodded. "And you're a team player, right?"

"Yeah, that's right." Oliver took another long sip of coffee and winced at the bitter taste. He lit another cigarette, and then grinned sheepishly. His face turned red. "I'm not going to smoke much longer. Just until this stuff blows over."

Pat nodded. "Just one more question. Are you sure what you saw was a deer?"

"Yeah, I'm sure. I'm not as much a city boy as most people think. I was raised on a farm. We had deer all over the place. It was definitely a deer. A stag to be accurate; quite handsome."

Pat picked up Oliver's cup of coffee and drained it. She put the cup back down and patted his hand laying on the table. "Thanks. You've been a lot of help," she said with an edge of sarcasm she couldn't quite keep out of her voice.

She started to slide out of the booth. Oliver grabbed her arm. "Let it go, Pat. You'll have a much happier life."

Pat extricated his fingers from her wrist. "I'd like to. I just can't." She turned and walked out of the coffee house.

OLIVER SAT PUFFING on his cigarette long after Pat had left. *I should have told her*, he thought as he studied the thick cloud of smoke which hung like a veil in front of him. Maybe she could have explained why the deer had been bleeding and what had been sticking out of its neck. And perhaps, she could have told him why those two details had been left out of the report, although every other minuscule little point had been included.

He crushed the cigarette out in the ashtray and left its corpse with its companions. No, he had done the smart thing. What was important to remember was that the report had been censored. Someone had decided not to include the details about the deer. Someone on the team more important than himself.

"I better take my own advice," he muttered as he slid out of the booth and dropped a couple bucks on the table. "Shut-up and go with the team."

Part Two

The Miracle of Birth

C-Section
Monday, June 7, 2003

T he giant dog waddled into the exam room. For a moment, Dr. Allan Pritchard thought the dog would get stuck in the doorway because her mid-section distended, and as wide as the door. But she passed with a couple of inches to spare.

"Looks like a cross between a St. Bernard and a double-wide mobile home," he said with a smile to the petite lady being dragged along by the hemp rope tied to the dog's neck.

"Oh, but such a sweetheart she is," Alice Parker replied. "She wound up on our doorstep a couple of weeks ago, in a motherly way. She was wet, cold, and hungry. One look with those soft brown eyes and I was hooked. She's come close to eating us out of house and home since then, but I can think of worse ways to end up in the poorhouse."

Alice and her family had been clients of Dr. Pritchard ever since he'd opened his practice in Waynesboro six years ago. Like most of his clients, the Parkers were good ole southern folk, not high on the cuff of life financially but with a wide-open heart. Somehow they always managed to pay their bills, although maybe not as quickly as he'd like all the time. At last count, Alice had three other dogs and no telling how many barn cats, and her two-footed family was almost as large. If the truth was known, a hundred-pound pregnant bitch was the last visitor they needed on their doorstep, but for some reason, Providence seldom stopped to consider such details.

Allan noticed two of her strapping teenage sons standing awkwardly outside the door. *Thank goodness for strong help.* He'd already called Dawn, his receptionist, and right-arm assistant, but it would be another twenty minutes before she would be dressed and at the clinic. Hopefully, by then he'd know whether a C-section was in the making for the early morning hours or not.

Gazing down at the rotund mid-section of the dog, he suspected that would be the case.

"Boys, how 'bout coming in here and giving me a hand. Given the size of mamma dog here, I don't think we'll lift her on the table. But I'd like to check to see if she has a puppy in the birth canal. She's less likely to drag us into the next county if you two help hold while I do it."

Dr. Pritchard turned to Alice and smiled at her. "No offense ma'am, but I'd like you to take the bow. Get in front and talk to her. All this is really frightening to her, and she could use your comforting."

"No offense taken, Doctor Pritchard. Lord knows, I ain't got much control over her. I'm no more than a fly pestering at her neck with this here rope."

Alice relinquished the rope to her two sons and slipped in front. She knelt down in front of the dog and spoke softly in her ear. "It'll be alright, Molly. Doc here is going to take good care of you."

She looked up at Allan with a sheepish grin. "Don't rightly know what her real name is, but she reminded me of Molly O'Brien when she was carrying her triplets. Since she don't come to any other name, we figured Molly was as good as any."

"And better than some," Allan replied as he slipped the long fingers of his right hand into the latex glove. "I'm going check to see how far along she is and see if I can tell if we've got a pup lodged in the canal."

"If she's breech, does that mean you'll have to cut the puppy up to get it out of her?" Buster, Alice's younger son, asked.

"Where'd you get such an idea?" Alice asked, her eyes growing large at the thought.

"That's what Doc Williams had to do with Jimmy's milking cow a few months ago. She couldn't have the calf, so he went in and sliced it up and yanked it out piece by piece."

Alice turned to him, her face white with fright. "I don't care so much if we save the pups, that's not what's most important here, but you won't have to put Molly through such an ordeal, will ya Doc?"

Allan smiled reassuringly. "Don't worry, Alice. Small animal practice is a bit different from a farm practice. I'm just going to see what's what in here first. If we have a breach, we'll simply do a C-section. Molly will be asleep, and she won't feel anything. But let's not jump to conclusions." He smeared the glove with lubricant.

"Hold her real still, fellas. This may be a bit uncomfortable for her."

A soft groan of anguish worried Allan at first as he inserted the gloved finger into the dog's vagina, but he relaxed a little when he realized the sound came from Molly's concerned owner. Molly continued to stand patiently, apparently unconcerned by the invasion of her privacy.

"It's times like this that I'm glad I have such large hands," Allan said to no one in particular. He felt around for a few seconds and didn't like what he found. "There's a pup in the canal, no doubt about it, and it feels huge. How long did you say she'd been in labor before you called me?"

"I'd say a good two, maybe three hours," Alice replied. "At least half that time she's really been straining, but she wasn't having any luck."

Allan pulled his finger out, slipped the glove off his hand, and tossed it in the trash can. "Well, we could take an x-ray to confirm what I suspect, but all indications point to a C-section."

"To tell the truth, Doc, if it's all the same to you, I'd just as soon avoid the extra expense of the x-ray. As it is, I'll have to pay for the surgery over time, but you know I'm good for it."

"I'm not worried about that, Alice. You just sit here with Molly and make her as comfortable as you can. I'm going to get the surgery suite set up so we can begin as soon as Dawn gets here. We'll take good care of mamma and the pups."

Alice patted the dog's broad head, and Allan noticed her eyes glistened more than usual. "Take good care of her, Doc. I've gotten real attached to her. Like I said, I'm not so concerned with the pups. If it's a question of her or the pups, save old Molly here."

Allan understood what Alice was saying. There were to be no heroics trying to save the puppies if they were in trouble.

"KEEP THE ANESTHETIC as light as you can and still keep her down, Dawn. I've already used a local so she won't feel the incision," Allan said as he started to drape Molly's newly shaved and washed belly. "We want to get in and out as quickly as possible and get her awake."

Dawn nodded and smiled. Allan knew what she was thinking. In the six years she'd worked with him, she'd heard the same speech many times before. More than once he'd used her as his sounding board extolling the virtues of quick surgery. Not so fast that you were sloppy, but not so darn fired slowly that you lost the patient from too much anesthetic. She squeezed the bag of the anesthetic machine, then refilled it with fresh oxygen.

The two worked like a well-oiled team. They both knew what to expect from each other. That's why even though Allan had two other fully trained and qualified technicians, he still called Dawn for the emergency surgeries. Besides, she lived the closest to the clinic, and she was divorced with only a teenage daughter. She didn't mind the late-night calls. At least that's what she told him whenever he asked.

Allan finished clamping the last drape in place and reached for the scalpel. He made a bold incision along the midline between the two rows of engorged mammary glands and watched as the blood mixed with the milk of one of the glands where it had been nicked. It always fascinated him that tissue could bleed milk as well as blood. He sponged the incision for a moment before making a second incision through the connective tissue of the midline of the abdominal muscles.

"It feels more like I'm operating on a horse than a dog," Allan said to Dawn as he finished the incision and laid the scalpel down on the instrument tray. "Do you have a box and towels ready? In just a minute, we'll be up to our knees in squirming yelping pups."

"All ready, Dr. Pritchard. You start tossing them out, and I'll start catching them. Don't worry about the umbilical cords. I've got the suture material ready to tie them off."

Allan smiled behind his mask at Dawn's formal use of his title. It didn't make any difference how often he told Dawn it wasn't necessary to call him doctor after hours. Old habits die hard, and since she'd been in human medicine for five years before starting with him, she was trained to use the formal title long before she came to his clinic. Besides, as she often said, "once you're a doctor, you're always a doctor."

He reached into the incision and began to pull the right horn of the uterus out. As he did so, Molly's side collapsed to almost normal size. "Whoo-wee, we've got some large puppies here. I wonder if she mated with one of old man Jacob's Shetland ponies."

He rested the thick tubular uterus onto the surgery drape and worked to free the left horn from Molly's abdomen, looking for an area without major veins coursing through it to make the next incision. Blotting the glistening surface with several gauze sponges, he reached for the scalpel.

"How's she doing, Dawn?" Allan asked as he prepared to cut through the muscular organ.

"She's stable, and the color of her gums is nice and pink."

"How 'bout increasing her I.V. drip just a little. This is about the time her blood pressure is likely to drop."

"It's done," she replied in a few seconds.

"Good. Well, get ready for some pups that might resemble Shetland ponies." He slid the scalpel smoothly across the body of the uterus so he could pull all the puppies from both horns through the one incision.

Allan was always thankful when he cut into a uterus for his years of training at the emergency clinic where C-sections had become a routine piece of surgery. A cut too deep could leave one or more puppies missing a toe or worse. He made the incision lightly through the uterus, deftly stopping just short of the fetus that lay beneath.

Placing the scalpel back on the tray, Allan reached into the incision to pull out the first puppy. His hands made contact with the creamy white surface at the same time his eyes told him he was touching a huge pulsating maggot. Without thinking, he yanked his hands away and stepped away from the table, feeling an involuntary shudder course along his back.

"What is it, Doctor? What's wrong?" Dawn asked at the sudden movement. "Did you hit a bleeder?"

Allan stood frozen to the spot, a good two feet from the table, his hands clutching the surgery gown at his chest. A wave of nausea passed through his body and up his throat. He swallowed once, twice, tasting the foul stomach acid.

"No, no bleeder. Everything is fine—I think," he finally managed to say.

He felt a droplet of sweat trickle down his temple and had the absurd urge to ask Dawn to wipe his brow but refrained. Taking a final gulp, he stepped back to the spot he had so recently vacated. He stared into the incision at the pulsating mass partially hidden by the pooling blood that seeped from the incised uterus but didn't take his hands from where they were glued to his gown.

"Are you okay, Dr. Pritchard?" Dawn asked as she started to rise from the stool she sat on next to the anesthetic machine.

"I'm fine; stay where you are," he said too brusquely. "I'll let you know when I need your help," he added in a softer tone.

Taking the longest forceps from the surgery tray, Allan gently prodded the blunt end of the mass. It retracted itself away from the probe. As it did so, he could see what appeared to be a similar mass lying beneath the first one. *How many of these horrible things could there be*? He wondered. As the shock of the discovery subsided, the inquisitive mind of the scientist began to emerge. *How could these things have gotten inside her? Were they parasitic? Had they eaten the puppies that should have been in there?*

Allan noticed the pool of blood slowly expanding, seeping from a medium-sized vessel. He clamped it off with forceps then cleared the pool with a wad of sponges. Molly still needed help in delivering whatever it was inside her. With another shudder, he reached into the incision and gently cupped his hands around the swollen lump. It had a firmer feel than he had expected and was warm to the touch. Still feeling the pulsating motion through his gloves, he fought a strong urge to withdraw his hands.

Allan pulled the mass out of the uterus. It slipped out with a sucking sound like pulling a shoe out of the mud. At about eight inches, it was much longer than he had imagined. Pulling the wormlike mass out of Molly's abdomen, Allan looked for some sign of an umbilical cord but couldn't find one. As the other end reached the surface where he could see it, he noticed it was lightly attached to the inner lining of the uterus and was a little more sharply tapered. *Could this be its head*? He wondered. He wiped the glistening surface with the partially blood-soaked sponges and as he did, heard a gasp of astonishment escape from Dawn's lips.

"Oh my God!" she whispered when she finally found her voice. "What in God's name . . . ?"

Allan gently laid the larvae-like mass in the towel-lined box that Dawn had prepared—the box that had been intended for cute, cuddly puppies. The lump wiggled much like a newborn pup, but there was no chance of confusing the two.

"I don't know what in God's creation it is, or if it even is of God's doing, but there are plenty more where that one came from," Allan replied as he pulled the second squirming mass from the incision. By this time the beads of sweat dripped from both sides of his face, but he ignored the tickling sensation. He was repulsed by the eight-inch maggot-like masses and at the same time drawn by curiosity.

Surely they can't live, he thought. *But what if they did? What would they grow into, and from where did they come? How could nature be so arbitrary with such a miracle as birth?* He continued to pull them out of each horn of the uterus until six white sausages laid in a row in the box.

Finally convinced he had the final one, he looked up for the first time at Dawn's pale face. He tried to smile and was glad the mask hid the feeble attempt. "Well Dawn, aren't you going to goo-goo over the little bundles of joy like you always do?"

"No way!" she almost screamed at him, an edge of hysteria in her voice. "I'm not touching those horrid things, whatever they are." She stared down at the box despite herself. "What are they, anyway?"

"Well, they might be the ugliest litter of pups ever recorded, but I kinda doubt it." Allan joked in an attempt to lighten up the atmosphere of the room. "All I can guess is they are some bizarre parasite that somehow made its way into Molly's reproductive tract. Not that I've ever seen or heard of such a thing."

"What are you going to do?" Dawn asked.

"I'm going to finish this piece of surgery, first. Alice wanted me to go ahead and spay Molly if possible. Given what we just delivered, I think it's an excellent idea."

"But what are you going to do with those?" Dawn pointed to the box, a look of disgust still glued to her face.

"I don't know. I suppose we could save them for a barbecue this weekend." He knew as soon as he said it that it was a mistake. He'd been accused more than once of having a sick twist to his sense of humor.

"Dr. Pritchard! Sometimes you say the most horrid things—really."

"Well, don't worry about them. I'll dispose of them. I'm sure whatever they are, they don't have a chance of living."

Several minutes went by without either one talking as Allan concentrated on the surgery. As he finished removing Molly's enlarged uterus, he paused and looked at Dawn. "Alice wasn't concerned with saving the puppies as much as she was with Molly. I think it might be best just to tell her the puppies were born dead. No reason to have her all worried about something we can't explain."

"You don't have to worry about me, Doc," Dawn replied, glancing down at the box one last time. "As far as I'm concerned, the less said about this night, the better."

Mother Molly

Despite the unexpected development of the surgery, Molly came through with flying colors. Dawn's masterful handling of the anesthesia had her chewing at the endotracheal tube as Allan tied the last skin suture.

"She'll be up and around in no time," Dr. Pritchard said as he snapped his gloves into the trash can. "You are one fine anesthetist, Dawn. Despite our surprise, you maintained her at just the right level. I might have to start paying you for these late nights." He smiled at her and laid his arm around her shoulders.

"Damn right you're going to pay me," she chided back. "Any more like this and you won't be able to pay me enough to come in."

Walking into the prep room, Allan slipped out of his gown and, folding it into a ball, tossed it in the general direction of the clothes hamper.

"If you don't mind, how about going up front and let Alice know Molly is doing fine. I'll be up in a few minutes after I clean her up a bit. Tell Alice we'll be keeping Molly overnight but to call us in the morning around nine. No, better make that ten. Considering the hour, I might be in a little later than usual."

"Do you think we can keep you out of here until at least after eight?" Dawn asked. The entire staff was always giving their boss a hard time about the long hours he kept.

"Well, we'll see," he answered as he turned to walk back into surgery then stuck his head back out the door. "Remember, the pups were born dead, but Molly is doing great. Tell her she can come back and say goodnight to her in about ten minutes. Then come back and help me get her off the table."

Allan walked back into the surgery room, untying his mask as he went. He tossed the disposable cap and mask in the general direction of the trash can and watched as they fluttered in the air like two wounded ducks, then fell short of the can by about a foot. As he stood looking at them lying on the floor, he could hear Laura's voice reverberating in his mind. Although his wife had been dead for four years, she was never far from his thoughts.

"Allan Pritchard, if you aren't the messiest man I have ever seen. Why in the world would God be so cruel as to have me fall in love with such a messy man?"

"Probably has something to do with keeping balance in the world, sweetie," he'd answer back. "If we were all as neat and perfect as you, He'd not have any fun watching us."

Allan caught himself staring at the cap and mask lying next to the trash can. Four years since the fire that took Laura and Todd and their presence was still so strong. *When will it end?* He wondered. Would the pain of his loss ever leave him alone? When would he stop hearing their voices and seeing their faces every time he missed a trash can, or cleaned the dishes, or did any of a hundred other mundane, day-to-day activities? How long would he have to detour around Waynesboro Elementary School whenever he traveled north out of town?

He strolled over to the debris lying on the floor, picked it up, and placed it in the can. *That's for you Laura, to let you know I still love you.* As he straightened up, his eyes fell on the delivery box. He wasn't surprised to find three of the white sausages had already turned a pale gray and were no longer moving.

It's just as well, he thought. *It saves me the trouble of figuring out how to put them to sleep.* But as he continued to stare at the box, he noticed something about the three that were still alive that had escaped his first inspection. Towards the tapered end, what he imagined was the head end, were two dark splotches, less than a centimeter across. Allan bent lower to get a better look. Sure enough, each of the living larvae had the marks, but they were missing from the dead ones. What could it mean?

The scientist in him began speculating. *It could mean that is the hind end, and those are developing gonads indicating that those three are males*, he thought. *It would make sense the males would live longer than the females*; he kidded with himself. But no, he was pretty sure that was the front end, assuming the front end would be the one attached to the uterine lining for nourishment.

Ok, if he assumed the dots were at the front end, what did they represent? *Of course*, he thought, *those must be primitive eyespots. But if that was the case, then why didn't the other three larvae have them?*

He took one of the towels from the pile and used it to pick up one of the dead larvae. For some reason, he was not anxious to handle them without something between him and their white skin. He turned it over in his hands, confirming there were no marks. Inspecting the other two revealed the same information.

"Very interesting, Doctor," he said softly to himself. "But what does it mean?"

As though to answer, a low moan startled him so much he almost dropped the larva before realizing the sound came from Molly. He took the three dead larvae and placed them in a plastic trash bag. He started to tie it shut but stopped. He still needed to decide what to do with the other three. Molly moaned again to remind him that she needed his attention first.

Allan placed the trash bag next to the box and began untying Molly from the surgery table. Laying her on her side, he placed a few clean sponges against her incision to absorb the seeping blood. He stood there for a couple of minutes, stroking the soft fur behind her ear.

"Poor Molly, you're going to wake up expecting to be a mother, and you're going to be awfully disappointed. I guess you'll just have to give all that love to those kids out there. Maybe they can be your pups instead."

He heard Dawn come back into the treatment room adjacent to the surgery suite. "Here comes the cavalry to help this old doctor get your large carcass off the table and into a cage. Lord help me not to throw my back out again."

Dawn pushed the surgery door open and propped it with the rubber wedge. "Are you sure you don't want me to get those boys back here to help us with this?" she asked. Dawn knew the long history of her doctor's back ailments.

"No. I don't want to take any chance of them seeing those things." He pointed to the box and bag. "They'd have fun scaring the dickens out of their mom. I promise to be careful and to bend at the knees. Let's just put her in the recovery cage in the treatment room. We can move her to a run in the morning when she's awake enough to walk out there on her own."

After moving the half-awake dog to her cage, Allan straightened up slowly and was relieved to feel only a mild twinge in his back. It'd be a little sore in the morning but nothing he couldn't handle.

"I see half of them are already dead," Dawn remarked as she walked into the surgery room to clean up.

"Yeah. I doubt the other three will be far behind."

"You are going to put them to sleep, aren't you?" Dawn said with a note of surprise in her voice.

Allan hesitated before answering. He hated to lie to Dawn, but putting animals to sleep was one thing he hadn't been able to do since Laura and Todd's accident.

Dawn walked over to him and touched his arm. "You want me to do it?" She asked in a soft voice. He felt her shudder as she said it.

"No. It's alright. You just go home and get whatever rest you can with what's left of the night. Marva can clean up in the morning. I'll leave her a note."

Dawn stood there for a couple of seconds, her hand still resting on his arm, as though trying to think of something else to say. Then she sighed softly and dropped her arm.

"You're the boss, Doc. Don't stay here the rest of the night cleaning up though. I know your tricks. I'll be mad as a wet hornet if I find out that's what you did."

He smiled at her. "I promise to be a good little boy and go home and get some sleep. You run on home."

Allan started back into surgery then remembered the Parkers.

"Did they want to see Molly?" He asked.

"No. They said if she were still sleeping they'd just wait until morning. They were real tired too."

"Good night, Dawn, and thanks — really."

"Anytime, Doc. Just not for a couple more days, okay?"

He laughed. "I promise."

After Dawn left, Allan walked back into surgery and gazed down at the three living lumps. They continued to pulsate and squirm next to each other just like three newborn pups.

But they're not pups, he thought. *They're probably not even mammals. God only knows what they are. Probably would grow up to be giant flies. They'd be frustrated all their lives because they'd never be able to find a large enough heap of cow dung to fly around.* He smiled at his ridiculous thought.

He knelt down in front of the box and felt another warning twinge from his back. He continued to stare at them for a couple of minutes. Finally, he reached out with his hand. Like what would they feel? They'd been warm when he'd removed them from the womb, but that would have been expected. The uterus was a nicely regulated incubator. His hand continued to close the gap. Two inches from the closest one, he stopped as a shudder formed between his shoulder blades.

Oh, go ahead. Don't be silly. He touched it and was surprised to find it felt like a hairless puppy. It was warm and soft. *Well, it sure the hell isn't cuddly,* he thought. *But two out of three isn't bad.*

Allan watched in amazement as the lump turned its "head" in the direction of his hand. It knew he was there. It was responding to his touch. He suddenly realized what it was looking for. The tapered end sucked in and out, looking like a fish out of the water. It brushed against his hand then reached for his small finger.

It was trying to suckle his finger! He jerked his hand back and cracked it against the surgery table above his head.

"Sorry guy. I'm not your mamma. I don't know who is, but I know it isn't me."

Allan watched the three small lumps of life as they continued to wiggle next to each other. Could they be puppies that just hadn't fully developed? The thought was ridiculous. As much as he had hated embryology class in vet school and despite the number of hours he'd spent asleep in it, he'd learned enough to know there was no larval stage in the dog's fetal development.

Well, the choice is simple, he thought. *I can either put the tiny creatures to sleep and stay up the rest of the night with a guilty conscience, or I can let them live and spend the evening trying to figure out how to keep them alive.* Either way, it didn't look like sleep was on the agenda, but as he considered the alternative he knew which one he'd choose.

Whatever they were, they had made it this far, and they had every right to live. If they died, it wouldn't be at his hands. And until he knew more about them, he'd treat them like three orphan puppies. He couldn't see putting them back with Molly. His entire staff would probably quit on him if they walked into the clinic in the morning to three eight-inch maggots suckling on a hundred-pound hound.

He could give them some of Molly's milk though. She had plenty, and if they had been pups, that first milk would be important. Dr. Pritchard walked back into the treatment room where Molly lay on her side in her cage, snoring softly. He took a small bowl from the cabinet and began milking the thick colostrum from Molly's glands. She opened one big brown eye and stared without much enthusiasm at him, then closed her eye and went back to sleep. He collected enough to give each of the pups at least a couple of feedings. He noticed as he gathered the milk, he had suddenly shifted how he thought about them. They were no longer unknown lumps but had suddenly become puppies.

"Very strange puppies, but puppies," he muttered to himself as he poured the warm milk into a baby bottle. *If Dawn comes back and finds me feeding these little things, she'll probably have me committed, and I wouldn't argue with her.*

He walked back into surgery with the bottle. Would he have to hold them in his hands to get them to nurse? The thought made him feel a little queasy. Although he'd decided they should have a chance at life, they were still repulsive. He picked up the towel lying next to the box and picked the largest one up with the towel, placing the nurser in front of its "head." Immediately the suckling motions resumed as the white lump of life tried to drain the bottle.

Amazed at the appetite and the volume of milk it could hold, he realized he'd have to milk Molly again if he was going to give them two feedings of the colostrum as he'd planned. When the bottle was about a third empty, he placed the pup back into the box and picked up the next one. It also tried to suck the bottle dry, but when he picked up the third one, the smallest of the litter, it refused to take the nipple.

"Not a good sign, little one," he said as he tried to stick the nipple in its small orifice. "Let's see; I do have the right end, don't I?"

He checked and found the eyespots. That wasn't the problem. He continued for another ten minutes with little results. Finally, frustrated with the battle, he took an infant feeding tube from the next room and fed the remaining milk through the tube.

"If you think I'm going to feed you in that manner every time, you better rethink it," he told the tiny pup as he placed it back with the other two. "You're too ugly for such special treatment."

He walked back into the treatment room and glanced at the wall clock. Almost 2:30. He rubbed his tired eyes. With a little luck, he could still get a couple of hours of sleep. He quickly milked another bottle of colostrum from Molly then grabbed a couple more towels and a heating pad, placing everything in the box with the pups. As he started to leave, he noticed the garbage bag with the three dead pups. He picked it up and dropped it into the special can reserved for deceased pets for animal control to pick up.

It didn't occur to him until late the next morning that it would have been a good idea to save the bodies for autopsy, but by then, animal control had already made their rounds.

Biogentrix
Tuesday, June 8

Allan slept a dreamless five hours and awoke groggy and grumpy. He stumbled into the bathroom and was in midstream of emptying his bladder when his eyes fell on the three white sausages lying in the box next to the tub.

He staggered back in shock, the stream of warm urine spraying the carpet next to the john. Allan grabbed one of the spare towels he had brought home from the clinic and cleaned up the mess. As he did so, he remembered the previous evening's occurrences. Filling the sink with cold water, he soaked his head until he was able to open his eyes without them crossing. He hated mornings. A large part of staying up at all hours was because he knew when he finally gave in to sleep, it would mean going through the hell of waking up.

It hadn't been that bad when Laura and Todd were around. Todd was usually the first one to wake up. Allan remembered many mornings when his young son would sneak into his parents' bedroom and slide beneath the covers between the two of them. He missed those mornings. He missed a lot of things about those days.

When he could hold his breath no longer, Allan lifted his head out of the water and felt a familiar twinge of pain course down his lower back and into his right thigh. *Damn, not yet forty and already falling apart. Life isn't fair,* he thought, then chuckled. *Typical early morning thoughts. If any of my clients saw me in the morning before I'm fully awake, they'd think I was Dr. Jekyll and Mr. Hyde. Could this be the kindly Doc Pritchard, who coos over the puppies and kittens and extends credit to everyone who needs it?*

Allan shook his head, sending tiny water droplets spraying around the room, then reached for a fresh towel, being careful to pick up one of his own and not one from the clinic to save him from the displeasure of picking animal hair out of his mouth the rest of the morning.

He bent over slowly, partially supporting himself with his hands on his knees, and gazed into the box. He immediately realized the smallest pup had died during the night. He wasn't surprised.

"I wouldn't be surprised if they all croaked," he muttered. *Well, good morning Mr. Sunshine. Aren't we in a great mood this morning?* He decided to take a shower before feeding the remaining two pups. In his present attitude, he'd probably choke them to death. A shower and a cup of coffee had wondrous effects on his morning temperament.

Twenty minutes later as Allan returned to the box, he noticed the remaining two pups didn't look the same.

"Why I'll be . . . " he said as he set his coffee cup on the back of the john and bent over to pick up the larger pup. It took him a couple of seconds before he realized he had picked it up without a towel, but it didn't seem to matter nearly as much now since the small lump had transformed itself during the night. It no longer looked like a giant maggot. It now had features that suggested it really was a puppy. Not a normal pup by any means since none of the features were fully formed, but where the dark eyespots had been, they were now tiny slits. He thought he could make out two tiny holes where the nose should be, and the mouth had shifted to one side.

Allan picked up the second pup and studied it. It too had altered its structure during the night although not as completely as the larger one. Were those tiny nubs at the tip of the head going to be ears? The body itself hadn't changed as much as the head, but even there it looked like it had been molded. No legs, but on the larger one there were tiny bumps where it looked like legs could be forming.

He placed them back in their box and walked to the kitchen for their milk. *Fascinating*, he thought, shaking his head. *Whatever the tiny creatures were, they were altering their shape at a miraculous rate.*

As he returned from the kitchen, Allan stopped for a moment in the den. It was one of his favorite rooms in the sprawling log cabin, probably because of the rows of pictures that lined the walls. Each one showed Todd and Laura at some special moment: Todd's first birthday; Todd swinging on the swing set that Santa had given him when he was four and that had put his young parents in hock for months; Todd going off on his first day of school. Only one room had more pictures in it—Todd's room. It was Todd's room even though neither Todd nor anyone else had slept in it since the accident. The den would be a better place than the bathroom to keep the pups. It was warmer and less drafty. Allan pushed a recliner a foot or two farther away from the wood stove to make room for the box and tossed a couple of new logs onto the coals. The nights and mornings had been nippy even for early April. For some reason, it seemed very important that the remaining two pups stay alive. Suddenly the morning didn't look quite so grim.

After feeding the pups, Allan placed their box in its new location next to the stove and realized his stomach was urging him to the kitchen for breakfast. He glanced at his watch. Almost eight o'clock. Usually, he'd be at the clinic by now reviewing the appointment and surgery books. Breakfast was not a normal part of his routine, but today was different in many ways. He grabbed the portable phone on his way to the front door. He punched in the speed-dial number to the clinic. Dawn answered the phone as he was bending down to pick up the paper, grunting as another shockwave reverberated down his back and right thigh.

"Hello, Waynesboro Animal Hospital, this is Dawn."

Allan straightened up and cradled the phone against his neck. "Hey Dawn, this is Doc."

"I thought that was a familiar groan," she replied. "Your back bothering you this morning?"

"Maybe a little," he lied. In truth, it was hurting like hell. He closed the front door and started to the bathroom for his bottle of aspirin and muscle relaxants. "I'm calling to let you know that I'll be in a little late. How about checking the appointment book...."

"Don't worry, Doc. It's already taken care of. You're clear until 9:30 when Ms. Talmon is bringing in her poodle for shots and to check her ears. We can take her in as a drop-off if you like."

"You're a gem, Dawn. Now I know why I keep you around. Keep Ms. Talmon down for her appointment. I'll be in before then." Allan began to tell Dawn about the two live pups but stopped, deciding to wait until he saw whether they were going to make it or not. Somehow, he didn't think Dawn would be too keen on him keeping them alive.

"How's Molly?" He asked instead.

"She's doing wonderfully. She's up and around, and she ate all of her breakfast. Alice has already called to check on her. I told her she'd probably be going home later today."

"Great. I'll check her when I get in." He shook a couple of aspirin and a muscle relaxant into his hand and took them with the lukewarm coffee.

"Are you sure you should be coming in this morning?" Dawn asked. "You know how your back can flare up."

"Don't worry. I'm taking good care of it right now. I promise to hang in my torture chamber for at least fifteen minutes before I come in." Allan's "torture chamber" was a gravity boot system he used to help stretch his back. Hanging upside down like a bat did wonder for straightening his spine and relieving the pressure on the pinched nerves.

Allan walked into the kitchen, the phone still cradled against his head. He finished the call and set the phone and paper down on the table; his mind focused on a big batch of French toast. As the paper hit the table, it fell open to the front page. He glanced down at it, and the headlines caught his attention.

Biogentrix Denies Charges
Says Genetic Engineering Projects Meet Federal Guidelines

They're at it again, he thought. Biogentrix was not the largest employer of Waynesboro, but they were the one most often in the headlines. The feud had raged ever since the company had moved into the area three years ago. They virtually brought their entire staff of 850 people from the outside, rather than hiring locals as the Waynesboro founding fathers had suggested.

On top of that, Biogentrix was very hush-hush about projects they were working on, something else that made the rest of the community uncomfortable. A small town like Waynesboro loved to gossip but preferred to have a few facts to seed the stories. In recent years there had been a lot of talk about the genetic engineering projects, rumored to be a large part of Biogentrix's research. Most of the locals, both merchants, and farmers, saw such experimentation as dabbling in work rightfully belonging to God.

Finally, the townspeople made such a fuss, the federal agency responsible for monitoring such experiments decided to inspect Biogentrix's facilities. According to the paper, the final verdict was still out, but Biogentrix was pleading not guilty to all charges.

Allan's thoughts flashed to the young forms resting quietly in his den. His mind toyed with the idea that there may be a connection. *But no, surely not. How on earth could there be?* But the nagging thought persisted like a kernel of popcorn lodged in the back of his throat.

Alice had said Molly had been a stray. Could she have escaped from Biogentrix's facilities? It didn't seem likely. Most labs used much smaller dogs, like beagles, to cut down on the care and feeding costs. Of course, that could vary, depending on the project. But what kind of project could they be up to that would result in eight-inch-long maggots?

Okay smarty, if not from Biogentrix, from where did Molly's surprise package come? He spent the rest of breakfast munching on French toast and pondering the question.

Marva the Mouth
Tuesday, June 15

A week later, Allan found the smaller of the two puppies curled up next to its littermate, cold and stiff, having died during the night. Again, he wasn't surprised. It hadn't done well for the past two days, and although it had continued to look more like a real puppy, its transformation remained far behind the larger one, which was by now almost indistinguishable from the real thing.

The remaining pup's eyes opened on day ten, right on schedule, and started taking solid food at the end of the third week, which was a little ahead of schedule. Allan was thankful since he had been skipping out three or four times during the day, driving the seven minutes to his house, feeding the pup, and running back for the next appointment. Such action didn't go unnoticed by the staff, particularly his full-time technician, Marva Chamblis. He overheard a typical conversation she had with Dawn one afternoon as he slipped quietly into the clinic through the back door.

"Come on, Dawn, play the game with me. What do you think Dr. Pritchard is doing when he runs home every day? Do you think he's got a mistress stashed away? Maybe he met her down at Quincy's."

"Marva, I don't want to play your silly game. It's none of my business what Dr. Pritchard is doing, and neither is it yours," Dawn answered with an icy tone that sent goosebumps down most people's backs and usually shut up all further gossip from them—but when it came to gossiping, Marva wasn't most people. She was an award winner, and she saw Dawn's cold response as a challenge to her title, so she continued the game.

"Maybe it isn't any of our business, but aren't you the least bit curious? I mean, suddenly in the last couple of weeks, every time we turn around we see his backside going out the door. You have to admit that's pretty strange for someone we normally can't drag out of the clinic during regular hours."

"Marva, you ask more questions than any black person I've ever known," Dawn replied. Allan knew when she referred to Marva's skin color the shit was about to hit the fan. Dawn's Southern Baptist upbringing in the mountains of North Carolina had left her with a thin yet deep streak of racial prejudice, one that usually remained well hidden but was about to surface.

"I'm going to say this one more time, and that's it. Dr. Pritchard is your boss. He was nice enough to take a chance with you when no other veterinarian in this area would. I need not remind you that you'd been fired from three other places for gossiping when Dr. Pritchard took a chance. If you don't want to find yourself back out on the street living on food stamps, I suggest you find a way to curb your tongue even if it means *cutting it out*." She added that last bit with a biting emphasis. "Do I make myself clear?"

Allan smiled despite himself. Dawn rarely got angry, but when she did, Lord protect anyone in her path. He found himself feeling a little sorry for Marva.

"Yes ma'am, I understand." Marva's meek reply was almost too soft to hear. "You know how much I need this job, Dawn. You wouldn't tell Dr. Pritchard on me, would you?"

"Marva sweetie, I love you to death, I really do. But unrestrained curiosity will be your downfall." Dawn's mothering instinct had already replaced her anger. "Now, I suggest you keep your nose squarely in the center of that pretty face of yours and out of other people's business. You'll make everyone a lot happier."

Allan reopened the back door and closed it again, harder this time. He coughed a couple of times to be sure they heard him as he walked into the clinic. The conversation came to a sudden stop, and by the time he walked into the reception area, Marva was busily dusting the dog food display, and Dawn was filing records, something he suspected she had been doing while talking with Marva. He thought he smelled the stale odor of tobacco smoke and wondered where Marva had stashed the forbidden cigarette but decided not to press the issue.

Allan stopped next to the counter, fully intending to tell both of them about his little houseguest, but as he gazed at Marva busily dusting the same row of cans for the third time, he knew that telling her would be like placing a full-page ad in the Waynesboro Chronicle. No matter what he said about keeping it a secret or what he threatened, Marva would not be able to be quiet about it. It wouldn't be that she wouldn't try to keep quiet. He knew Marva really liked working for him and wouldn't do anything to hurt him or intentionally breach his trust. But asking a chronic gossiper to keep a secret was like expecting a dog to share his food with a strange dog freely. It was simply against the laws of nature. Allan decided he'd tell Dawn about it later when she was alone and elicit her assistance in coming up with a harmless white lie to appease Marva.

MONDAY, JULY 12

The puppy was five weeks old when Allan began to notice further alterations in its appearance. The changes, subtle at first, became more noticeable as the weeks passed. The nose, which had grown into a short muzzle, began to shorten again; the earflaps became smaller and slid down the sides of the head. The tiny toes on the front feet elongated and looked more like fingers. It was the hands that gave it away. The small vestigial dewclaw which generally remains the smallest digit grew like the rest of them and by week eight had taken its place next to the other four fingers. The pup was growing an opposable thumb.

During this time Allan kept the puppy a secret. Each day he'd go into the clinic fully expecting to tell Dawn about the miracle of life that was evolving at his home, but each evening he'd leave the clinic making a new agreement with himself to tell her the next day. By the tenth week, Allan gave up the game. It was at the same time he bought a used bassinet from the Goodwill Store and moved his 'baby' from the den into Todd's room.

As he placed the small bundle onto the soft cushion of the bassinet, Allan felt a familiar warm glow in the pit of his stomach. It had been years since he'd felt it, not since the last time he had tucked Todd into bed and read him a chapter of Aesop's Fables. He continued to stare into the rich brown eyes that had locked onto his own. It was as though they were playing a game to see who could stare at the other the longest. Allan lost.

He strolled into the den and took Todd's baby picture off the wall where it had been hanging over the cardboard box next to the wood stove. He took it and another picture of Todd at two years of age from the coffee table and returned to the bedroom. He removed the hand-stitched embroidery pictures, one of a puppy and the other of a kitten that his mother had stitched for her only grandson, from the wall over the bassinet and replaced them with the pictures of Todd. And then he waited—waited for the miracle of life, of a life he didn't understand to unfold.

Nanny Kendra
Monday, August 2

By the eighth week, Allan had started showing videos he'd taken of the real Todd whenever he was home, several of which also had Todd talking and singing. It seemed to work as the likeness to his son grew noticeably. At the same time, Allan realized he needed help. Todd had kept him up several nights with his crying. Added to that, Allan had two late emergencies that pulled him back to the clinic after eleven. He felt more and more uncomfortable about leaving Todd at home alone. What if he climbed out of the bassinet? He could break his neck. Allan solved part of the problem with another trip to Goodwill, returning with a baby crib and playpen. Allan shopped at Goodwill for these articles, not to save money but because it was on the far side of town in an area seldom visited by his clients, and so his purchases remained a secret; not an easy feat for a town the size of Waynesboro.

But he knew he had to tell someone. He needed help and didn't know where to get it. Dawn seemed a natural choice. He even toyed with telling her the truth. Surely if anyone would understand, she would. Even so, when he really considered it, he couldn't imagine anyone really understanding what he was doing. He didn't understand himself. He was raising a little boy that looked just like his son but had come from a stray dog's belly. When he stopped and thought about it, he doubted his own sanity. He couldn't expect anyone else to believe the story.

Allan decided his only choice was to lie to Dawn for the first time since he'd known her, almost seven years. He called her into his office to avoid Marva's elephant ears for gossip. Dawn closed the door on his instructions and sat on the edge of the chair across from his desk. He noticed she wrung her hands as she sat there trying to look calm and wondered what she must think, being called so unexpectedly into his office.

"Relax, Dawn. This isn't about you or your work, which by the way is out-standing. It's personal, very personal, and I'm asking you to treat it with the utmost confidence. Do you understand?"

"Oh sure, Dr. Pritchard," she answered as she visibly relaxed. "I was just certain that I had done something wrong."

"You've done nothing wrong except to continue to call me 'Dr. Pritchard' when we're in private. Do you think you'll ever be able to call me Allan?"

Dawn smiled. "I've tried Doc. I've tried, but it always comes out the same. I'm afraid I'm a creature of habit, and it's an old habit that just won't die."

"Okay, I guess I can accept it." Allan hesitated, unsure how to begin the well-rehearsed lie. "This is a matter which is rather difficult to discuss, Dawn. I'm sure you've been wondering why I've been running home so much the last several weeks."

"Well, the thought did cross my mind, as well as some other minds." She nodded in the direction of the outer office where Marva sat manning the phones.

"Yes, I'm sure it's driving Marva crazy, poor girl. Unfortunately, it'll have to be that way for now. I'm going to tell you what's going on, but under no circumstances is Marva or anyone else to know."

"I understand."

Allan took a deep breath. "I am temporarily keeping my three-month-old nephew while my brother and his wife work out some marital problems."

"Your brother from Maine?" Dawn asked, a look of surprise on her face.

"Yes, he drove down a few weeks ago on his way to Florida." He plodded along with the made-up story, feeling as though the words were stuck together with peanut butter. Dawn knew little about his brother, only that the two of them didn't see each other very often. The fact was they never saw each other. They hardly acknowledged the other one's existence. For that reason, Allan thought the story would hold. It was unlikely his brother would actually visit him.

"But I didn't think you ever saw your brother?" Dawn asked with a confused look on her face.

"Well, we don't, or didn't," Allan stammered. "The truth is ... " his eyes flitted to the blotter on the desk and back to Dawn. "... we've been getting along a little better lately since his problems at home started. Warren doesn't have many friends, and I guess when your marriage is breaking up, you need to talk to someone. I'm the someone for Warren. It certainly shocked me."

"Why didn't you say something sooner?" Dawn continued to ask questions that forced Allan to dig himself deeper into the lie.

"Warren asked me not to say anything to anyone," he replied. He was alarmed to find the lying was becoming easier. "He thought it would only be for a week or two at first, but now it may be for months." He bit his tongue to keep from saying that Kitty, Warren's wife, had been caught fooling around with another man. Once the lying started, it was difficult to cut it off.

Dawn smiled. "So you're a father again. Well, I'll be. I shoulda guessed, the way you've been dancing around here. Why that's just wonderful." She was beaming now. "But you don't mean to tell me you've been keeping that little boy; you did say it was a boy . . . "

He nodded.

"... You've been keeping that little boy all alone at your house with no one to look after him during the day."

Without hesitation, Allan answered with another lie. "Warren was here for most of that time, but he had to head out to Florida the other day. I don't know when he'll be back. He asked me to look after . . . " He suddenly realized he hadn't thought of another name for Todd. He sat there with his mouth open, panic gripping him by the throat. *This isn't going to work*, he thought. *She sees right through this sham. She's just playing along to see how much rope I'll take before I hang myself.*

Allan's eyes finally focused back on Dawn, and he saw the poster behind her with the words Upjohn Pharmaceuticals boldly printed across the front.

"... John." He finally finished the sentence. "But we call him TJ. It's a little difficult looking at the little bundle and thinking of him as John just now." *Nice recovery,* he thought, but he was aware how close a call it had been. What other questions did Dawn have to trip him up?

Before she had the chance to think up a new one, he grabbed the initiative. "Warren left suddenly, as is his nature, and I now realize that I need someone to help out while I'm here at the office. I thought you might know of someone who could handle this very discreetly. I don't want my name or Warren's becoming the popular gossip."

Dawn pondered the question for a moment, her brow knitted in thought. Then her face brightened with a smile.

"How about Kendra? She's out of school for the summer. She's planning to sit out a semester while she decides whether to go to college or not. To tell you the truth, I'd love to get her out of the house for a while. She's beginning to drive me crazy."

Kendra was Dawn's seventeen-year-old daughter. Allan had watched her grow from a scrawny adolescent into a young woman. There was no doubt in Allan's mind she was capable of looking after his new son. But could she keep a secret even from her mom? It was risky, but it seemed to be his best bet.

"Do you think she'd do it?" Allan asked tentatively.

"Are you kidding? She'd fly to the moon for you. Besides, she loves to babysit, if the kid is fairly well behaved. How is TJ?"

"Oh, he's very easy to care for," Allan answered. *If you don't mind him changing shapes in front of your eyes*, he thought. It raised an important question. If Todd, alias TJ, continued to grow as quickly as he had been, how would he explain it to Kendra? His plan was developing holes in it—large ones.

He'd have to figure it out as he went, Allan concluded. Kendra was the best choice he had. She adored her "Unc-Doc." Even at home Dawn had perpetuated the formal title. He hated to do it, but if necessary he felt he could bring Kendra into the conspiracy without her spilling the beans. At least until he thought of something else.

"Well, does she have the job?" Dawn asked, shaking Allan out of his thoughts.

"Yeah, great. It would really help me out. Speak to her tonight and let me know."

"Oh, don't worry. I know she'll jump at the chance. And I don't want you paying her more than the going rate for babysitters. I know how you like to spoil her." Dawn stood up to leave. At the door, she stopped and looked back at her boss. "When do I get to visit your little nephew?"

The question sent a cold chill down Allan's back. "Uhh, not for a little while, if you don't mind. He's just getting over a bad cold, and I want to keep his exposure to other people to a minimum. I'll let you know when."

"Okay, but don't think you can hide him from his Aunt Dawn forever." She started to leave again but paused once more. "What's it like after all this time to have a baby in the house?"

Allan smiled at her as he leaned back in his chair. "It feels a bit like the old days." But as Dawn left the office his mind was racing. It was nothing like the old days. Everything was moving too fast. Todd was growing too fast, and it seemed only a matter of time before someone would find out the truth.

The thought struck him funny. *The truth? What was the truth, really?*

TJ's Disorder
Wednesday, October 13

Allan turned into the driveway of his log cabin and cut the engine of his Chevy Blazer. Through the twilight of the early summer evening, the light from the kitchen window caught his attention. Kendra's figure was highlighted on the other side. For a brief moment, Allan experienced a painful stab of déjà vu as he was reminded of the many similar nights he had come home late to his home but with a different figure waiting in the kitchen for him.

He shook his head to bring himself back to the present. No, it was not the same. Kendra was not Laura and Todd was not his real son. The first was easy to remember. Kendra was only seventeen, not thirty-five, and although she had begun to spoil Allan as much as his wife had, he never confused the two. Though at five feet, six inches, she was tall for her age, she wore her brunette hair pulled back in a perky ponytail, while Laura always kept her blonde hair too short to pull back. Todd, on the other hand, was an entirely different matter. As the weeks flew by, it seemed more and more natural to have his son back — maybe too natural. So, when it came time to introduce Kendra to the baby she'd be helping to take care of, he called him TJ — part Todd and part...what? He'd not come up with an adequate answer to that question.

He pulled the bag of groceries out of the back seat and walked towards the back door that led into the kitchen. Was he going crazy? The thought had popped unexpectedly into his mind a number of times lately. Or was he already a bona fide nutcase? Trying to raise someone or something that had come from the uterus of a mutt dog but was obviously not a puppy but that was taking on the unmistakable identity of his deceased son. *Sounds pretty certifiable to me*, he thought as he reached the door.

As he strolled into the kitchen, Kendra stopped rinsing the dishes and placed the last one in the dishwasher. She held the portable phone cradled against one cheek.

"Dr. Pritchard just came in. I'll need to call you back later tonight, Mimi."

As she hung up the phone, she turned, a troubled look on her face, obvious to Allan even through the smile she used to try to mask it.

"Who was that on the phone?" Allan asked as he set the groceries on the kitchen table and walked over to the refrigerator to get himself a beer.

"Mimi Rawlins. You know, she's Bo Rawlins' niece. She lives over in Foster Flats, but well, she's having some family problems, so she's been spending a lot of time at her uncle's. We've become good friends. I think she really needs a friend right now."

"Well, that's really nice of you," Allan replied.

"She's easy to be friends with," Kendra continued. "Even though she's a year younger than me, she's more interesting than most of my other friends. She wants to be a reporter when she grows up. Most of my classmates don't seem to know what they want past next week."

"How's TJ been today?" Allan asked changing the subject. "He hasn't been giving you any trouble, has he?"

Kendra wiped her hands with a towel and tossed it on the counter. She walked over to the kitchen table and reached into the bag of groceries. Then she stopped in mid-motion. Taking her hands back out of the bag without removing anything, she turned to Allan.

"No, TJ has been a little angel, as usual, Doc." Since turning sixteen, she'd dropped the "Unc" part of the name. "But something is wrong with him, isn't there?"

"What do you mean, sweetie? Isn't he feeling well?" Allan asked, a growing concern beginning to gnaw at his stomach. *Was TJ sick? Was he going to follow the path of the rest of the litter?*

"I thought it was just my imagination at first, but now I'm certain it's not." Kendra continued as though she hadn't heard Allan's questions. She sat down in the chair next to the kitchen table. She rested her hands in her lap, but they refused to sit still. *She's nervous or scared about something*, Allan thought as he pulled a chair out from the table and sat down facing her. The gnawing sensation in his stomach grew. *The jig is up.* He wondered what had happened today. *Had TJ turned back into a dog or worse? How could he ever have thought he could get away with this crazy game?*

"He's growing too fast," Kendra said simply. "Like I said, at first I thought it was me. Babies always seem to grow faster than they should. But not like TJ. I weighed him two weeks ago and again today. He's gained four pounds. That's abnormal by anyone's standards."

Allan nodded. He knew she was right. He'd suspected it would be only a matter of time before Kendra began to suspect something, so he wasn't completely caught off-guard by the comment. In fact, he felt a little relieved. So many other things far harder to explain could have happened. He took a long draught on his beer before answering. When he did, he spoke with the smooth tone of a professional liar. Why not? That is what he had become of late.

"I know, dear. You're right. I've been meaning to tell you, but I just haven't quite known how. TJ has a rare disorder. Doctors don't quite know what is causing it, but he is growing much faster than normal. There have been a few other cases similar to TJ's reported, but it is quite rare. It's part of what has caused the trouble between my brother and his wife. The two of them are under a lot of stress trying to cope with it. I should have told you sooner. I'm sorry."

The look on Kendra's face almost broke Allan's heart. Kendra had fallen in love with the little infant almost at once. To now hear that TJ had a serious illness was harsh news to deal with for a seventeen-year-old.

What am I doing? Allan wondered. *I'm just digging myself deeper. I'm only putting off the inevitable. Sooner or later someone else would have to know the truth. Why not just get it over with and confess to Kendra now? Have her call her mom and Marva and the newspapers. Get it all out in the open.* But even as he argued with himself, he knew why not.

They'd take TJ away. They'd want to study him — try to figure out what he really was and from where he had come. Allan just couldn't let that happen. He couldn't lose his son a second time. Not yet.

He turned his attention back to Kendra's troubled look. "It'll be okay, sweetie. TJ's dad is talking to as many doctors as he can. That's part of the reason he left TJ with me. We may have to take him to some specialists soon, but in the meantime, you just continue to do a great job caring for him. Everything will be alright."

Kendra brightened a little bit. "Do you think they can find a cure?"

"I don't know for certain, but modern medicine is making major discoveries almost every day."

Kendra walked over to the refrigerator and pulled out one of TJ's bottles. She took it over to the stove to warm. "Well, we'll just have to be sure he gets everything he needs in the meantime. I'll tell mom that I might have to spend more time over here to be sure he's getting the proper care."

"I'd appreciate it if you didn't say anything to your mom about TJ's condition. It would only worry her. TJ's parents don't want other people to know right now. You might just tell your mom he has a condition which makes it not a good idea to have visitors. We can't afford to have him come down with anything else."

"Oh sure, she'll understand. You're right. Mom is a natural worrier when it comes to babies. She wouldn't want to do anything to jeopardize TJ's health. I'll tell her without letting her in on our secret."

Allan finished his beer. He walked over to toss the can in the recycling bin. He felt elated. The lie had gone smoothly. *I'm getting really good at this.* The thought disturbed him. He was particularly concerned by the sense of pride and satisfaction that came with it. Proud to be a good liar? Into what was he turning?

He walked over to Kendra and put his arm around her shoulders and squeezed her.

"I really appreciate what a good job you're doing. And I know TJ thanks you as well. After giving him his bottle, you run on home. You must be getting hungry yourself."

Part Three

"People think the FDA is protecting them—it isn't. What the FDA is doing, and what people think it's doing, are as different as night and day." Herbert Ley, Jr. MD, former Commissioner of the FDA.

Vogt's Return
Saturday, October 23

Pat Vogt pulled her new Jeep Cherokee onto the shoulder of the state highway. She slipped it out of gear and pulled the emergency brake. With the engine and air conditioning still running, she climbed out of the car to stretch her legs and get her bearings. The ride of the Cherokee wasn't as comfortable as the Mercedes she'd traded in, but it was more her kind of automobile. The Merc had been fine in Charlotte. Her clients expected her to drive such a car. The owner of one of the most successful private investigation agencies in the southeast should drive a Mercedes, or BMW or Porsche. But deep down, Pat was more of a Chevy truck kind of woman, or a Jeep Cherokee.

She stretched her arms and legs and bent down to touch her toes, feeling the familiar pop of her lower back. For the first time in years, she'd missed her workouts this past week. Something she almost never did. Her hours in the gym were a sacred discipline. They were what kept her alive, as crucial as a policeman cleaning his gun or a surgeon sterilizing his instruments. But this week had been an exceptional week. Completing all her important cases and turning more routine matters of her agency over to her employees for an indefinite period of time was no small matter.

It always seemed to be more difficult than it should be, but then, delegating anything to anyone was so tricky. You just couldn't count on most people to do a good job. But the agency took a backseat to the case on which she was now working. Sometimes Pat thought the only reason she even bothered with her P.I. firm was to have a way to support the one case that meant everything to her. The case that had become her sole purpose in life — maybe even her obsession.

So, as difficult as the turnover of the business always was, Pat had gotten pretty good at it. In the past eight or ten years, she'd pulled herself out of the rat race of her own business at least four times that she could remember, each time without knowing how long she'd be gone. Some had been as short as a couple of weeks. Once she'd stayed on the road for six months, and the business had almost gone under. Tracking down clues on her own case — the Case of the Missing Alien, she affectionately called it — wasn't easy work. No one else knew where she went or for what. She didn't dare tell anyone.

B.I.U.F.O. had made sure she'd keep her mouth shut. She had been on the edge of being declared certifiably crazy by the time they let her out of the organization. The intensive therapy sessions that had all been recorded in her permanent files didn't help her mental state or her reputation. They'd done an excellent job of setting her up so, if by chance she went to the papers with her story, she would have no credibility. Not that all papers cared about their sources' credibility these days. Such papers as the *National News, the Sun Times*, and the worst one of all, the *Global Inquiry* out of Atlanta. Pat suspected few people read those papers' stories as though they were true, but they still had effect. Just to be sure Pat cooperated, B.I.U.F.O. had made it perfectly clear to her they would not hesitate to pull her back in for a long-term lease on a padded cell.

So Pat didn't dare tell anyone about The Case of the Missing Alien, not even her parents, which was tough. They never knew why she had left B.I.U.F.O. Her dad, who had been so proud of her when she'd gotten the position, was confused when she suddenly left. Both parents had been concerned when they found out about the therapy. She had finally told her dad that it wasn't as it seemed and although she couldn't tell him what had happened, she asked him to trust her. Without a moment of hesitation he had. He'd been around long enough to know about the political pitfalls one could fall into, but most of all, he knew and trusted his daughter.

Pat reached into the jeep and pulled the map off the dash. Opening it on the hood, she studied her progress. Only another thirty to forty minutes, she estimated, to the outskirts of Waynesboro. It was her third trip back to the quiet township that sat nestled in the foothills not far from the mountain of her nightmares. But she'd not been back in over five years. *Third time's the charm*, she recited another of her father's favorite sayings. *Well, it had better be*, she told herself, *because if I don't find anything on this trip, the Case of the Missing Alien will be permanently put to rest.*

Over the past couple of months, she had given it a lot of thought and had decided ten years was long enough to put her life on hold, waiting for something, anything to happen that would suggest the alien was still alive. Oh, there had been tidbits in the news from time to time. All of them had turned out to be someone's wild imagination. As far as Pat was concerned, this was her last trip to the mountains. A final goodbye to a stage of her life she was quite ready to move beyond. She promised herself, this time she would move on.

It would be interesting to see how much the little town had changed in the five years, if indeed it had. Many of the small towns in the North Carolina mountains seemed stuck in time. It was as though they grew to fit the size of one of the narrow valleys then stopped. With no additional land flat enough for new growth, Waynesboro had grown to its maximum capacity.

Pat folded the map in the open position in case she needed to look at it while driving. She was about to climb back in the Cherokee for the last leg of her journey when she heard a low moan, almost a whimper. She stopped dead in her tracks, her hand automatically reaching to the small of her back where she kept her revolver. As her hand touched the vacant spot, she remembered she'd placed it in the glove compartment so she wouldn't have to endure the discomfort of sitting on it for the three-hour trip.

Should she go fetch it now? The sound repeated itself. It didn't sound very threatening. She reached down and felt for the stiletto knife strapped to her ankle and as she often did when checking for the knife, she had a momentary flash of another time she'd reached for a different knife. The comfort of the cold steel reassured her.

She walked around the back of the jeep, pausing every few steps to listen. The sound repeated itself for the third time, a little louder. She continued her search. She pulled the knife from its sheath and used it to push away the dense underbrush along the road. As she pushed deeper into the thick bushes, the whimpering repeated, this time blending into a low threatening growl.

It was an animal. It had to be. The permanently implanted image of the alien as it towered over her in the ship flashed before her eyes. No, it couldn't be. What were the chances of her running into it along the side of the road like this? *Maybe not that one alien*, she thought. *But what about one of its offspring? What if in the past ten years, it had done nothing but continued to mul-*

tiply? There could have been a second alien of the opposite sex. Hell, who's to say the alien needed two different sexes. There were plenty of examples in the animal kingdom of asexual reproduction.

But I'd have heard of other people running into strange animals. I have been looking for such clues. Right? Still, who could say what was hiding in the bushes? She suddenly regretted leaving the revolver behind in the glove compartment. *It should be in my hand. Wouldn't dad be pissed to find out his daughter had been killed all because she hadn't gone back for her gun. He'd never speak to me again.* The ridiculous thought almost made her giggle. With a second low growl, the giggle caught in her throat.

"Easy boy, I'm not going to hurt you," Pat said in a low soothing voice. She'd grown up with animals around her and although the growling made her nervous, it wasn't going to stop her. She pushed a clump of low-lying branches to one side and took another step forward. The deep growl continued as Pat finally found its source. Lying partially hidden by the brush and with leaves and twigs hanging from its thick coat was a Golden Retriever. As it saw Pat for the first time, the growl turned back to a whimper and it wagged its tail.

A good sign, Pat thought. *It must be used to people.* She spoke softly to the dog as she bent down to take a closer look. "Good boy. I'm not going to hurt you. Take it easy."

She put the stiletto back in its sheath and held out her hand palm up, making sure it was below the level of the dog's head. After a moment, the dog took a sniff of her hand then a tentative lick. She let the dog check her hand out thoroughly before trying to pet its head. When he didn't shy away from her, Pat decided to be a little bolder. She quietly moved closer to the dog so she could get a better look at him. As she did so, he moved back deeper into the brush, exposing his left rear leg and the deep gash that had caused him to take refuge.

"Oh, you poor boy," Pat said as she stared at the nasty wound. "What happened? How did you get in such a mess?" Pat slowly moved around among the brambles in an effort to get a better look at the wound. It was a nasty one, deep and dirty. There was no doubt it would need a vet's attention.

Keeping her eyes on the stray, she carefully removed her belt from her jeans. There was no question she'd take care of the poor fellow. Pat had spent most of her life around animals, and it never occurred to her to abandon one in such obvious need. At the same time, she knew how dangerous an injured creature could be, and she wasn't interested in starting on this trip with a nasty bite.

She eased up closer to the retriever again and was relieved to see him wag its tail at her. The soft whimper did not turn into a growl. It was as though he was telling her he was ready to be helped out of his dilemma. Pat gently stroked the dog's head and scratched behind his ears for a few minutes, building his trust. She then slipped the belt around his neck, through the buckle, and then around his nose.

She'd have to pick him up and carry him to the car. If she moved the leg the wrong way, it could hurt him and his instincts would be to bite first and ask questions later. Still talking soothingly to the dog, she moved deeper under the bush and gently eased one arm under his belly. Still holding onto the belt with the other, she placed her knees well under her body and lifted up, being thankful for the many hours on the exercise machines that gave her the strength to help an animal in need. He was lighter than he had looked at first.

"You're nothing but a bag of bones, boy," she said to him as she adjusted his weight close to her body. The dog struggled for just an instant then relaxed in her arms.

"That's a good boy. We're going to take care of that nasty wound. Don't you worry. We'll get some food in you as well." She carried him back to the Cherokee and placed him in the back compartment.

"I wonder if Waynesboro is large enough to have its own vet?" She asked herself as she shut the rear hatch and smiled as the Retriever spun around a few times then lay down.

WAYNESBORO HAD GROWN, Pat noticed as she drove through the outskirts of the small town, but not enough that anyone living there every day would probably have noticed. She stopped at the first filling station and asked for the directions to the nearest veterinary hospital and was relieved to learn the town did indeed have its own. Two in fact. She asked if either one specialized in pets and was again surprised to learn Waynesboro had its very own small animal vet — Dr. Allan Pritchard. The gas station attendant said it with pride.

"He's my vet. I take all my dogs and cats to him. You won't find a finer one around. He's a little on the expensive side but worth it. Lets most people pay as they can, though I don't know about a stranger. You tell him Jake from the station told you about him. It might help."

As Pat pulled into the parking area of Waynesboro Veterinary Hospital, she was surprised for the third time. The building, although smaller than most veterinary hospitals she was accustomed to, was of contemporary design and had a well-manicured lawn. She pulled into the parking spot in front of the clinic door. There was only one other car in the area, a gray and black Blazer which she hoped belonged to the vet himself. She glanced at the lettering on the door, which gave the hours the clinic was open and frowned. The clinic closed at one, and it was already past two.

She glanced back to the Blazer, deciding it was the kind of car a vet might drive in a small town like Waynesboro. Leaving the engine of her car running to keep the cab cool, she walked to the front door and found it unlocked. She strolled into the small but impeccably clean waiting room. Along two walls were cushioned benches, the pastel blue of the cushions matching the small squares in the wallpaper. The corner between the seats was taken up by a small table, a set of recent dog and cat magazines neatly fanned out for display.

Set up for the next business day, Pat thought. Someone runs a pretty tight ship here. As the door closed behind her, she heard the muffled sound of a bell somewhere in the back of the hospital. In a moment a tall, lanky man in his late thirties to early forties came down the hall, wiping his hands on a towel. He wore a crisp white lab coat that came down to his knees. By the time he reached Pat, she'd decided she could trust this man with her parents' lives, much less any of her pets.

"Yes? May I help you?"

"Yes. I know you're closed now, and normally I would wait until your regular hours, but I have a stray dog outside that's been seriously injured..." Pat stopped as she noticed the man smiling.

"I'm Dr. Pritchard, Allan Pritchard. Most people around here just call me Doc but then, you're not from around here, are you? So you may call me whatever you're comfortable with."

"No, I've driven up from Charlotte, but I didn't know it was quite so obvious," Pat replied, returning his smile.

"It's not, not really. It's just what you said about regular hours. I don't think anyone else around here considers that I have regular or irregular hours. I'm pretty much always available. Anyway, let's take a look at your friend." He reached into the large pocket of his lab coat and pulled out a leather leash. They walked out to Pat's car.

"I do need to let you know one thing," Allan said with some hesitation. "My receptionist, Dawn, will kill me if I don't mention it. It's regarding taking care of a stray. If it's as serious as you've indicated, treatment may be rather extensive." He hesitated again. "In which case, I'll be happy to administer whatever first-aid is necessary, but . . . "

"Oh, don't worry Dr. Pritchard. I don't expect you to take on the financial obligation of a stray. I'll assume full responsibility for whatever needs to be done. I just couldn't think of walking away from a hurt animal."

The doctor noticeably relaxed. Pat smiled. *I bet he has a significant amount of money on the books*, she thought. She'd see to it that her bill didn't become a part of it. Between the two of them, they were able to get the retriever out of the car and into one of the exam rooms without hurting him further.

"I don't suppose you recognize him, do you?" Pat asked.

"No, can't say I do. The shape he's in, it'd be hard for even his owner to recognize him. Golden Retrievers are popular in these parts. It shouldn't be too difficult to find his owner. And if not and you decide not to keep him, I'm sure we can find him a good home. He looks like a purebred," he said as he slipped a muzzle over the dog's nose. "I'm going to clip and clean the leg which may hurt a little. If you wouldn't mind helping? My staff has already left for the day."

Pat moved to the front of the animal and put one arm around the dog's neck.

After a few moments of clipping the leg with a pair of electric razors, Allan looked up at Pat and smiled his warm smile again. "You hold him like a real pro. You're not looking for a new career as a vet technician, are you?"

To Pat's surprise, she found herself blushing at the smile and the remark. "No, I'm quite happy with what I currently do, but I'll certainly keep your offer in mind."

"By the way," Allan continued as he washed the leg wound, "what brings you to our fair town of Waynesboro, if you don't mind me asking?"

I'm looking for an alien who tried to kill me not far from here almost ten years ago. The thought almost leapt out of Pat's mouth. Instead she said, "I love the mountains and decided I needed a little time away from Charlotte to recharge my batteries. But I didn't want one of the usual touristy type places."

"Well, Waynesboro definitely isn't one of those." Allan laughed. "If you're looking for peace and quiet, we have it in spades. What do you do in Charlotte?"

"I run a private investigation agency," Pat replied, noting how unusual it felt to be on the other side of the questioning. This Dr. Pritchard would make a pretty good investigator himself. He seemed very competent at gleaning the information he needed without appearing to pry.

"I love my job but it can be pretty stressful at times." Pat moved a little closer to get a better look at the leg. After the clipping and cleaning, the wound didn't look nearly as bad as before.

As though reading her thoughts, Allan said, "Our fella here isn't too bad off. I'll dress the wound and get him started on some antibiotics for the infection. In a couple of days, if the infection responds as it should, I'll probably be able to stitch most of it closed. The rest will heal with a little time. He should be as good as new within a week to ten days. Were you planning to be around that long?"

Pat nodded. "I haven't decided how long my stay will be here. It depends on how well things go back at my office. If it stays quiet, I'll stay longer."

In truth, she knew the office could manage itself. She'd trained her people that way. What would really determine the length of her stay was what information she came up with from the mountain and surrounding countryside. She was at a blind end everywhere else. If she couldn't pick up some trail here, the ten year long investigation might come to a close.

Allan applied a yellow antibacterial ointment to the wound and began to wrap it with stretch gauze. "Do you plan to camp or stay at one of our fine hotels?"

"Probably a little of both. I was up here four or five years ago and found several nice camping areas. I also have found about three days of camping is as long as I can stay away from civilization and a hot shower. Is the Waynesboro Tourist Lodge still open?"

"Oh sure and still run by the Adkins family. Elma has turned most of it over to her daughter, Lorna, but it continues to plug along like the rest of us."

Allan finished wrapping the leg and patted the retriever on the head. "Well, I never like taking in a dog without knowing his name and since we aren't likely to learn yours, I guess we'll just have to make one up." He continued to rub the dog's ear but his eyes were on Pat.

"What do you say we just call him Lucky for awhile? It seems to fit." Pat found herself blushing for a second time as she gazed into Allan's steel gray eyes. "Yes. That fits him."

"And if you'll help me get him in a cage, I'd say we're about done. It looks like we might be seeing you a bit over the next few days."

"You can count on it. If you don't mind, I'd like to visit him each day."

Allan nodded and smiled. "Mind? No, I don't mind. That would be fine—just fine."

Hunting Trip
Friday, Nov. 5

Dawn stuck her head into the surgery room and interrupted Allan's humming.

"It's Bo Rawlins on the phone. He's calling again about your annual deer hunt. It's the third time in the last two days he's called. What do you want me to tell him?" Dawn asked, the unpleasant look on her face suggesting what she would like to tell him, but Bo was one of their most influential clients, particularly among the hunting crowd, a large number of which supported Allan's practice. Besides, Allan found Bo's down-home humor refreshing despite the fact it occasionally stepped over the boundary of good taste.

"Tell him I'll be with him in a moment." Allan said as he tied the next to the last suture. "I'm almost done in here. Oh, by the way, any word from Kendra?"

"Yes, she called a few minutes ago." Dawn replied, her look instantly transforming to a smile. "She said not to forget TJ's food, especially another box of Cheerios. He's eating you out of house and home, or something like that." Dawn laughed. "She really loves taking care of him. She says she's never seen a child eat so much or grow so fast."

Allan pulled his mask off and scratched the end of his nose where it had been tickling for the last five minutes.

"He is a growing boy," he answered, but the thought made him nervous. So far, since telling Kendra the fable about the growth problem, she'd kept her word not to say anything to anyone, but how long could she be counted on not to let something slip? He felt as though he was skating across a lake of thin ice, listening to the dull thuds of the ice cracking.

Living a life of lies was becoming increasingly uncomfortable. Allan sat down behind his desk, tossing the mask and cap onto the clutter of paper that habitually hid the desk's mahogany surface. He picked up the receiver and leaned back in the chair.

"Bo, good morning. What can I do for Waynesboro's finest hunter and fisherman?"

"For starters, you can keep throwing the blarney my way. Others might begin to believe it if an upright citizen like yourself keeps saying it. Secondly, you can join me and a few of the guys this Saturday. We're going deer hunting, and we'd like to invite you to come along."

"Well Bo, you know I'm not much of a hunter. I doubt I've shot my rifle since vet school."

"You say that every year, Doc. Neither have some of these other fellas, least not close enough to any game to make a difference on the ecology. It's mostly an excuse to get together and freeze our butts for a couple of hours. It's also a good excuse to indulge in a little 'medicinal' to warm the blood. We'll probably go down to Jake's after we're through hunting. Whatta ya say?"

"I guess you can count on me." Allan finally relinquished. It was the same every year. Bo would pester him to go hunting with "the boys" as soon as the season opened, and continue to hound him until he said yes. Once Allan went with him, Bo would feel his social obligation was over until next year. Allan had done it for the last three years and so far, had never even seen a deer or fired his rifle. He figured it was a good excuse to clean the old firearm if nothing else. It didn't hurt his business any either.

"Great! I'll pick you up at your place around six; how's that?"

Allan groaned. Six on a Saturday morning; there ought to be a law against it.

"I'll meet you at the clinic at 6:00 a.m. I'll need to check a couple of cases." The last person he needed down at his cabin was Bo. If he found out about TJ, it would be all over town before the sun set.

"Okay, it's a date—and Doc, we're going to get us a deer this year, you wait and see."

Allan hung up the phone but remained in his seat, shaking his head. *Get us a deer, would we?* He could hardly wait. He pushed the intercom button and in a few seconds, Dawn's voice came through the phone. "You rang?" She asked, her voice poorly disguised as a butler.

"Yes. I was wondering if we have Lucky cleaned up and ready to go. Pat, uh, Ms. Vogt will be here in a few minutes."

It would be Lucky's first excursion out since coming into the hospital. The leg had responded well to Allan's careful attention. Pat had asked to try him outdoors with her over the weekend while they continued to look for a permanent home.

"Yes, Dr. Pritchard. For the third time, Lucky is ready. I promise Ms. Pat will be very pleased. You will definitely be a hero in her eyes."

What was Dawn talking about? Be a hero in her eyes? He just wanted to be sure his newest patient and client received the proper care. He smiled to himself at the thought. Well, maybe he was being a little more attentive than usual.

Pat had made it a point to visit Lucky every day since he had been admitted to the hospital, and Allan had made just as much a point to be around to talk to her. Evidently, his actions had not been missed by Dawn's trained eyes. Well, so be it.

"Thank you, Dawn. That will be all for now." He cut the connection in the middle of her giggle.

A few minutes later, Allan's intercom beeped.

"Dr. Pritchard, Ms. Vogt is in exam room three. I thought you might like to go over Lucky's instructions for the weekend." There was a syrupy quality to Dawn's voice that was unmistakable. Allan chose to ignore the implication.

"Thank you, Dawn. I'll be right there." He returned the receiver to its cradle, grinning in spite of himself. He noticed a light flutter in his stomach similar to the sensation he experienced when he had to speak to one of Waynesboro's many civic groups. He knew the reason for the butterflies. The thought had been in the back of his head for the last two days. He'd allowed it to come to the foreground only twice, both times without any resolution.

Now, when the moment was upon him, he knew he'd made his decision. He would ask Pat out on a date for Saturday night. At least, he had decided that it was a good idea, something he wanted to do. Now, would he follow through? That was another question entirely. He remembered back to when he'd decided to ask Laura out on a date. They were both still in college. It had taken him a good two weeks to get up the nerve to finally ask. Surely, in the past several years he'd improved. He was now a successful veterinarian and businessman; as Bo said, a well respected 'pillow' of the community.

Yep, and I'm still as nervous as a cat about to have kittens around attractive women, Allan thought as he pushed away from his desk. Already, the palms of his hands were sweaty and his mouth dry. *Hell, by the time I get into the room I'll be lucky if I can even get the words out.*

Despite the discomfort, he had to admit he enjoyed the sensation. It had been a long time since he'd been interested in anyone of the opposite sex. He'd begun to think he might never be. Pat Vogt had changed all that. *Now, let's see if she'll be willing to go out with an over-the-hill widower.*

As he entered the exam room, he smelled the light scent of Pat's perfume. It was a fragrance he'd come to look forward to each day. Pat stood up as he entered the room. She wore a pair of faded jeans that fit snugly in all the right places. They were stuck down in the tops of a pair of well-worn hiking boots. Her flannel shirt had a multi-colored-checkered pattern which matched the light blue turtleneck underneath. Her medium length black hair was pulled back in a ponytail, revealing small ears. The blues of her shirt and turtleneck highlighted her blue eyes which now met Allan's gray eyes in a steady gaze.

After a couple of seconds, Pat's lips turned upward into a demure smile. "Is anything wrong?" She asked as Allan continued to stand frozen, staring at her.

Suddenly realizing how long he'd been studying her, Allan shook his head and returned the smile. "No, nothing. Nothing's wrong. You just look..." He lost the words to describe what he was thinking . . . "Lovely," he finally finished.

Pat's smile broadened.

"Why thank you, kind sir," Pat replied in an exaggerated southern accent. "You say the kindest things."

Remembering why she was here, Allan began to review the case with her, telling her how well the wound had healed and what to look for over the next couple of days. Pat listened intently, occasionally asking a question for clarification. When he was finished telling her how to care for Lucky, there was a pregnant pause.

"Well, I guess I'll go tell Dawn to bring Lucky up to you," Allan said awkwardly, but didn't move to the door. Instead, he stood frozen in place, the fluttering of his stomach intensifying. *Hell, I'm going to blow it. Go ahead, just ask her. What's the worst she can say? She can say no. She can say how inappropriate and unprofessional it is for a veterinarian to ask a client out. She could say . . .*

"Is there anything else?" Pat's words interrupted Allan's argument with himself.

"No. Yes. Well, what I mean to say is no. That's all I think you need to know about Lucky. Do you have any other questions?"

Pat smiled. "Well, yes. There is one question. I was wondering what there might be for Lucky and me to do on a Saturday night. I mean, we could just stay out at the campsite all night, but I thought if there was some place I could take him, I might find his owner or someone who would like to take care of him."

"Well, most people will be at the high school football game on Saturday. We're playing Morganton. They're one of our biggest rivals. I don't know. You might have some problem getting Lucky through the gate, but if you want to give it a try, I'd be happy to go with you. I'm pretty sure I could convince them to let Lucky in."

"Would you do that?" Pat asked. "That would be great. I haven't been to a high school game in ages."

"Do you enjoy football?" Allan asked, surprised at how easy it suddenly was to talk.

"No, not really. I mean, I'm not a great fan of the game, but I do love the excitement that's around it—especially with the right company."

Allan found himself blushing. "Well, is it a date?"

"It's a date. Why don't I just meet you here at the clinic around 6:30? That'll give us plenty of time to get to the game by 7:00."

"That's fine," Allan replied as he started to open the door to escort Pat into the lobby. Then he stopped, a confused look on his face. "How did you know the game started at 7:00?"

It was Pat's turn to blush. "Why I believe it came up when I was talking to Dawn a few minutes ago." She patted his cheek as she walked by. "See you Saturday."

ALLAN HUDDLED IN THE front seat of his Chevy Blazer, his rifle still in its case in the seat beside him. He had the engine running and the heat on full blast, but so far the stream of warm air had done little to warm the cab. He shuddered inside the down vest. Six in the morning was his accustomed time to rise during the week, but he usually spent the first hour warming himself next to the wood stove as he made coffee and toast. He hadn't realized how important that time was to his tired body. As he shifted in his seat, he could feel the familiar twinge along his lower back. It felt like a rusty door hinge in need of a good spraying of WD-40.

I'm like an old car, he thought. Okay once I warm up but not worth a plug nickel until the oil begins to flow. He thought of waiting in the clinic but as it turned out, he didn't have any cases to check over. There was a thick stack of paperwork waiting on his desk, but it would just have to continue waiting.

A beam of light from an approaching car drew Allan back to the real world. He glanced at his watch — 5:58. It was one thing you could count on about Bo. When it came to hunting or fishing, he was never late. Now bringing in his dogs for heartworm testing, that was a different matter.

Allan turned off the engine and grabbed the gun case. Hopefully, Bo's truck would be warmer since he had driven from across town. He locked the Chevy's door and waved to Bo as he pulled up beside him, then ran around to the passenger side of the brick red truck. He tried the door before remembering that it couldn't be opened from the outside. He waited while Bo leaned over and opened it.

"Sorry about that, Doc. Been meaning to fix that thing one of these days."

Allan smiled to himself. The door hadn't worked for at least the last three years. Bo's remedy for fixing something was to come up with a pat excuse that could be used whenever needed. He climbed into the seat next to the large man and was surprised to find the cab colder than his own.

"Oh, by the way. The heater went on the fritz a few weeks ago. Gotta get it fixed when I take ol' Nellie in about the door." Bo jammed the truck in reverse and started to back out.

"We could take mine," Allan offered hopefully.

"Nah, that's okay. Ol' Nellie's feelings would get hurt and my reputation would never be the same if I was caught in one of those new fangled yuppy-mobiles. No offense, Doc."

Allan huddled deeper into his vest and stuck his hands into its pockets, seeking even the smallest pocket of warm air to thaw his numb fingers. "None taken, Bo," he answered and watched as the fog from his breath collected on the windshield. Something told him it was going to be a long morning.

Allan glanced at Bo over the vest's collar. Bo was undoubtedly one of Waynesboro's most unique citizens. Despite all outward signs to the contrary, Bo was one of the richest and shrewdest businessmen in the county, possibly in the state. He'd made most of his money in real estate using his down-home-good-old-boy technique to keep his competition off stride. About the time they figured they had a real sucker, he usually found a way to turn the tables on them. Many a high-roller from the big city had returned home with their tails between their legs and with an expensive lesson they'd not soon forget.

At the same time, Bo was one of the most honest men Allan had met. He shot from the hip; if he liked you, he would give you the shirt off his back. If not, you would know it within ten minutes of meeting him. Allan felt lucky that Bo had taken a shine to him from the first.

"Oh, we're going to get us a deer today, today . . . " Bo started singing off key. "A deer we're going to get, oh yeah . . ." Singing was not one of Bo's strong suits.

Allan smiled. Maybe the day wouldn't be such a chore after all.

IT WAS AROUND 7:30 or 8:00 when the buck appeared on the crest of the hill, less than fifty yards from where Allan sat huddled next to a tree. He had been instructed by Bo to climb up the tree but had refrained. He wasn't sure his back was ready for such antics. He had just about dozed off when he heard the slight snap of the twig. He looked up, half expecting to see one of the other hunters approaching.

There it stood, silhouetted against the early morning sky. Allan counted at least ten points on its antlers, a marvelous specimen of deerhood. He raised his rifle and clicked off the safety. The deer remained frozen as though a statue one would place in the front yard. Allan squeezed the trigger, bracing himself for the kick of the gun. Then his finger froze just short of the critical point that would end the deer's life.

What are you doing, Doc? He asked himself. *Going to kill yourself a deer, huh? Mind if I ask you why? You don't particularly care for venison, as I recollect. Maybe you're thinking of mounting that gorgeous head. You could place it in the reception area. That would sure impress your clients, wouldn't it? No? Well, how about over the fireplace where little TJ can look up every day and see it. What silent lesson would that be for the boy?*

Allan lowered his rifle but continued to stare at the deer. *Go on, get outta here,* he thought. *The forest isn't safe today.* Allan raised his arm, preparing to scare the buck away. The deer raised its head at the motion, a split second before the explosion of Bo's rifle stopped Allan's heart for a few seconds and the buck's heart forever.

The buck leaped in the air as though to run down the ridge, but stumbled on the third step then stumbled again, falling forward on the carpus of its right then left front foot, tried to run that way but found it impossible. It fell into a clump of bushes and lay motionless.

Allan stood frozen to the spot, wondering from the pain in his chest whether he'd been shot in the same moment. He finally realized he had stopped breathing, took a gasp, then another, like an old car in need of a jump-start. Everything appeared in slow motion for the next few seconds.

He heard Bo yell, "I got me a good on' I sure did." Then Bo appeared from the brush about twenty yards to Allan's left, running up the slope towards his kill.

Allan suddenly felt nauseous. So this was deer hunting. Now he knew why every year he had been so reluctant to accept Bo's invitation. As he clicked the safety back on, the thought flashed through his mind to keep it off and see how good a shot he was on the moving target in front of him. He leaned the gun against the thick oak he'd been using for support and began hiking slowly up the hill.

Why was he walking in that direction? Did he think he could save the fallen deer? Maybe give it mouth-to-mouth until they got it to his clinic. Do emergency thoracic surgery to recover the bullet and sew up the gaping hole it had dug through the heart. No. He knew Bo's shot had been too perfect. The kill had been virtually instantaneous. The deer was dead in its tracks, the last few steps more of a reflex than anything else. Still he wanted to see—to be sure the deer was dead.

Like he had had to be sure when Laura and Todd were killed. Had insisted on going to the county morgue to view the charred remains. Had insisted
on studying the dental charts to verify what was no longer apparent by seeing the bodies. He had to be sure that the blackened twisted logs lying in the
morgue were his wife and child—were the remains of the two people who,
only hours before, had been his every reason for living.

Within ten minutes, the other hunters had gathered around the carcass
of the dead deer. There was Jake and Jeff Hawkins, father and son. It was Jeff's
first hunting trip and at sixteen years of age, to be this close to a fallen deer
was a rare treat. Suddenly, he had a new hero besides his dad: Bo Rawlins, the
great white hunter.

The other two men, Lee Reynolds and Larry Withers, were regulars with
Bo. They immediately began to compare the most recent kill with the dozens
of other deer Bo or one of them had killed through the years. After about ten
minutes of jarring, during which it was decided that this was about the most
massive and most handsome buck to date, Bo pulled out his hunting knife
and wiped the blade on his pant's leg.

"Well, if we want to get any decent meat out of this here carcass, I guess
we'd best get with cleaning and gutting it. Lee, how about you and Larry help
hold him steady while I slit the belly open. We'll field dress it here and then
take it into Bryce's Grocers for him to finish the job."

The two men stepped to either side of the deer and rolled it over on its
back. Starting at the sternum, Bo expertly stabbed the belly and sawed his way
down to the pubic bone. As he did so, the belly glistened open. They rolled
the carcass to one side, and the contents of the abdomen slithered out onto
the leaf-covered ground.

Allan had seen dozens of autopsies on animals both in vet school and
in his practice. Already the procedure seemed to diminish the magnificence
of the animal. Less than an hour before, he'd stood watching the deer, awe-
struck by its regal beauty. Now, it was rapidly turning into a side of meat: a
slab of dead, gamey tasting meat.

He started to turn away from the activity, suddenly disinterested in the
hunt. But a brief glimpse of a familiar white glistening lump pulled his eyes
back to the contents of the abdomen.

"What is that?" Jeff Hawkins asked as he leaned closer to the spectacle in front of him, pointing to the white mass that had drawn Allan's attention. As he pointed, the contents continued to roll onto the ground revealing four similar lumps—larvae.

"Must be some sort of worm or parasite," said his father, the least knowledgeable of the group when it came to animal innards.

"No type of worm I've ever seen," replied Bo, as he poked gingerly at one of the lumps with his knife.

The larvae were smaller than the first set Allan had seen. He estimated they were not more than four inches across. *Immature, not fully developed*, he thought. *Probably won't live. May not have any signs of life yet.* He continued to study the small lumps as each pair of eyes turned to him for an answer to Jeff's question.

Noticing he had suddenly become the center of attention, he stooped down on his haunches and studied the lumps closer, as though seeing them for the first time. He took Bo's knife from him and pushed one of the larvae away from the others, rolling it over as he did.

"Not any type of parasite I've ever seen either, but that doesn't mean a whole lot. Deer autopsies are not my forte. They could be some form of liver fluke or some such that I'm not familiar with. Strange, they're floating free in the belly like this."

"Well, the important question, Doc, do you think the meat will be okay to eat?" Bo asked in a worried voice.

"I can't say for certain, Bo, but I don't see any reason why not," Allan replied. His mind was suddenly racing. *What if they find out about the other larvae? They'll find out about Todd—they'll take him away and study him. Don't be a fool. How are they going to find out? Just take care of these larvae, and everyone will forget about them in a few days.*

"Go ahead and finish dressing the animal, Bo. I'll take these back to the office and do some checking into them. I'll let you know if I find out anything."

One of the men handed him a plastic bag left over from a couple of biscuits packed by his wife. Allan placed the four small lumps into it and pressed it shut.

How many more animals are running through the countryside with larvae inside them? Allan wondered. What would happen if they started popping up elsewhere? Dawn would undoubtedly hear about it sooner or later and make the connection with Molly's strange C-section.

Could he cover it all up? Could he shelter Todd from discovery? What would he do if they found out that his young nephew wasn't what he seemed? As Allan walked back to Bo's truck, he had the strangest thought of all. What would Pat think of what he had done?

High School Football
Saturday, Nov. 8

As Allan pulled into the parking lot of his clinic, the alarm of his quartz watch beeped six o'clock. Pat's car was already parked near the front entrance, but Pat and Lucky were nowhere to be seen. He pulled his car next to hers and cut off the engine but left his lights on.

As he opened his car door, the inside light highlighted the bright bouquet of flowers resting in the passenger's seat. *Dumb. Bringing flowers were dumb,* Allan thought. *She'll think I'm a country hick. Long stem roses might do, but not these flowers.* The local florists had closed early because of the game. Their son was a star defensive back and so despite the loss of business, they always closed early for home games.

So Allan had had to settle for an assortment of cut flowers from the largest grocery store in town. *She'll hate them. I just know she will. Maybe I should just take them into the clinic for the staff. Dawn and Marva would like them.*

Allan started back to the car to fetch the flowers just as Lucky bounded around the side of the clinic with Pat not far behind. *Too late. If I try to tell her the flowers aren't for her, she'll really think I'm a jerk. Relax, man. Maybe she'll like them.*

Pat waved to him as she trotted up to the cars. Her cheeks were flushed from running in the cold night air. She was wearing a thick bright turquoise sweater with a full turtleneck and corduroy pants. Allan thought she was the most beautiful woman he'd ever seen. *Why in the world is she going out with me?* He wondered, then mentally kicked himself for such a thought. After all, he wasn't such a bad date. He was still young, reasonably attractive, and a successful doctor and businessman. There were dozens of eligible young ladies who would be insanely jealous of Pat when they saw the two of them walk into the football stadium. Many of them were his clients. One of Dawn's favorite games was to point out to her boss which of his young and sometimes not-so-young lady clients were flirting with him.

Well, here goes nothing, he thought as he reached into the car and withdrew the flowers.

"Ahh, how sweet," Pat said as she broke out into a gorgeous smile. "It's been quite a while since someone has given me flowers." She slipped up next to him and gave him a quick peck on the cheek, then twirled around him, her arms grasping the flowers to her chest and Lucky prancing beside her, barking.

"It's been such a great day, and now I get to cap it off with flowers, a football game, and being escorted by one of Waynesboro's most eligible men."

Allan blushed. "Just how long did you and Dawn talk on Friday?"

"Oh, long enough. I had to find out if it was safe to accept your invitation," Pat replied with a light giggle. "She assured me that it was, although she cautioned me that I might develop several lifelong enemies of the female persuasion."

The three of them piled in Allan's car and drove to the game. As they approached the high school, the traffic became increasingly thick.

"Wow. I didn't know there were so many people in Waynesboro," Pat remarked as they waited for one of the local police officers to wave their line of traffic forward.

"There isn't, really. A lot of these people have driven in especially for the game. This is the biggest game of the year. Morganton is just up the road about thirty miles. Their high school is almost twice our size but for some reason every year, our boys give them a run for their money." Allan gazed in the rear view mirror at the long line of lights behind him. "And I imagine nearly half of these cars are from Morganton's fans. They always have a good showing."

Pat turned in her seat to Lucky who was sitting quietly in the back seat and patted his head. "This looks like the perfect place to find your owner or to find someone who would like to be your owner."

"How did he do today?" Allan asked.

"He was marvelous. He's obviously been well taken care of. He's very obedient and learns fast. In some ways, I'd like to keep him myself but with my schedule, I just don't see how I could."

They arrived at the stadium with ten minutes to spare. "Let's see how much clout as a veterinarian I have in this town. Dogs are normally excluded from being part of the Waynesboro cheering section, but I made a couple of phone calls late Friday and explained to Frank Whiting, the head of security, what we wanted to do." Allan reached into his shirt pocket and pulled out a pair of dark sunglasses.

"Here, put these on. I told Frank that Lucky is your seeing-eye dog."

Pat's hand went out for the glasses, then stopped a few inches from them. Her eyes darted from the glasses to Allan and back to the glasses.

"Are you sure we need to do it this way?" She asked, a look of concern and confusion on her face.

Unable to keep a straight face, Allan burst out laughing. "I'm sorry. I couldn't help it. It was just too good a story not to try it on you." He put the glasses on the dash.

"Why you old kidder, you. Dawn didn't warn me about this side of you," Pat said joining in on the joke with her own smile. "I was beginning to think I was going to have to watch the game through glasses too dark to see anything." The two of them laughed at the thought. As they did, their eyes met and captured each other for a brief moment. *It's going to be an excellent evening,* Allan thought as he studied the fine details of Pat's face. They broke the momentary gaze, and Allan went around the car to open Pat's door.

"Thank you kind sir," Pat said as she exited the car, turning to help Lucky out over the seat. She clipped the leash to his collar, and he obediently came to her left side.

"Good boy. You look pretty for the people tonight, and see if you can't find your real owner. Okay?"

"We need to go to the south gate to get in. Frank said he'd be sure to be stationed there. He has a note for us just in case anyone tries to raise a fuss. We should be just in time for the pre-game show."

Pat stepped up beside him and took his arm. "Thanks so much for inviting me to the game. I really feel like part of the community. It's nice. I've lived in Charlotte for years and haven't felt as much at home as I do here tonight."

"It's the small town atmosphere. It'll get you every time if you give it a chance," Allan replied. They joined the crowd entering the stadium.

FOR A SMALL TOWN HIGH school, Waynesboro boasted having one of the nicest and largest places to play football, and on this particular evening, the Eagle's Nest, as it was popularly called, was jammed to capacity. The Waynesboro Eagles and the Morganton Bulldogs were still in their respective locker rooms. The Morganton band was marching off the field at one end while the Waynesboro band lined up at the other, preparing to make their entrance for the pregame show.

"This is a beautiful facility," Pat remarked as Allan turned over their tickets to a tall lanky fellow wearing a crisply starched security uniform.

"Why, thank you ma'am," Frank replied as he handed the ticket stubs back to Allan. "You might get a chance to tell our benevolent benefactor what you think. He's here tonight; somewhere."

"Oh? Who's that?" Pat asked.

"Why Dr. Fredric Homlin, president and owner of Biogentrix, of course."

"Did you say Dr. Homlin is here tonight? That's unusual," Allan remarked.

"Not really," Frank replied. "His 'Honor' usually makes an appearance at all the big home games. He thinks it's good P.R. Just like he thinks donating all the money to build this stadium gives him the right to do whatever he wants in this town and out there in that damn lab of his." The sarcasm in Frank's voice was only slightly masked.

"Dr. Homlin doesn't seem to be the most popular guy in town," Pat said as they wound their way to their seats. "Despite trying to buy some popularity."

"No, I'd have to agree with you there," Allan replied. "I've never met the man face to face, but despite donating a lot of money to Waynesboro in one way or another and despite the fact Biogentrix is one of our larger employers, most people aren't settled about having them here. Most of the people who work there transferred in. It was great for the economy here, but not everyone saw it that way."

"How long has Biogentrix been here?"

"Only about three years. It's been a hornet's nest from the very first. Lately, it's gotten worse. That's why I was surprised to hear that Dr. Homlin has decided to walk among the common folk."

"I'd like to meet the man," Pat said with an edge of intensity that startled Allan.

"You are here for a vacation, aren't you?"

Pat laughed. "That's right. Still, once a detective, always a detective. He sounds like an interesting fellow, that's all. Don't worry, you're my date for the entire evening."

Allan smiled. "Thanks. It wouldn't do my reputation much good to have you leave me for someone else in front of so many people."

They came to their seats on the thirty yard line. Lucky brought immediate attention to them as the three of them sat down. Allan had purchased three tickets to be sure they'd have plenty of room for Lucky. Several of the kids around them immediately came up to Lucky and started patting him. Lucky ate up the attention.

"Neat. We have a new mascot," one of the teenager's said. "But he's not wearing the school colors." Within moments, the problem was remedied. Someone found an old Eagle's sweatshirt for Lucky. Allan helped Pat slip the shirt over Lucky's head and thread his front legs through the arms of the shirt. Everyone howled with laughter and Lucky joined in with a chorus of his own.

"Well, I guess we don't have to worry whether Lucky might fit in or not," Allan said as they finally settled in to watch the game. The two teams streamed onto the field, and the game was underway.

PAT GLANCED UP AT THE scoreboard at the end of the field. "Fourteen, fourteen. Can't ask for a closer game. I can't remember the last time I had so much fun at a football game." She turned to look at Allan. "Can we walk around during the halftime? I think we should try to find a spot to exercise Lucky."

"Sure. Could I interest you in a cup of coffee or hot chocolate?" As Allan asked the question, his breath formed a momentary cloud between them.

"Oh, I'd love some hot chocolate."

The three of them walked down to the refreshment stand, pausing frequently to give several kids in the crowd time to pat Lucky's head. The refreshment stand was crowded with other people intent on warming themselves up. The mood of the crowd was festive and light. Their team had held their own against the larger high school, and the Eagles were known as a second-half team. The stage seemed set for an upset.

Allan and Pat were almost to the front of the line when they heard a commotion behind them. As they turned to watch, a large man who towered a good four inches over anyone else in the crowd pushed his way through the crowd.

"Out of the way folks. Get out of the way," the man said repeatedly as he pushed the crowd to either side. Several people grunted their complaints as they were shoved out of their spots, but no one attempted to get in the big man's way. As he approached them, Pat stepped purposefully in front of him, planting her left heel into his instep with painful force.

"Excuse me. I'm so sorry. I didn't see you bullying your way through. May I help you?"

The man cursed under his breath but kept his self control. Through tearing eyes, he glared at Pat. "I need to get through here and get Dr. Homlin some coffee," he said as he attempted to wave Pat to the side, but Pat's heel was still on his instep, and she merely shifted her weight forward again and the man winced in pain once more.

"You don't mean 'the' Dr. Homlin? Not Dr. Fredric Homlin? Is ol' Freddy here tonight?"

"That's right. Now if you'll excuse me . . . "

But Pat didn't budge from her spot. She simply applied a little more weight to her left foot. "Why don't you go on back to your boss. I'll be happy to get ol' Freddy a cup of coffee and bring it to him."

The big man hesitated for a moment, unsure whether to proceed with his assignment or not. His attention was finally drawn to the fuming crowd around him as though he noticed for the first time that there were other people around. Pat ground her heel into the tender area of his foot one last time.

"Go on now. I'll be over there in just a moment with Freddy's coffee."

The thug finally pulled his foot out from under hers and retreated. "Dr. Homlin doesn't like to be called Freddy," he said under his breath. "He's over there next to the restrooms." He pointed to a small group of men, all dressed in dark cashmere coats.

As the man turned his back on them, Allan slid up next to Pat. "You're really something."

She turned to him, surprised at the comment. "Whatever do you mean?"

"You not only averted a mob scene single-handedly. You completely cowed that giant and got yourself a meeting with the eminent Dr. Homlin."

Pat smiled. "Well, I did say I wanted to meet him. Do you mind?"

"No, not at all, as long as you bring me along."

"Of course, silly. You're my date."

As they reached the front of the line, they purchased two hot chocolates, a coffee, and a hotdog for Lucky.

"It's terrible for my reputation for this many people to see me feed such trashy food to a dog, but since the next closest small animal vet is thirty miles away, I don't imagine it'll cost me too much business." Allan bent down and fed the hotdog to Lucky. "Now, let's go meet this Dr. Homlin."

They jostled their way through the crowd, Allan and Lucky leading the way with Pat following behind in their wake with the extra cup of coffee. As they approached the group, all the men turned to watch their arrival. Pat stepped forward with the cup of steaming coffee.

"Hello big guy," she said to the man she'd stopped in the crowd. "Here's the coffee I promised."

One of the men stepped forward to take the cup, but Pat ignored him. Instead she stepped around him and handed the cup to the shorter man standing next to him.

"Dr. Homlin, I presume," Pat said as she handed the cup to him. As she did so, Lucky stepped forward and took a sniff of Homlin's pant leg. The hairs on the back of his neck immediately bristled and a low threatening growl grew in his throat. Allan immediately pulled him back, but Lucky continued his threatening stance.

Dr. Homlin glanced first at Pat and then to Lucky and back again to Pat. "Your dog?" He asked as he nodded in Lucky's direction.

"No, not really. He's a stray I'm taking care of for a few days," Pat replied with a cold smile. She felt her own hackles rise on her back. She'd been a private investigator long enough to learn to trust her instincts. This man was to be watched carefully.

"Fine looking beast, though a bit silly looking in that garb. Perhaps I'd be interested in him." As he spoke, he took a couple of steps back.

Lucky calmed down a little but continued a barely audible growl in the back of his throat.

"Thanks for considering it. I'll let you know," Pat replied without much interest in the offer. She'd already decided Dr. Homlin was the last man on earth she'd ever give Lucky to. She continued to study him as Allan introduced himself. The owner of Biogentrix looked to be in his mid-forties although he had a face that made judging his age difficult. He was an attractive man. What one would call distinguished, dark hair with a dusting of gray at the temples.

Pat was most interested in Homlin's eyes. They were cold yet intense. She had the thought as she studied them that he could literally freeze you in your tracks with one stare. The slight crow's feet at the edges gave them a sinister quality. Pat felt the goose bumps tingle along her arms and understood why Lucky continued to growl. The dog had good judgment.

"I appreciate the coffee." Dr. Homlin directed the comment to Pat. "You must come out to my place someday soon, and let me return the hospitality."

Pat noticed the momentary look of surprise that flashed across the face of the large man who appeared to be Homlin's bodyguard. It appeared the invitation was an unusual one for Homlin to make.

"Why, I'd love to come out and see what goes on at Biogentrix. Perhaps Allan and I could make it out some afternoon for a tour."

Dr. Homlin laughed but there was no humor in the sound. "No, no, my dear. I'm afraid you misunderstood. The lab is off base. No one is permitted through there, even one so lovely as yourself. No. I meant my home, Waverly Place. It was once a game preserve. I bought it a few years ago and have been fixing it up. You'd be most welcome there."

Pat smiled at the correction and decided she must check out the Biogentrix lab as well as its mysterious owner.

"I am a bit difficult to reach right now, but you could give Allan a call at his clinic. He's taking care of Lucky right now, and so I'll get the message through him. Is that okay with you, Allan?"

"Sure, no problem. I have next Wednesday afternoon off. If that would work in your schedule, Dr. Homlin."

Pat appreciated Allan's willingness to come along. The thought of being alone with Homlin had only added to her goosebumps.

"I'll need to check my schedule. I can let you know by the first of the week," Dr. Homlin replied. Pat had the distinct feeling he was not excited about including Allan in the invitation, which was just fine with her.

Dr. Homlin tipped his coffee to them as though to make a toast. "Well, here's to an exciting second half. Enjoy the game." And with that, he and his entourage turned and walked away.

Only after he was out of sight did Lucky finally stop growling. "Well, it's for sure, ol' Lucky didn't have much use for the president of Biogentrix," Allan said as the three of them started back to their seats.

"No. I'd say Lucky has very good taste in people. I have to admit, Dr. Homlin gave me the creeps as well."

"Then why did you accept his invitation?" Allan asked, a note of surprise in his voice.

"Because he does give me the creeps. I've got a gut feeling something is off about the man, and I intend to find out what it is. I appreciate your offer to come along, but if you would rather not, I'll understand. I'll be fine."

"Are you kidding?" Allan replied. "I'm simply coming along to protect my own interest. After seeing how you handled yourself tonight, I'm sure you'll be fine. If anything, I'm more worried about Homlin. Just remember, you're on vacation."

"Yes, well, I think the vacation has just been turned into a working one." Pat took Allan's arm. "But for the rest of tonight it's all vacation, and I'll not have another thought about Dr. Homlin. Promise."

Unfortunately, it was a promise she found herself breaking several times throughout the rest of the evening.

Dissecting Larvae
Sunday, Nov. 9

The sharp scalpel blade slid across the glistening white tissue. Being accustomed to seeing a thin line of blood mark where the blade had traveled, Allan was surprised when the red streak did not appear. Of course, the larva had been dead for at least twenty-four hours. You wouldn't expect much bleeding this long after death. Then again, who was to say the damn things even had blood or that the blood would be red?

He wiped a drop of perspiration from his temple with the upper part of his arm. Why was he sweating so much? It couldn't be more than seventy degrees in the treatment room. *You're cutting open one of the things that turned into Todd*, he thought. *It's okay to feel a little strange, even to sweat a little. Your life has taken a bizarre twist lately. This is peculiar behavior even for Halloween.*

He continued to dissect into the deeper layers of the larva, surprised to find only a homogeneous mass of off-white tissue—but not entirely homogeneous. Throughout the layers were subtle markings, tissue a bit off-colored, as though it might one day have differentiated into organs.

In his years as a veterinary student and then as a practicing doctor, Allan had dissected many strange animals from starfishes and mud puppies to horses and cows. He'd never seen anything quite like the larva. There just wasn't much to look at. The closest thing it reminded him of was cutting through a brain. You knew it was a complex organ, the most complex of the body, yet when you cut through one about all you saw was white tissue.

Could the larva be just that—an undifferentiated brain waiting for a body to be formed around it? No, the first larvae hadn't formed a body around themselves. They had become the body, first a puppy like form then a human baby and last of all a reproduction of his son.

Allan had dissected the remaining larvae. Each one was like the first. What conclusions could he draw from his hour or so of work? Not much.

The larvae were definitely not like anything he'd ever run across. He'd known that from the start, and the dissections had only confirmed it. They appeared to be blank slates with very little of their inner workings predetermined. It made sense. Maybe that's why they were able to adapt to different forms so easily. Their genetic makeup wasn't preset. It seemed like a likely hypothesis.

Allan took the remains of the four larvae,

and triple bagged them. He then placed the bags into a sturdy cardboard box, taped it shut, and placed the box in the freezer reserved for animal pick-up. The city would be around in the morning to pick up whatever was in the freezer. They would simply think it was another dead animal waiting for disposal and would burn the whole thing: box, bags, and larvae.

Allan felt like an accomplice to a crime. Destroying evidence to protect a loved one. Well, perhaps it was true. He was protecting Todd. He had to. What would they do to Todd if anyone ever found out where he had come from? They'd haul him off to some governmental lab, and a dozen or more scientists would end up doing to him what Allan had just finished. They'd test him, draw all sorts of different samples, x-ray him, and eventually cut him open to see what made him tick. Allan shuddered at the thought. Not to his son they wouldn't.

He walked into his office and picked up his ski jacket off the desk where he'd thrown it when he'd first come in. As he put it on, his thoughts wandered from Todd to Pat. He had invited her to dinner on Wednesday after they were through visiting Homlin's place. He toyed with the idea of introducing Pat to Todd, except it couldn't be Todd, it would have to be TJ. It was a crazy thought. It could only complicate matters, the more people who knew about his secret.

But for some strange reason, he didn't want Pat to know just about TJ — not the fabricated story but the truth. All of it. Maybe she'd understand what he was going through. Maybe she would be able to shed some light on the mystery. After all, she was a private investigator.

The thought sent a cold chill down his back. That's right, she's a P.I. She'd love to know about such a story. But what would she do with it? Could he actually trust this woman who he'd only known for a couple of weeks? Or would she run to the authorities, or worse yet, report him to the mental health people? It was too dangerous. He couldn't take the chance. But the burden of carrying his secret around on his own was becoming overpowering. He had to tell someone soon or he'd burst. And if he was going to tell anyone, Pat would be the one to tell. He didn't know exactly why, but he trusted her.

How could he go about it? The question haunted him as he shut out the lights and turned the heat back. He had until Wednesday to figure it out. He had to tell someone, soon.

WEDNESDAY, NOV. 12

Allan pulled the latex gloves from his hands and threw them in the trash can.

"Give her two cc's of penicillin, Marva. We'll keep her in recovery until she's fully awake. Please have Dawn call Ms. Curtis and let her know Missy is doing fine and will be able to go home in the morning." He glanced at the work roster and then at his watch. "It's been a good morning. I love it when the day actually goes as you plan it."

He walked into his office, removing his lab coat as he went. It was almost one p.m., closing time for the clinic on Wednesday. Pat would be pulling into the driveway in a couple of minutes. They were scheduled to meet Dr. Homlin at two o'clock. That would give them just enough time to get a quick bite to eat before driving to the old animal reserve that had in the past three years become Homlin's private property and another reason for Waynesboro's citizens to complain about the mysterious owner of Biogentrix.

Although Allan was looking forward to seeing Pat again, he wasn't excited about going out to Homlin's. The man seemed cold and ruthless, and he didn't trust Homlin's motives at all. *If he makes a play for Pat I'll slug him, bodyguards or no bodyguards*, he thought as he glanced at the telephone messages Dawn had neatly laid out on his desk. Only one needed to be called today. He reached for the phone. May as well get it out of the way before he left. Then he'd call Kendra and let her know he'd be home around four so she could plan the rest of her day.

On his first call, a message machine answered, and he left a short message regarding one of his patients. Then he called his home. Kendra picked up the phone on the second ring.

"Dr. Pritchard's residence. Who's calling, please?" Kendra sounded a lot like her mother answering the clinic phone.

"Hey, Kendra. This is the Doc. How's TJ doing?"

"Hi, Doc. TJ is doing fine. Had a bowl of Cheerios. I've never seen a kid so crazy for them. He's napping at the moment. I can't believe how well he's walking already, and talking...he's talking up a storm. He even asked for his 'Dada' a few times before nodding off. So cute. Hope your brother doesn't get upset when he learns his son is calling you Dada. What's up?"

"Nothing much. I just wanted to let you know I'll be home around four today, and then I'm going to let you have the rest of the day off."

"Great! I've been meaning to ask you for some time off. I have several errands I need to run."

"Well, today is the day for them. Be sure TJ is dressed in something cute, will you?"

"Of course. I always dress him nice for his favorite uncle."

The comment caught Allan off guard. He didn't think of himself as TJ's uncle. He was his dad. After a funny pause, he said good-bye to Kendra and hung up the phone. As he did so, he glanced out the window and noticed Pat's car pulling into the parking lot. He glanced at his watch again. 12:58. He loved a woman who was prompt. He took his corduroy blazer from behind the door and stepped into the waiting room.

Meeting TJ
Wednesday, Nov. 19

Allan glanced at the clock on the kitchen wall; five-thirty. Only an hour before Pat was due to arrive. He'd finally made up his mind he would introduce her to TJ and tell her the whole story. He couldn't keep it a secret any longer. His "son" was still growing at an incredible rate. It was getting more and more difficult to hide the truth, much less keep him from wandering around. Sooner or later, Kendra would say something to Dawn about how large TJ had grown, or something else would happen to blow TJ's cover. Then what?

Allan had no way of knowing where that would lead. He also knew Pat wouldn't have any idea either, but the stress of worrying about it alone had become too much for him. At least with Pat knowing everything, he'd have someone he could talk to about it. Talking things out always helped. At least that's what Laura had always said. And deep down inside, Allan felt there was some hope that between the two of them, they could figure something out — some way to introduce TJ to the rest of the world without him being looked on as a freak or as dangerous.

When Allan had arrived home around four o'clock, TJ was still napping. Allan walked over to the refrigerator to see what he could find to warm up for his son.

He's not your son, a small voice said in the deep recesses of Allan's mind. *Your son is dead, and what you have napping in his room is a mutant larva that you pulled out of a stray dog. He's not your son. He's not even human. You don't know what he is, but he's not your son.*

"So what," Allan said out loud. "He's close enough."

As he said this, he spied the plastic container of food that Kendra had prepared for TJ's meal. God bless her. She sure made his life with TJ easier. Who was to say that this boy wasn't human? He looked human — looked uncannily like Todd looked when he was three. He eats human food. He talks like a human. He seemed to have a better vocabulary than Allan remembered his son having at three. Other humans, at least one other, related to him as human. So, for all practical purposes, he was human. Right?

Allan took the plastic container out of the refrigerator and stuck it in the microwave, loosening the lid as he did. He had learned the hard way about firmly applied lids in a microwave. After a minute, the bell to the microwave alerted him that TJ's meal was ready. He took it out and removed the lid to allow it to cool a little. He then walked in to waken him. By the time TJ was fully awake, the food would be cool enough for him to eat.

Allan entered TJ's room — the room that had been transformed from a shrine to his deceased son to his replacement son's nursery. Allan stopped in the doorway. *Something is wrong*, the nagging voice said even before he turned on the overhead light. *The crib looks empty...but it can't be...it's empty, I tell you.*

Allan flipped on the light and stared at the empty crib, the sheets and blanket pulled back as though whoever had been sleeping in the bed had suddenly thrown them off. The railing was still up. Allan's eyes flitted to the open window at the other end of the room, a light breeze ruffling the curtains. *Someone has taken my son*, was his first thought. *No — that's not possible. No one knows about TJ except Kendra and Dawn.* He was certain of that and equally sure neither one of them would have kidnapped him.

The bitter truth hit Allan in the pit of his stomach like a blow from a boxer pounding on his opponent's body to weaken him. TJ, or whatever TJ really was, had escaped on his own. He'd left by the window so as to go unnoticed, knowing Allan would have stopped him. But where had he gone and why?

Allan sat on the chair next to the crib where he usually sat to read bedtime stories, tears rimming his lower lids and then breaking over them. For the second time he'd lost his son and for the second time he felt the hollow sensation throughout every fiber of his body.

He could simply be outside playing. His mind told him. *You don't know what has happened. He might be back. Go look for him, you idiot. He may have just left.* But even as Allan rose from the chair to go find his flashlight, he feared he'd seen his son for the last time.

He started his search underneath TJ's window and, sure enough, found small footprints that matched TJ's foot size. He followed them across the lawn towards the woods, but before the trail made it to the woods, the pattern changed from child footprints to paw prints.

Allan stared down at the set of prints. *Still believe this is your son?* He asked himself. *Since when did Todd know how to transform himself into a dog?* Allan could feel the energy drain from him. Shoulders slumped, he slowly walked back to the house, obliterating the trail as he went.

"I REALLY APPRECIATE your coming back on your afternoon off," Pat said as she took the leash back from Dawn.

"Think nothing of it. Lucky is comfortable in his run, and I was planning on dropping by this afternoon to check on Mrs. Avery's two cats anyway. It was no trouble at all," Dawn replied with a smile, then added, "How's it going with Dr. Pritchard?"

"Well, with your help, it's going great. You were right, he really is a nice guy. We're having dinner in just a few minutes."

Dawn walked around the counter and escorted Pat to the door. "I'm so glad to hear it's going well. I'm not much for meddling in other people's affairs, but you two seemed made for each other."

She paused at the door, her hand on the lock. "I think the world of Dr. Pritchard. He's been good to me and my family. I'd do anything to see him happy." She smiled again. "He's happy when he's around you. I'd say you're good for each other."

Pat returned the smile, suddenly a little embarrassed by what Dawn was saying. Good for each other? Yes, she guessed they were.

As she turned out of the clinic's driveway heading towards Allan's house, the conversation with Dawn haunted her. She looked at herself in the rear view mirror. If Allan was happy around her, the feeling was mutual. She'd noticed it herself. Despite everything that was going on with the investigation, she was more relaxed and contented than she could remember being in the last ten years. It even showed on her face. Yes, Allan Pritchard was also good for her. She stopped at a traffic light a few blocks from the clinic and pulled out the directions Allan had given her to his place. When the light changed, she turned right.

Take today for instance. The visit to Homlin's private sanctuary could have been a nightmare. But having Allan there had made a big difference in how she viewed it. *Funny*, Pat thought. *He doesn't even know what's going on and he's making a difference. What might be possible if I told him what I was really up to?*

The thought surprised her. What was she up to? She wasn't even sure herself but something deep down inside, the little voice she had learned to listen to, kept whispering to her that somehow Homlin was connected to the Case of the Missing Alien. Maybe he had found the alien, saved its life, and was now in cohorts with it. Maybe the alien had died and Homlin was trying to use its genetic material in some way? The voice hadn't come up with many possibilities — at least not any that made sense. Still, it wouldn't let the matter rest.

Oh, so now you're going to tell Allan about what you've spent the last ten years of your life on? Tell someone about the Case of the Missing Alien? Someone you've only known for a couple of weeks? Are you crazy?

Why not? She argued with herself. *You just said Allan made a lot of difference at Homlin's today. What if the two of us were partners in this? Two heads are better than one.*

No way. How do you know he won't go to the authorities? If B.I.U.F.O. ever heard you were in these parts, what do you think they'd do? No, the risk is too high. It could blow the entire investigation. You just can't trust people to keep their mouths shut. You just can't trust people, period.

Pat suddenly realized she'd missed her turn. She pulled over to the side of the road to turn around. As she waited for the traffic to clear, the debate continued. For ten years she'd been quiet about what had happened on that mountain, convinced that if she told anyone, it would somehow get back to B.I.U.F.O. and before she knew it, she'd be locked up for life. It wasn't just that she did not relish the idea of spending the rest of her life in some room with quilted walls. If they put her away as they had threatened to do, who would be on the watch for the alien? She had to stay free. Sooner or later the alien would surface and when it did, she had to be ready to stop it.

No, as much as she liked Allan and wanted to trust him, it was just too dangerous. There was simply too much at stake.

━━━━━━+++\\ᕻ±+━━━

AT SIX-THIRTY WHEN Pat pulled up in front of his house, Allan was still outside looking for TJ. He heard the approaching jeep and walked around the house, flashlight in hand.

"Hello?" Pat said, a troubled frown on her face. "Is something the matter?"

Her P.I. radar is already on, thought Allan. "No, not really. Just thought I heard something in the backyard. Come on in the house."

In the last half hour, he'd been debating with himself whether to go ahead with his original plan to tell Pat about TJ, but his disappearance changed everything. Was there really a need to bring her into this now? Given her profession, it was likely she would view his son's disappearance as a possible kidnapping and would want to call in the police and FBI if she even believed his story. Without TJ, there was very little reason to expect she would. It was just too dangerous. As they entered through the kitchen door, Pat gazed around as though a potential buyer being shown the house for the first time by the real estate agent.

"Very nice. Cozy. It has that lived-in feel without being messy. I approve." She strolled into the living room where the wood stove and overstuffed furniture added to the warm, lived-in feeling. She glanced at the wall of pictures and then back to Allan, a surprised look on her face. She continued to walk around as Allan stood in the center of the living room, unsure what to do or say. She walked past the partially open door that led into TJ's room, and Allan held his breath. He had failed to come back into the house and prepare it for Pat's visit. His mind raced. *What to do? If she goes into TJ's room, she'll know something is up. I've got to stop her.*

"How about some dinner?" He blurted out too loudly.

Pat stopped a few feet from TJ's room and turned to look at Allan, a confused look on her face. "Aren't you going to show me around first?"

"Well, the rest of the house is a bit messy. I'd rather wait until another time when it's clean, if you don't mind."

Allan walked past her and pulled the door to TJ's room closed. "I've also changed my mind about eating in. There's a new place on the edge of town that opened up a couple of weeks ago I've been meaning to try. I doubt it'll be too busy this evening. Why don't we try it?"

Allan took Pat's arm and gently guided her back to the kitchen. "I'll just get my coat and be right with you." He left her in the kitchen and ran to the hall closet to pull out his blazer.

As he walked back into the kitchen, he found Pat standing in front of the microwave, its door open. In her hand was the plastic sectional plate with TJ's dinner. She turned and stared at Allan. The two stood a few feet apart, frozen in place by the mystery between them. Finally, Pat broke the silence.

"What's going on Allan? You can tell me. I'll understand."

"What do you mean?" Allan replied lamely. He didn't know what else to say.

"You're outdoors with a flashlight. The empty unmade crib in the other room. Everywhere I look, signs that a child lives here — including dinner," she said, holding the dish of baby food out to him.

Their eyes locked onto each other. Would she understand? Allan doubted it, but whether she did or not, he had to tell her. It was too much to keep between them. He laid his jacket on the back of a kitchen chair.

"Sit down, Pat. It's a long story. I don't know if you'll understand. I don't know that I do, but I'll tell you the whole thing." He sat down in the chair where he'd laid his jacket. Already, a heavy burden seemed to be lifting from his heart.

Pat sat down in the chair next to him, placing the plastic plate on the table beside them. She reached out and took his hands in hers and squeezed them gently and waited for him to speak. Allan started with the emergency C-section months ago.

"... WHEN I WENT INTO the room to wake him up, he had gone through the window. God only knows where." Allan finished the story with a heavy sigh and a shrug of his shoulder. He studied his hands that Pat still held in her own.

After a few moments, Pat pulled one of her hands away and lifted his chin with it. "Allan, I know this is going to sound strange, but I believe every word of your story. I can't explain what's going on either, not fully, but I suspect what brought me here is somehow connected to what has happened to you."

"What do you mean?" Allan asked, shaking his head. "I thought you were here on vacation."

Pat shook her head. "I'm afraid I haven't been sincere and upfront with you either."

She stood up and walked over to the kitchen window. She stared out into the night, struggling with herself. After almost a minute, she turned around and looked at Allan but still didn't speak. Another thirty seconds went by.

Finally she said, "I've never told anyone what I'm about to tell you. To tell you the truth, I had decided earlier tonight that I wouldn't tell you either, but what you just shared changes all that. If you can keep such a secret...well, I'm just going to trust you." As she said it, she exhaled a deep sigh.

"It's your turn to sit back and hear my unbelievable but true story. After we're both caught up with what is happening around here, maybe, between the two of us, we can figure out what or who is causing it.

"This is not the first time I've been to these parts," Pat began as she walked back over to him and sat down. "The first time was ten years ago when I worked for an organization called B.I.U.F.O. . ."

"... I'VE SPENT THE LAST ten years waiting for the alien to turn up. Anything that sounded suspicious, I'd check it out. So far, every lead has gone nowhere. I finally decided to come back here to the scene of the crime, so to speak, to see if I could pick up anything new. Until a couple of days ago, I'd had no luck."

"What happened a couple of days ago?" Allan asked, a look of wonder mixed with confusion on his face.

"I met Dr. Homlin. I still don't know what the connection is, but I know he's connected in some way. Maybe he found the beast ... the alien. In my mind I think of it as a beast—a vicious killing machine. Anyway, I don't know how, but I'm sure Homlin is connected in some way. And I suspect — no, I know the copy of your son is connected as well."

Allan flinched at the word 'copy'. He realized it was an accurate description, but he wasn't ready to think that way — not yet. Pat patted his knee. She stood up and walked over to the counter where Allan's coffee maker sat. "Do you mind if I make us a pot of coffee? For some reason, I think this might turn into a late evening."

Allan nodded. "Everything is in the cabinet over the coffee maker."

As Pat filled the coffee maker with water, she glanced over her shoulder to Allan who continued sitting at the kitchen table, studying his hands clasped together in front of him.

"You know Allan, this is going to sound awfully harsh of me, but I think it needs to be said." She paused for a moment. "Your son, Todd, died several years ago. Whatever has been living in your house isn't your son. I know you'd like it to be, but it isn't."

Allan nodded but didn't reply. After about a minute he walked over to the refrigerator and pulled out a carton of milk for the coffee. "You know, I used to never keep milk in the fridge. I don't drink it very often except in coffee. A quart would go sour on me but when Todd . . . TJ . . . whoever — I don't even know what to call him...it...when he came, I started keeping half gallons.

"I know what you're saying is true," he continued. "I've been living in a fantasy, knowing all along, sooner or later I'd have to wake up, but the dream was so sweet, I just didn't want to face the morning."

His eyes began to tear and Pat took a step closer and put her arms around him. He stood rigid for a few seconds then relaxed into her embrace. He laid his head against her neck and shoulder. After a moment, Pat felt his body shudder and his tears moisten her neck. They stood huddled together for several minutes as Allan quietly wept.

Neither one spoke for several minutes. Pat continued to hold Allan in her arms but even as she comforted him, she wondered. *What had been staying with him?*

A LIGHT TAPPING ON the study door brought Homlin's head up from the pile of papers on his desk. "Yes, what is it?" He asked gruffly. Hadn't he told them he was not to be disturbed?

The door opened and Alex Yadkin, Homlin's right hand man, stuck his head and shoulder in through the crack. "I'm sorry to disturb you, but it's rather important. There's a small boy here to see you. About all we can get out of him is his name. TJ—TJ Pritchard," Alex said with an amused look on his face.

"I don't know anyone by that name. Find out what he wants ... wait a minute. What did you say his name was?"

"TJ Pritchard." Alex repeated.

"Any relation to that ass, Allan Pritchard?"

"He says he's Dr. Pritchard's son."

"Oh, he does, does he?" Homlin shut the file in front of him and rose from behind the desk. "I didn't think Pritchard had any children."

"That's the interesting thing." Alex replied. "He doesn't, although our research on him revealed he did have one who died in a fire a few years ago. His name was Todd."

Homlin glanced at his bodyguard. "What's going on here? What are you smirking at?"

"You'll see in just a moment," Alex answered.

"This had better be good or you'll be answering to me. You know I don't care for practical jokes."

"Oh, you'll enjoy this one. I'll stack my next three days off on it."

The two of them walked down the stairs to the library. Alex opened the door and stepped aside to allow his boss to enter first. As Homlin walked through the doorway he saw the child sitting in the center of the plush sofa, his legs dangling in mid-air, a confused, worried look on his face. When Homlin first entered the room, the boy was looking all around, as though he'd never been in such a large room, but then his eyes drifted over to Homlin and stayed fixed. The boy's furrowed brow relaxed, and his face took on the calm composure of someone nestled in his loved one's arms.

Homlin studied the small infant for several seconds before turning his attention to his amused escort. "Why didn't you tell me? He's one of us!"

IT WAS WELL AFTER MIDNIGHT. Allan had lost all track of how long they'd been talking. He lay on the sofa in the den enjoying the warm cozy heat of the wood stove. His head rested on Pat's lap, and as they talked, her hand lightly stroked his temple. Despite the intensity of the conversation—how their two stories might fit together—Allan couldn't remember a time when he'd been more at ease. It felt so natural. It was hard to believe he'd known this woman for such a brief time.

As the evening progressed, the talking grew softer and less frequent. Allan found his attention drawn to Pat's light caresses. He studied the fine details of her face—the slightly upturned nose, the full lips, the high cheekbones, the creamy texture of her skin.

Slowly, Allan raised himself up on one elbow and brought his eyes level with Pat's. For the moment, all thoughts of mysterious larvae and alien space-ships evaporated. The only thing Allan was aware of was Pat's slightly parted lips. So lovely, so sensual, drawing him in so much. It had been so long since he'd allowed himself to think about being with a woman. He had tried dating a couple of times in the past two years. Both had ended in disaster. He'd simply not been ready. But with Pat it was different. This didn't feel like a date. This felt as natural as if they'd been together for years. She belonged here in his den and he belonged in her arms. That's just the way it was supposed to be.

His lips lightly touched hers once, twice. He turned his head slightly and kissed her again, harder this time, then harder still. The passion mounted like a freight train rumbling down the side of the mountain. Pat's supple body pressed against his, a willing player in the love game. They explored each other at will — two children discovering that their best friend isn't exactly the same after all.

Finally, when Allan felt like he would burst, Pat gently pushed him away for a moment. "Not on the couch. Let's go to your bed." Her face was flushed and the look of desire matched his own.

Allan was suddenly uncertain. It wasn't that he didn't want to make love to Pat. He did, more than anything he could think of at the moment. The question suddenly shot into his head. *Could he?* It had been so long. He'd always been a satisfying lover to Laura, but that had been years ago and the two of them had practically grown up together. What would Pat expect? She was probably used to experienced lovers with special talents that came from sleeping with many different women. Meanwhile, he was just a small town boy who could count on one hand, maybe two, the number of women with whom he had slept.

Pat seemed to notice his hesitation and patted his cheek. "Don't worry honey, we're just going to bed. Who knows what will happen. We might just fall asleep." Her warm smile and light teasing reassured him. True, he didn't know what Pat liked and finding out would be half the fun.

As they entered Allan's bedroom, he was momentarily embarrassed to find he'd not made up his bed, but Pat didn't seem to even notice. She excused herself and walked into the bathroom. As soon as the door closed, Allan rushed to put the bed linens in some order, before stripping his clothes off. Pajamas? Should he put something on? Hell, he didn't even know if he still owned a pair or not. Certainly, Pat wouldn't have any gown to put on. Not unless she had a teddy secretly hidden in her handbag.

He decided against looking for pajamas. *What the hell, go for broke*, he thought as he stripped off his underwear. It felt funny to suddenly be so self-conscious about what he did or didn't wear. He pulled the sheet and bed-spread back and slipped into bed. The cool sheets felt good against his warm body. Despite his sexual arousal, he felt a calming drowsiness start to play at his eyelids. Wouldn't Pat be shocked if she came out of the bathroom to find him snoring away in bed. She'd probably never forgive him. There was no chance of it happening. His body was too tingly—too aroused.

In a moment, Allan noticed the crack of light under the bathroom door disappear, and a moment later the door opened and Pat strolled out towards the bed. She wore his bathrobe she'd found behind the bathroom door. She approached the bed, her slender form silhouetted by the light coming through the bedroom door from the other room. She stood next to the bed for a moment, gazing down at him, then slowly pulled the tie loose from her slender waist. She slipped the bathrobe from her shoulders and let it drop to the floor. The light from the other room cast an eerie glow across her slender shape.

Allan slid himself to the other side of the bed, giving Pat room to slide into the warm spot he'd just vacated. As she pulled the sheet over her, she turned towards him and pulled his head to her breasts. Allan inhaled the sensual fragrance of her perfume mingled with the aroma of arousal. He closed his eyes and enjoyed the visual fireworks discharging behind his eyelids. His hands and tongue danced across the dance floor of Pat's body as her hands did their own dance across his.

Allan smiled to himself. *Making love is a little like riding a bike*, he thought. *Some things you just never forget.*

Poaching
Sunday, Nov. 23

The buck raised his head, sniffing at the air for possible danger. Noticing no change, he resumed his grazing at the edge of the open field. The muscles of his shoulders twitched slightly. He stepped from patch to patch of the dry grass, seemingly unconscious to his surroundings. Suddenly his head lifted again, a large tuft of grass still in his mouth. Before the buck could take a step, the arrow entered his chest, penetrating deeply through the lung, puncturing the heart.

Despite the fatal wound, the buck flung himself back on his rear legs and leaped into the air, galloping across the clearing. With each beat, the heart pumped the life-giving blood into the chest cavity. At the middle of the field, the deer stumbled, righted itself and stumbled again. Ten yards into the woods it crashed to the ground, already its brown eyes glazing over. By the time the hunter reached it, the heart had stopped pumping its blood through the wrong channel.

"Damn, what a shot!" "Convoy" MacMillan shouted, then realizing where he was, clamped a hand over his mouth. He ran across the edge of the clearing keeping his eye on the spot where the deer had disappeared into the woods. He wasn't worried. The arrow from his crossbow had traveled straight and true to its mark. He would not have a long search for this one. God only knew how he was going to get it out of here by himself. But he wasn't that far from the opening in the fence and his pickup truck. He'd field-dress it as quickly as possible to reduce the weight and drag the remains out. It would be worth the hard work. He could already imagine the look on Bo's face when he drove up to his place with the buck in the back of his truck. The look alone would be worth the effort.

As Convoy entered the far edge of the woods, he slung the crossbow across his back and pulled the hunting knife from its sheath. It would pay for him to be quick with his work. One could never be too careful when poaching on a game reserve. *Especially this one*, Convoy thought. Ever since the strange doctor had taken it over, it gave him the heebie-jeebies to hunt there. He'd seen the patrols, each man with an automatic rifle that looked like it came from a Rambo movie. He suspected the men were the type who would shoot first and ask questions later. He wasn't interested in finding out if this was true. Best just to move fast, take the spoils and vamoose.

As he spied the still carcass only a few yards into the woods, Convoy smiled. *What a shot!* He thought again. He loved hunting with a crossbow. It was the weapon of a true sportsman. It took cunning, patience, and a high level of skill. Not like hunting with a rifle where you could take a beast like this one down from a hundred yards. Anyone could do that. Hell, even Bo got lucky on occasions.

Convoy pulled the deer onto its back and jammed the knife into the warm belly. As the knife penetrated the cavity, steam rose from around the opening, and the glistening innards pushed their way through the wound. Convoy continued to saw across the thick muscle of the abdomen, working his way towards the chest. Concentrating on his work, he missed the quivering lump of white tissue until one of them fell out of the wound and landed on his boot.

At first, he glanced down nonchalantly at his foot to see what had hit it. Spying the still moving mass, he jumped back from the buck, dropping his knife in the leaves.

"Holy mother-of-pearl. What the hell. .? Shit! Not those damn things again. What is it with you guys?" He addressed the question to the dead buck. "Really. This is disgusting. How can you all look so damn healthy and be eaten up inside with such disgusting worms, or whatever the fuck they are?"

He wiped the boot the larva had landed on in the leaves. He stopped for a moment and considered his next move. What had Bo said about these things? He'd seen them too, hadn't he? And it had been from a deer outside the reserve. That vet friend of Bo's had been there and had seen them too.

What had Bo said about it? Hell, they'd been drinking a good while by the time the subject had come up. His mind was a bit foggy about the whole conversation. The vet hadn't known what the damn things were either. Wasn't that what Bo had said? They'd taken the carcass and dressed it anyway, but no one had dared try the meat yet. Fuck! What was he to do?

He stared down at the deer's carcass. Maybe he could take it over to the next county and sell it to some of his buddies over there. It was doubtful anyone over there had heard about these things. Yeah, that's what he'd do. He'd cut the head off and have it preserved and he'd sell the meat, or if he couldn't sell it, he'd trade it for some 'shine. He'd get something out of his hard work besides a queasy stomach.

He kicked the quivering lump with the same boot he'd been trying to clean and watched the white mass sail into a clump of bushes several feet away. As he watched the mass disappear into the bush he suddenly realized he was not alone. Standing a few yards deeper into the woods behind the bushes where the lump had disappeared was a thickly muscled brute, his automatic rifle resting comfortably in the crook of one arm. The cold smile on the man's face turned Convoy's stomach for another loop.

I'm in deep shit now, he thought as he found his lips stretching into a fake smile. All thoughts of the meat and the rack of antlers evaporated into the cold winter air. Survival was the only thing that mattered now. Get the fuck out of the reserve without ending up like the buck. He turned in the opposite direction of the man and started tearing through the bush, zigging from side to side. As he ran, he thought he could hear the man behind him raise the gun and cock it. Still, he ran, the cold air burning deep into his emphysemic lungs.

He'd begun to think the man had been all threat and no action. *Hell, he's one of those who can't pull the trigger*, he thought, just before the burst of gunfire lifted him off the ground and crashed him into a tree. It was his last thought before the shattering pain enveloped him followed closely by a wave of darkness.

———————— ⁜⁜∖∖⌿⌿ ————————

HOMLIN LEANED BACK in the plush leather chair and pulled deeply on the cigar. *A strange habit*, he thought for the hundredth time, as he enjoyed the sensation of smoke entering his chest. Nowhere else had he ever heard of any civilization that inhaled smoke as a pastime. It was even stranger that he had adopted such a habit. He leaned a little further back in his chair and stared at Alex through the thick haze of smoke.

"Well, what do you have to report on our Ms. Vogt?"

Alex didn't respond at once. He'd learned to choose his words carefully when reporting to his superior. Homlin was not above killing the messenger for being the bearer of bad news. It could get dicey sometimes, even when the news wasn't so bad, as in this instance.

"I have two of my best men on her in twelve hour rotations. She has moved into the Waynesboro Inn and is no longer camping out. For the most part she just seems to be enjoying her vacation. Nothing suspicious to report at this point."

"Good. But I don't want your men to relax. She's unpredictable," Homlin replied, remembering all too well his almost fatal first meeting with Pat Vogt. "She's a very cunning member of an equally cunning species. Don't relax, do you understand?"

Alex nodded, hesitated for a moment again, then decided to go for it. Homlin appeared in a good mood. It wasn't any harm in giving it a shot. "There's one thing I don't understand," Alex started tentatively, as though testing the water with his toe before jumping in.

"Yes? Go ahead," Homlin urged.

"Well, if this woman is so dangerous to our plan, why not just snuff her out? I mean, after all, she is the only human who might be able to figure out who you are. Why not get rid of her? I'd have no problem . . . "

Homlin suddenly righted himself in his chair and leaned forward across his desk. He opened his mouth, a quick retort ready to put Alex in his place, then stopped, the first words hanging in his throat. Instead, he stood up and walked over to where Alex sat. "Even though I know you are here not to think but to act on my thinking, I'm feeling benevolent today so I'm going to explain the situation to you." He smiled down at Alex who visibly relaxed, then strolled towards the window.

"Vogt is dangerous, no question. She's very dangerous. As you said, she's the only human who actually saw me when I first landed. But the entire situation is dangerous at this point. We are at a critical time. Until we get the FDA approval for FreeForm, everything is in a very sensitive balance. One wrong move could jeopardize the entire project. I need not remind you what that could mean for our race."

"Killing a human right now, any human, could tip the balance. The one thing I do not need right now is to have attention drawn to this area or to Biogentrix or to myself. Not yet. I'll be flying back to Washington in a few days. I expect by this time next week everything will be in place for the final approval. It'll be downhill from there. But for right now, we are at a critical point. Very critical."

Homlin turned from the window and faced Alex. "Therefore, I want you to do only one thing. Follow my orders. Thinking on your own right now is very dangerous." Homlin smiled. "When the time is right for our Ms. Vogt, I'll let you know. I'm quite aware of your interest in her. You be a good soldier, and I'll be sure you get your reward."

Alex started to rise from his chair. Before he could do so, there was the sound of someone running down the hallway outside and a moment later a loud rap on the door.

"Come in," Homlin said, turning back to his desk.

Lenny, Alex's second officer in charge of the guards, burst through the door. One look at his face raised the hackles on the back of Homlin's neck. Now what had happened? He was only seconds from finding out.

"I'm sorry to barge in like this . . ."

"What is it?" Homlin interrupted him.

"There's been some trouble on the southwest quadrant of the grounds," Lenny replied, staring nervously at his two superiors.

"What kind of trouble?" Homlin asked as he flipped the ashes from his cigar.

"One of our men caught a poacher," Lenny continued.

Homlin relaxed at the news. He continued to his desk and sat down.

"Okay," he said in a more relaxed manner. "That's not so bad. You know what the procedure is for poachers, don't you?"

"Yes," Lenny replied. "I know, but I'm afraid one of the men panicked. The poacher was shot and killed."

"What!" Homlin and Alex shot out of their chairs as though pulled by the same string. "You've got to be kidding. You can't mean to tell me after all the warnings I've given your men, that one of them had the nerve to disobey me."

Homlin felt the veins in his neck bulge and his face grow suddenly warm. "Of all the stupid, avoidable accidents..." Homlin struggled to find the words to express his anger.

"Who was the poacher, do you know?" Alex asked.

"Yes. His ID was recovered. His name is Daniel MacMillan."

Daniel MacMillan? Homlin searched through his memory. He didn't know a MacMillan. He turned and glared at Alex.

"Well?"

"The name sounds familiar yet it doesn't quite fit," Alex replied. "MacMillan? I know of a MacMillan but his first name isn't Daniel. Wait a minute." Alex turned to his second in command.

"Was he wearing an old blue cap with some trucking emblem on it?" Alex asked as Homlin paced back and forth between the desk and the window.

"Yes, that's right," Lenny replied.

Alex let out a big sigh. "I don't think this is going to be as bad as it looks." He glanced first to Lenny and then to Homlin.

"Why not?" Homlin and Lenny asked at the same time.

"Well, I happen to know about our poacher. He's a no-count drifter. Seldom has a steady job. Drinks like a fish. It's not unusual for him to go on benders all the time. Might disappear for months on end. No one will be surprised if he suddenly disappears. Hell, I doubt anyone will even notice."

Homlin considered what Alex had said. He chewed on the half smoked cigar like it was meant for eating rather than smoking. "Are you sure?"

"I'll go down and verify who he is," Alex said. "But if he's who it sounds like, yes, I'm sure. No one will miss him."

Homlin continued to chew on the cigar. Finally he replied, "Okay. Go check it out and let me know for sure. Then I want you to pull everyone together. I'm going to get the point across once and for all. I'm not going to have our entire mission jeopardized by some trigger-happy idiot. And I want you to get a message to your two 'experts.' Under no circumstance are they to touch a hair on Vogt's head. They are simply to watch her and report all actions to me. Is that clear?"

Alex nodded. "Very clear." He rose from his chair. "I'll take care of it right away."

After the two men left, Homlin sat behind his desk and considered the situation. Everything would be fine if only he didn't have to depend on such idiots to get the job done.

Then he smiled as he lit his cigar and blew a new cloud of smoke. *Not much longer*, he thought. Soon, the most critical part of his job would be accomplished and he could relax. Then he would be able to give Alex the treat he so much longed for. Maybe he would arrange to watch the fun.

Homlin's Home
Saturday, Nov. 27

Pat pulled off the road onto the narrow driveway and found the road blocked by a formidable wrought iron gate. *It's about time I get a look beyond that gate*, she thought. Homlin had managed to put her and Allan off several times, offering various excuses, but once again her persistence — some might call it stubbornness — had paid off. A guard stepped out from the small house next to the gate and walked up to the jeep.

"Hi. I'm Pat Vogt and this is Dr. Allan Pritchard. We have a two o'clock appointment with Dr. Homlin."

"May I see your driver's license? Both of them," the guard replied coldly.

Allan and Pat glanced at each other as they pulled their licenses out and passed them to the guard who studied them carefully before passing them back.

"Drive straight to the house. It's .6 miles from here. Do not stop along the way for any reason. Drive fifteen miles per hour. No faster or slower. They will be expecting you. Is that understood?"

"Oh yes, quite well. You have a nice day now," Pat answered sweetly.

As the gate opened, she threw the jeep in gear and slammed her foot down on the gas pedal. The rear wheels kicked stones in all directions as they fought for traction. The jeep leaped ahead, passing fifteen miles per hour in the first few seconds.

Pat turned to Allan. "Did he say fifty miles per hour? That seems a little fast on such a narrow road." But she kept her foot to the floor.

Allan grabbed instinctively for the handhold above his head and smiled nervously.

They arrived at Homlin's home in less than a minute. Pat waited until the last second before slamming on the brakes. The jeep squealed to a stop in a cloud of dust and burning rubber, inches from the front porch. The front door burst open and four large men poured out onto the porch, automatic rifles and revolvers in their hands.

"Well, what a warm reception," Pat said as she undid her seat belt and opened her door. She started walking towards the house, then stopped to look back at Allan who continued to sit in the jeep, grasping the strap over his head. Pat walked around to his side and opened the door.

"Relax, Allan. I promise not to get us killed. I just want to play with them for a little while." She'd already proven her point. Dr. Homlin had something to hide. No one had so much security just for the fun of it. The question was, what was he hiding?

As she walked towards the house, she held her hands high in the air. "Don't shoot, don't shoot. It's just us. The guard said at the gate that we should go exactly fifty miles per hour until we got to the house. I thought it was a bit too fast, but who am I to argue with house rules?"

As she passed one of the guards standing on the first step of the porch, she lowered her hands and patted the automatic rifle he held in his hand. "Nice pea shooter you have there, Charlie. Do you know how to use it?"

Allan slowly exited the jeep, a sheepish grin still on his face. "Hello boys. No hard feelings, huh?"

When no one responded, he stepped up his pace and caught up with Pat.

"Take it easy, will you? You're not making any friends at the moment."

"You wouldn't want these gorillas as friends, anyway," Pat answered loud enough for the "gorilla" holding the door to hear.

As they entered the foyer, they were met by the man who Pat had first confronted at the ball game walking down the wide, spiral staircase that led to the second floor. *Quite a place Homlin has here,* Pat thought as she smiled politely.

"Ms. Vogt and Dr. Pritchard. How nice of you to pay us a visit. Dr. Homlin is on a long distance call at the moment. He'll be with you in a few minutes. In the meantime, if you'd like to step into his study..." He pointed to a set of double doors to the right.

Pat and Allan nodded and entered the study that had apparently been a sitting room in its former life as a game reserve. The room was large and spacious. Lining three walls were bookcases from floor to ceiling. Most of the fourth wall was taken up by a large picture window lined with heavy drapes that could be pulled shut to exclude all light. At the moment the drapes were open letting in the breathtaking view of the game reserve forest. Visible through the trees was a large lake.

"Could I fix you a drink while you wait?" The bodyguard asked with more manners than it seemed natural for him. *Obviously, Homlin has instructed him to be on his best behavior*, Pat thought.

"Do you happen to have lemonade?" Pat asked with a flutter of her eyelashes.

"Why yes, uhh, in the kitchen," the temporary host answered. "I'll go see if I can find it."

Pat nodded and watched as he left the room. As soon as the door closed behind him, she was in motion prowling around the room like a bloodhound on a hot trail.

"What are you doing?" Allan asked with a note of surprise in his voice.

"I'm just checking out Homlin's interest in reading material. The books in a person's library often say a lot about them." She continued to study the shelves of books.

After a few moments, she seemed to lose interest in the study and walked over to the window. "Well, what's the verdict?" Allan asked as he picked up a book at random from one of the shelves.

"If he's read all these books, he's very well read," she answered. "There doesn't seem to be a particular pattern which is unusual. Most people have one or two favorite subjects or types of books they read and collect. Homlin doesn't. There is a high concentration of classics, but they span the entire Dewey Decimal System in subject. The fiction is just as varied."

After a few more minutes of gazing out the window, she turned with a puzzled look on her face. "What do you think is out there?"

"What do you mean?"

"Out there." She pointed out the window. "In the game reserve? Our instructions were to not stop on the road. I dare say if we had been more than a minute or so late, we'd have been quickly sought out. What is out there that Homlin doesn't want us to see?"

"It's the rules," came a voice from the study doorway. Homlin stepped into the room, a smile on his face that sent a cold shiver down Pat's neck.

"I hired this protection agency after I received some threatening phone calls. My research is controversial as I'm sure you are aware if you read the paper. The agency agreed to protect me only if I followed their rules. Coming straight to the house at *fifteen miles per hour* is one of the rules. That's all."

Homlin gazed first at Pat and then at Allan as though checking to see if they were buying his explanation. As he spoke, he strolled over to the over-stuffed leather upholstered chair and motioned them to a matching sofa.

"Your drinks will be here in a moment. I apologize for not being available to welcome you personally, but it was an important call I've been waiting for all morning. To answer the question you were posing, I have maintained and added to the game reserve. What is out there . . . " He waved one arm in the direction of the picture window. " . . . is game. Quite an assortment of game, both indigenous to the region and some that are not, but they do well in this climate. I have a strong interest in preserving nature, especially the endangered wild animals. How about you, Ms. Vogt? It seems I've met you somewhere before. I was wondering if it could have been at some meeting on wildlife preservation?"

"No, I doubt it," Pat replied. "I've only a passing interest in it. Like many people, I'm an avid animal lover, but I'm not what you'd call an animal activist."

"Strange. I seldom forget a face, particularly such a charming one. Do I not ring a similar bell with you?" Homlin stared intently at Pat as she replied.

"No, I'm quite sure I've never met you," she replied with a casual shrug of her shoulder. "I am also very good at remembering faces and names." But as she smiled sweetly back at their host, she felt a strange feeling that she was lying even to herself. She had never met this man and yet at the same time there was something strangely familiar about him. But what?

"Have you lived in these parts long?" Homlin continued to question her but before she could answer, Homlin's bodyguard entered with their drinks. She waited until he was finished serving before answering.

"No, actually I'm visiting for the first time," Pat said and was relieved when Allan gave no indication otherwise. "So, unless you spend a lot of time in Charlotte, I'm afraid we've never met."

"Well, it's really not important," Homlin answered, but Pat was unconvinced by the statement. Homlin was not the type of man to ask such questions if they were not important. Something about Pat troubled him almost as much as he troubled her.

With that statement, Homlin turned his attention to Allan for a few moments, asking polite questions as though to cover up the fact that it was really only Pat in whom he was interested. After a few minutes, he turned the conversation to a more general direction. Each time Pat tried to ask anything about his research at Biogentrix, Homlin deftly sidestepped the question. After forty-five minutes, Pat knew little more about Homlin or his company.

He's good, Pat thought. *He's as slippery as I've seen when it comes to giving away information. I'm damn good at prying people open, but he's as tight a clam as I've ever run into. Whatever I find out won't come directly from him.*

Finally, Homlin glanced at his watch. "Oh, I'm sorry to have to cut this pleasant visit off so abruptly, but I'm expecting another important phone call in just a few minutes. It's likely to take quite some time so I'm afraid I'll have to say adieu for now. Alex will escort you to your car." He nodded to his bodyguard who had been standing quietly in the shadows and who now stepped forward.

Homlin shook Allan's hand then walked over to Pat. Taking her hand in his, he gazed intently into her eyes. Still holding her hand, he said, "It was a pleasure to see you again, Ms. Vogt. It may be that we have never met, but I trust this won't be the last time we see each other."

Pat forced a smile and a flicker of her long lashes, meanwhile fighting back a shiver. Homlin's hand felt like the appendage of a cold carcass laid out in some mildewy morgue. She turned to leave, then noticed Allan holding onto the banister of the staircase, staring at something above them.

"What's up," she whispered as she nodded in the direction he was looking.

"Oh...nothing," he replied, but continued looking towards the top of the stairs. "I just thought I...but it couldn't be." Noticing he was drawing unwanted attention to himself, he turned back to the group. "Very nice place you have here...very nice indeed."

Homlin bowed out, leaving them to Alex's care. He reminded them again to leave directly traveling at fifteen miles per hour this time, not fifty. Pat promised she would and surprised herself by keeping her promise.

ALEX WATCHED THE JEEP pull slowly out of the drive. As it turned the first bend he heard Homlin's voice over the intercom paging him to his office.

He entered the upstairs office. Homlin stood there gazing out the window at the path the jeep had recently traveled.

"I want you to put a couple of your best men on her," Homlin said without turning to look at Alex.

"You still think she might remember you?" Alex asked.

"I don't know for sure. I doubt it, but I can't take any chances. She almost had me convinced, but then she lied. She's been in these parts at least once before and there is no way in hell she could have forgotten it. Watch her closely. Let me know if she does anything out of the ordinary. If she starts snooping around Biogentrix, I'll just have to have her killed. It's that simple."

Alex nodded. If such an order was issued, he'd make sure he handled it himself. He'd enjoy snuffing the bitch out. He could have a lot of fun with such a fox before he finally did her in. A lot of fun.

They were almost back to Allan's house when Pat reached over and patted his leg. "What's up?" she asked.

"Humm...nothing," Allan replied. "What do you mean?"

"Well, you've not said three words in the last fifteen minutes. It's unlike you," Pat replied. "What did you see back there?"

Allan thought about the question for a moment before replying. "I'm not sure. I mean it's crazy, and I just caught a glimpse, and then it was gone."

"What was gone?"

"Well, if I didn't know better, I'd say it was..." He hesitated again. "...I think I saw TJ."

"Your son...I mean...you know what I mean," Pat replied, glancing at him.

"Yeah, I know what you mean. But he was older...much older than I'd expect him to be. I mean, it's only been a week or two since he disappeared."

"What do you make of it?" Pat asked.

"I don't know what to make of it." Allan shrugged. "It appears he may have found a new home with Homlin." He made a face, as though just saying the words left a bad taste in his mouth.

After another minute, Pat asked, "Are you okay?"

"I'm not sure," Allan replied, but he was sure — sure that he was not okay with Homlin raising his son. Not okay at all.

FDA Approval
Tuesday, Dec. 2

"I'm sorry to disturb you Dr. Pritchard, but Bo Rawlins is out here to see you." Dawn's voice just barely hid her agitation. "He insists on seeing you."

"Sure Dawn. Ask him to step on back here. I'm just finishing up on some records," Allan replied with a smile. Dawn was the best receptionist he could ever want, except when it came to Bo. *Well, no one is perfect*, he thought.

Bo pushed the partially closed door open, knocking lightly as he did. "Hope I'm not disturbing you too much," he said as he entered the room, his hunting cap firmly gripped in his hands.

"No, not at all. It's good to see you again. Had any luck hunting lately?" Allan closed the record in front of him and sat back in his chair, motioning to the chair next to the desk for Bo.

Bo sat down, shaking his head. "No, not much luck of late. It's kind of what I've come to talk to you about though." Bo twisted his cap between his hands.

"Well, if you've come for some hunting tips, I'm afraid you're barking up the wrong tree," Allan replied with a laugh.

Bo smiled but it appeared forced. "No, not looking for any tips, but I am looking for some information, Doc. You remember those ugly ol' bugs we pulled out of that deer a few weeks back? I was just wondering if you've heard anything from the state lab."

Allan hoped his face didn't show the alarm he felt by the mention of the larvae. He'd been counting on Bo's wispy memory to not remember anything about the larvae. It looked like he'd been hoping for too much.

"No Bo, as a matter of fact, I haven't, but I'm not surprised. The state lab has been known to take months on such matters, especially if it's anything out of the ordinary. Why do you ask?" He tried to ask the question nonchalantly.

133

"Well, I was jawing with an old hunting buddy of mine a while back. You might know him. , MacMillan?"

"No, I can't say I've had the pleasure."

"Well, no matter. Convoy and I were sitting around sipping on the juice, swapping hunting stories. I eventually got to telling him about those weird bugs we found in that buck. Much to my surprise, Convoy said he'd shot a buck a while back with them inside it as well. He described them to a tee. I was just wondering if we got some epee-demic going around or something."

As he spoke, Bo continued to pull and twist his hat. Allan couldn't remember ever seeing him so nervous and worried. Seeing Bo act this way was making him nervous as well.

"Well, I don't know, Bo, but I kind of doubt it. It's probably just one of those strange coincidences that happen from time to time. But if you like, I'll give the state lab a call and see if I can rush things along."

Bo's hands relaxed a little, and he smiled. "Yeah. I'd really appreciate it. I have to admit, I hate to think there might be something jeopardizing our wildlife. I know I'm a hunter and all, but like most hunters, I really love the outdoors. I wouldn't want to see anything happen."

"Well, I'll see what I can find out. In the meantime, try not to worry." Allan rose from behind the desk to show Bo out. "You might not want to say too much about this until we have some facts. You know how people can make stuff up out of nothing."

Bo laughed. "You can say that again. I have to confess, I mentioned our hunting trip to my niece the other day. Hell, she's always drilling me with questions. Says she's practicing being a reporter. But not to worry. Mimi is just a kid who's curious about everything and with a big imagination. You should hear about some of the wild stories she tells about the weird things supposedly going on over in Foster Flats. She writes it all down in her little black notebooks, but that's as far as it goes."

I sure hope he's right about that, Allan thought growing more nervous by the minute.

"She probably gets that imagination from me," Bo continued. "Hell, Convoy and I were supposed to get together a couple of days ago. When he didn't show, I started making up all sorts of shit. But the truth of the matter is, Convoy isn't the most reliable friend I have. He's probably locked up in the next county for too much carousing."

Suddenly, Allan was worried again. "Did Convoy happen to mention where he shot the deer he was telling you about?" Bo stopped at the door. "Well, yeah he did. You promise not to say anything to anyone?"

"Sure. I'm not out to get him in trouble," Allan replied.

"Convoy is a free-spirited sort. Not dangerous or anything. He just doesn't like to be confined by rules, if you know what I mean. He told me he snuck into the old game reserve a few weeks ago with his crossbow. Said he couldn't believe the number of deer he saw. It was like shooting fish in a barrel. Even said he might try it again. I tried to convince him to stay away, but he's not always the easiest person to convince."

Homlin's place. The deer Convoy had shot was on Homlin's reserve. *Oh boy, Pat is not going to like this*, Allan thought. In some strange way, it was beginning to make sense. It was like Pat has suspected. Homlin was the key. The question was, the key to what?

HOMLIN STARED OUT THE window, enjoying the view of the Washington Monument, as the five-doctor panel of the Food and Drug Administration filed in behind him. It was his third meeting with the panel in almost as many weeks. So far, everything had progressed as planned. The five doctors had not yet granted him permission to disseminate FreeForm to the other research facilities across the country, but neither had they thrown him out.

It took a vote of approval from four out of the five doctors to proceed. So far three of them had said yes. It took only one more to see it Homlin's way for his plan to proceed. Once that occurred, he'd be unstoppable. The FreeForm would be all across the country within a week of the vote.

Homlin chuckled to himself. Life was easy when one was willing to work inside the system. Anything could be accomplished when you went with the flow. Even if occasionally you had to manipulate the system just a little to get the flow to move in your direction.

A polite cough from one of the panel members notified Homlin they were ready to begin. He continued standing with his back to them for just a few seconds longer than was polite. Mustn't give up control. It was a cardinal rule when dealing with bureaucrats. Finally, with one last appreciative gaze out the window, Homlin turned and took his seat across the mahogany table.

"So good to see each of you again." Homlin started right in as though it had been his idea to call the meeting instead of the other way around. "I trust all your research is checking out. Are we ready to move on to the next step?"

"Not so fast," answered Dr. Ralph Connolly, one of the two doctors still opposing Homlin's proposal. Interesting, Homlin noted, Connolly and Lenair, the two doctors still opposing his request were seated together at his left. Wrightwall, Harrison, and McNeilly were in front and to his right. It seems the battle lines were clearly drawn.

"I would like, for the record, for you to quickly review your proposal, so we can be absolutely certain we understand what you are asking us to make a motion on."

"Certainly, Dr. Connolly. It's very simple, really. As you know my company, Biogentrix, has successfully manufactured a genetic material which has incredible adaptive properties. One could call it the modeling clay of life. We are a small lab with limited research funds. I realize that scientific progress could be made much more rapidly if more researchers could work on the material."

"And you've named the material, FreeForm. Is that right?" Connolly asked, then added, "For the record, Dr. Homlin."

"Oh, indeed, for the record. Yes, the product which I am speaking about has been registered under the trademark name of FreeForm."

"And the products and discoveries which are likely to come out of the research of others, you are proposing that Biogentrix be credited with fifty percent of the proceeds. Is that correct?"

"Yes, that is correct. We will supply the 'raw material' as it were. Each facility will apply their particular specialty and whatever new products come out, Biogentrix will be an equal partner," Homlin replied.

"And what are some of the products you suspect will come from such a collaboration?" Lenair asked, staring at the report over a pair of reading glasses propped on his nose.

"The sky is the limit, gentlemen. FreeForm is truly amazing and highly adaptive. I suspect some of the early products will be agricultural in nature.

Like blight resistant corn, and grass that grows to only three inches and never needs cutting, and cows that produce more milk, and beef cattle with lower cholesterol. Who knows after that?"

"Exactly my point!" Lenair shouted, slapping the report down on the table. "Who knows what could come of this? If this FreeForm is one tenth, hell, one hundredth as adaptive a material as Dr. Homlin claims, how is it to be controlled? Sure, we'll start with the simple stuff first, but how long will researchers be satisfied with messing around with beef cattle. How long before someone decides to try to clone the perfect woman or man? Then what?"

"Dr. Lenair, please." Harrison spoke up from the other end of the table. "We'll get to the questions in just a moment. We all realize you still have some concerns . . ."

"Damn right I do! Not the least of which is the fact that you three don't seem to be the least troubled by Dr. Homlin's proposal. Why, it's preposterous to think of distributing such a substance as this FreeForm to over a thousand other research facilities across the country with such scant preliminary data as he's presented to us."

"I understand your concern, Dr. Lenair," Harrison continued in a soothing voice. "It's not that we don't appreciate there are some risks involved. It's just that we see the possible benefits to all of mankind far outweighs the unlikely complications."

"Dr. Harrison," Dr. Connolly spoke up. "I believe what Dr. Lenair is pointing to is that the complications are not so unlikely. They are in fact very likely to arise and before we can approve of such a proposal we must have a firm set of guidelines which will address as many of these complicating questions as possible."

"Hell, that could take years." McNeilly now entered the discussion. "In the meantime, hundreds of thousands will continue to starve, millions will continue to suffer needlessly while we continue to stand in the way of the greatest scientific breakthrough in history."

"Better to stand in the way than to mindlessly open Pandora's box simply because it looks like it holds all the answers." Lenair's glasses threatened to fall off the tip of his nose.

Homlin sat across the table, quietly enjoying the heated debate. *For the record*, he thought, *Yes, for the record it's going very well*. He stared at the two doctors who continued to oppose his plan. Which one would come over to his way of thinking? Lenair was the spunkier of the two. It might be interesting to have him on his side...a bit less predictable than if Connolly came over.

As it turned out, today's meeting was important, after all. He had changed his mind. He liked Lenair's spunkiness, and there was the chance the nearsighted doctor might continue to cause trouble even when he was outvoted. It made more sense to have Lenair in his camp than outside raising a ruckus.

Homlin leaned back in his chair and rested his hands behind his head. As far as he was concerned, the meeting was over. He'd made the only really important decision. All the rest was just for the record.

"I'M BEING FOLLOWED."

"You're what? Are you sure?" Allan leaned across the table to Pat and grabbed her hand, as though fearful she might suddenly be taken away, the thought of a pleasant, uneventful lunch forgotten.

"Yes, sweetie, I'm sure. Remember a large part of my business is following other people. After a while you learn to read the signs when someone is doing it to you. Besides, they aren't very good at it. I suspect you'd be able to tell, yourself. By the way, are you being followed?"

"I don't know. I don't think so. Who would want to follow me around? It would get pretty boring. To the clinic, back home, to the clinic, back home, lunch with you. That's about it."

"Well, they may not be following you. They may have decided that I'm the only one that needs watching. After all, I'm the one with the tendency to stir up trouble."

"You mean Homlin's thugs?" Allan asked.

"Well, I certainly don't mean Lucky's old owners," Pat said, patting Allan's hand.

"I don't like this. This is getting out of control. What if they decide to do something besides just watch you?"

Pat squeezed Allan's hand. "You're cute. You really are. I think you're beginning to care about me."

"Don't be silly." Allan smiled. "I cared about you the minute you walked in my clinic. It's gone a lot farther than 'caring.'"

"Well, try not to worry. I'm not so concerned that they'll try anything with me. I think they're mostly concerned that I not try anything. Which, by the way, I plan to do."

"What do you mean? Pat, I think we're getting in over our heads. Maybe it's time to call in some help. I know the local police aren't the most crack shot in the world, but they're a start. Surely they'd be able to call in the SBI and probably the FBI."

"Think about it, Allan. What are we going to say? We want you to arrest Dr. Frederick Homlin, the owner and president of Biogentrix, on the grounds that he's connected with an alien spaceship that landed in this area ten years ago. And by the way, he has something to do with turning a larva that was pulled out of a stray dog into an exact replica of this man's son. They lock people up with stories like that. Remember, I've already had dealings with the federal government.

"No, without some proof, solid proof, we can't tell anyone and expect anything but a lot of strange looks. That's why I've got to get into Biogentrix."

"You've got to be kidding. Are you crazy? What do you expect the person tailing you to do? Simply report to his boss that you've broken into their secret facility? No way. It's far too dangerous." Allan's eyes darted around the restaurant like a married lover on a secret rendezvous.

"I haven't figured it out yet," Pat confessed. "Somehow I've got to lose my tail for a day or so. Maybe you could put on a wig and let them follow you for a while," she teased Allan.

"If I thought it would work, I'd be happy to do it. But I'd probably just get arrested for walking around in drag."

They both laughed, easing the tension a little. They sat quietly, deep in their own thoughts. Finally, Allan snapped his fingers, startling Pat.

"That's it," he said with a broad smile.

"No, Allan. You were right the first time. They'd never fall for the masquerade. But I appreciate the offer."

"Not me, silly. I'm not letting you out of my sight. I'm going with you to Biogentrix. We'll let Dawn wear the wig."

Pat immediately started shaking her head. "No way. Nix. Uh-uh. I wouldn't consider it. Dawn's a sweetheart of a person, but I couldn't ask her to do something like this for me."

"You won't have to. I will," Allan replied. Then leaning forward he added, "Listen, Pat. You said it yourself. This is important stuff. If Homlin is connected with the alien in some way, our entire country's security is at stake."

"I know what I said," Pat replied testily. "We'll just have to find another way. And you're not coming with me either. I appreciate the offer, but I'm not dragging you or Dawn into this any further."

The two lovers stared at each other, neither one willing to budge. Finally, Allan shook his head. "A couple nights ago you had me take a long hard look at myself. You helped me face something I had been avoiding. I'm now going to ask you to do the same."

Pat started to turn away but Allan grabbed her arm. "Listen to me," he said sharply, then in a softer voice he added, "please."

Pat turned back facing him.

"You've got to start trusting people."

"I do . . ." Pat tried to interrupt but Allan placed a finger on her lips.

"No, you don't. Not really. This is a perfect example. You're trying to do it all yourself, carrying the weight of the whole world on your shoulders. Well, you've managed to carry this alien thing around for the past ten years. And you've done a fine job of it, I'm sure. But now it's time to let go. Just like I had to let go of my illusions about TJ. You can't do this all by yourself. And even if you could, why bother? I'm here to help. I want to help. And Dawn will want to help as well. She doesn't have to know all the details. We'll tell her just enough so she can be you while we take a peek inside Biogentrix. Trust me on this one, Pat."

Pat sat there for several minutes considering what Allan had said. She had heard other people accuse her of the same thing before. Even her father used to tell her that her strong suit of being so self-reliant was also her blind spot. It had been one of the few things he had said that she had never been able to take to heart.

But now, it looked like she had to, somehow. Allan was right. There was too much at stake. She couldn't afford to blow it this time. Like she had the first time she'd been in these mountains. Oliver had said the same thing in his own way. She had interpreted his remarks as giving in to the establishment, but there were other ways to play on a team. Maybe the reason she was so driven to find the alien was that deep down inside she knew it was her fault that he was out there in the first place. She had tried to do it all herself. Be the big hero, but all she had been was dangerous. It had almost cost her her life, and it had cost two men theirs.

Pat felt the warm tears trickle down her cheeks. Allan offered her a handkerchief. Shaking her head, she reached for her purse to find her own, then, realizing she was doing it again, accepted the one Allan offered.

"It's not easy for a leopard to change her spots," she said as she wiped the tears away.

"I know. We'll take it one spot at a time," Allan replied. "I'll talk to Dawn this afternoon."

Pat nodded and smiled. With a little practice, she thought she could get used to having Allan around.

HOMLIN SAT IN THE FAR corner of the smoky tavern, his own cigar adding to the musty atmosphere. In front of him sat a half-finished mug of beer, only the second one he'd ever had. He now remembered why. It tasted foul, and the alcohol in it did not agree with his metabolism.

After a few minutes, the door to the bar opened and a tall man in a gray trench coat entered. He stood in the doorway for a moment then strolled towards Homlin's table. He slid into the booth across from Homlin, not bothering to remove his coat.

"So good to see you again, Dr. Harrison," Homlin said as the man unbuttoned his coat and slid it off his shoulders. "Quite an interesting show today, wouldn't you say?"

SATURDAY EVENING, DEC. 4

Allan glanced at his watch just as it beeped twelve midnight. *So far so good*, he thought. Earlier today, they had made the switch with Dawn smoothly. It had been simple. Pat had strolled into the clinic a few minutes after closing. A few minutes later, Dawn, dressed in Pat's clothes and wearing a black wig, had walked back out, gotten in Pat's car, and driven out of the parking lot. And sure enough, Allan had seen the gray sedan pull out behind Dawn and follow her down the road, both on their way to Charlotte. Watching the sedan tagging behind her had given Allan cold chills; he was careful to hide his concern from Pat. They had decided to have Dawn drive to Charlotte, as though Pat were checking on business matters. It was plausible and would at the same time give them flexibility as to how long to continue the scam.

Now, the two of them sat in Allan's Blazer outside the boundary fence of Biogentrix as Allan watched Pat apply the final touches of black smudge to her face.

"Okay, I'm all set. Remember, you are to stay here only as long as it remains perfectly calm and quiet. Any lights, alarms, or commotion of any sort and you are to hightail it out of here. No heroics. Understood?"

Allan squirmed in his seat. They had spent most of the afternoon arguing about who should be the one to go in. Allan accused Pat of being too self-reliant again and not letting him help out, while Pat pointed out that she was the one trained in such matters. When Allan had suggested they go in together, Pat explained, with an edge to her voice that made Allan wince just remembering it, that they could not afford to run the risk of them both being caught.

"We're the only two who knows that anything funny is going on. If we're both caught, there won't be anyone left to stop Homlin from completing his plans — whatever they are."

Allan hated to admit it but everything Pat said made sense. It still didn't mean he had to like it. He started to voice his concern once more, but before he could speak, Pat placed a finger to his lips. "No more discussion on this one, Allan, my dear. Straight to the police, you understand? If they grab me, which they won't, but if they do, you'll then have something to report. No alien stories, just that I've been missing and you know who has me. Are we clear?"

Allan nodded.

"Okay, great. I'll be in and out before you know it. Try not to fall asleep. I wouldn't want anyone sneaking up on you."

"The likelihood of my falling asleep in my present condition is so infinitesimally small as to not be a part of the equation. It's more likely someone will hear my heart pounding and decide to look for the source of it."

Pat leaned over and gave him a firm, moist kiss. "I won't be long," she said as she opened her door and slipped out into the darkness, leaving behind the subtle fragrance of her perfume and the pleasant sensation on Allan's lips.

Allan squinted through the windshield trying to make out her passage to the fence, but her black clothing was an effective camouflage. He could see nothing.

He noticed his hands had found their way to the steering wheel, which they were firmly gripping. He began tapping lightly with his thumbs on the cold metal. *This is going to be a long night, even if she's only gone for twenty minutes*, Allan thought. Why had he given in to this harebrained idea? What was he doing out here in the middle of nowhere while his new love broke into a top-secret laboratory? Was any of this really happening, or was he just suffering from overwork and stress? He could remember TJ but already the memory was fading. Had that really happened? It seemed too incredible, too surrealistic. Perhaps none of it had really happened. Maybe Pat had made her story up as well, and now the two of them were simply living out a fantasy—a very dangerous fantasy.

And now he had managed to drag Dawn into it as well. Not with the real story but a fabricated one. It hadn't surprised him how readily Dawn had been willing to help them out. She'd hardly needed any explanation at all. All they had said was they suspected one of Pat's old boyfriends might have put a tail on her, and they needed to verify it.

Allan didn't like lying to his long time employee and friend even though he knew it was crazy to think they could tell her the truth. They'd cautioned Dawn not to blow her disguise no matter what, but otherwise just to take a leisurely trip to the big city and to enjoy herself. Such a natural approach would be more likely to convince Homlin's men that they were still following the right person.

Allan glanced at his watch and was surprised to find it was only five minutes after twelve. It seemed like Pat had been gone for at least twenty minutes. His instructions were to wait for an hour. If Pat was not out by one, he was to go straight to the police and file a missing person's report, claiming that

Pat had been missing not for an hour but for three days and that she'd last been seen with Dr. Homlin. He prayed he wouldn't have to tell yet another string of lies, especially to the police. He was beginning to worry that his nose would start growing from such a steady diet.

THE WIRE CUTTERS, AN old pair borrowed from Allan's surgical supplies previously used for cutting the heads off of bone pins, had worked well on the chain link fence. The passage through the opening had raised no alarm, nor had the crawl across the open expanse to the first building.

Having reached the rear door where she planned to enter the lab, Pat stopped long enough to remove the backpack. She returned the wire cutters to the bag and removed a small electronic device. Mailed to her by special overnight delivery, the device was the finest electronic decoder money could buy on the black market. Pat had only needed it once before but in both cases, the instrument was worth its weight in diamonds.

As her preliminary investigation had revealed, the rear door, like all the other doors of Biogentrix, was electronically locked and required a special sensing card for entrance...*or a black market decoder*, Pat thought as she applied the sensors of the box to the flat surface of the door lock. She flipped a switch then waited a few seconds as the decoder searched for the correct code sequence. The almost silent click of the door indicated a successful entry.

Pat removed the sensors and gently placed the decoder back into her pack. So far so good. No signs of guards, no alarms, no disturbance of any kind. She entered the building, letting the door close behind her. Better to keep it closed just in case they had it wired to detect any breach of security. It appeared Homlin depended mostly on electronic security, in place of human personnel. If so, it would be to Pat's advantage. At the same time, it would be stupid to assume there weren't any security guards around. Stupid and deadly.

Once inside, Pat was uncertain where to go next. She'd not been able to get a floor plan of the building. No one in the area seemed to know who had built the building or even designed it. All the work had come from outside the community. All there was to do was to check as many different rooms as possible in the time she had...and pray for a little luck.

Behind the first four doors she checked, she found simple offices or labs, the type found in hundreds of research facilities across the country. The fifth door she came to was the first that had its own security lock. Pat tripped the lock with the decoder and silently slipped through it, closing it behind her.

She found herself in a small anteroom of an office. *Interesting*, she thought, *that they would have a security lock on this room.* As she entered the adjacent room she saw why. She shined the flashlight around a plush executive office. The beam reflected on a brass name plaque lying on the desk:

DR. FREDERICK HOMLIN

Bingo, Pat almost shouted out loud. Homlin's office. *What a stroke of luck*, she thought as she closed the door behind her. She directed the beam of light around the room again until she found on the far wall the line of filing cabinets. Walking over to them, she quickly opened the top drawer and leafed through the files, mostly receipts and invoices for supplies. She went on to the second one. About half way through the file she spied an interesting heading—FOOD AND DRUG ADMINISTRATION. She pulled the file out and walked over to Homlin's desk, leafing through the file's contents as she walked.

The most interesting item was a letter dated the last week of September from a Dr. Harrison. As Pat read the letters, a knot began to form in the pit of her stomach. The letter was an invitation for Homlin to meet with a board of FDA officials to discuss his plans for FreeForm and its dissemination to other research labs throughout the country.

FreeForm? What in the hell is FreeForm? She wondered. For some reason she didn't think she would like the answer to the question. Pat studied the rest of the file's contents and found a second letter dated the first of October in which the same Dr. Harrison requested a second meeting to further explore Homlin's "interesting proposal." Whatever Homlin was promoting, it looked like the dumb ass bureaucrats were actually thinking of taking him up on his plan. The knot is Pat's stomach continued to tighten.

She sat down in Homlin's chair wondering what to do next. *What if Homlin was a legitimate businessman and researcher? This FreeForm might be nothing. On the other hand, why is every fiber of my body telling me that Homlin is up to no good?* As she sat there, her eyes slowly focused on the papers lying on Homlin's desk. A familiar piece of stationery brought her eyes sharply in focus.

It was another letter from the Food and Drug Administration, dated Dec. 2, 2003. Only two days ago. Under the letter was the overnight express container in which it had been mailed and on top the letter, brief and to the point, read:

Dear Dr. Homlin,

We enjoyed meeting with you yesterday and feel that we are coming closer to a decision with each discussion. I feel confident that with a final meeting next week we can give you a much better idea whether your proposal can be accepted. We'd like to meet with you on Wednesday, Dec. 8, at 9:00 am. Please call my office to confirm this date and time.

Sincerely,

Dr. Leonard Harrison

Pat frowned. December 8th was only four days away. If Homlin was up to no good with this FreeForm, she was running out of time.

Pat laid the letters out on the desk. She turned on the desk lamp for additional lighting then photographed each document, then returned the file to its correct location in the filing cabinet.

She turned back to the desk to turn the light out. As her hand reached out for the short chain, a glare of light reflecting off a piece of shiny paper caught her attention — a stack of photographs. She looked more closely, a feeling of familiarity starting to grow. What would Homlin be doing with photos of a small child — a disturbingly familiar child. She looked more closely. They looked uncannily like the pictures she'd seen in Allan's home. Could it be? She glanced at a few of the others, obviously of the same boy but older by at least three or four years. No doubt about it. It had to be TJ. She thought about taking one of them but decided it was too risky, so she took a picture of the stack instead. It would have to do.

She was about to turn off the light again when another object partially hidden under the overnight packet made her heart race. The knot in her stomach hardened and she found it hard to breathe. Her hands suddenly felt cold and damp.

It couldn't be. How was it possible? Her hand released the chain and gently pushed the overnight mailer out of the way, revealing the tip of a knife — the blunt tip of the knife her father had given her as a graduation present; the knife she had used to get into the alien ship. She had last seen the knife sticking out of the alien's neck where she had thrown it in a desperate effort to save her life.

Pat picked the knife up to inspect it more closely. As she felt the familiar grip of it in her hand, the scene of those last few seconds in the ship flashed before her again. The same scene she had awoken to night after night, lying in bed, the sheets damp, her body drenched in a cold sweat.

How had Homlin come upon the knife? Had he found it in the woods? Had the alien given it to him? Surely, this proved the two were somehow connected. The question was how?

Her mind raced with questions, trying to piece all the loose ends together. The sound of footsteps and muffled voices yanked her from her thoughts.

Sneaking Around
Saturday Evening, Dec. 4

Allan stared at his watch for what must have been the twentieth time. He couldn't believe twenty-five minutes could pass so slowly. Where in the hell was she? Why had he ever agreed to let her go in alone? What if she had been caught? At this very minute, someone could be holding her, waiting for Homlin to show up to interrogate her. Or they might have decided to take her to Homlin instead and he was just sitting out here like a lump on a log waiting for nothing, except maybe a carload of Homlin's thugs to drive up behind him. If they caught both of them, no one would ever know what had happened except possibly Dawn. And if they'd already caught Pat in the lab, they would already know they were chasing a decoy. It would be simple enough to capture Dawn and end the whole deal.

I should go check on Pat, Allan thought for the tenth time in the last ten minutes. He glanced at his watch again. 12:35. He would wait five more minutes, that was all. After that he was going in after her. It didn't matter what he'd promised her about going for help. By the time the Waynesboro police could get back out here, Pat could be dead.

12:40 and still no Pat. He was going in.

IN ONE MOTION, PAT grabbed the knife from the desk and turned the light off. She crouched behind the desk, suddenly feeling as trapped as she had that day on the ship...the last time she'd depended on the knife to save her life. *He's out there*, she thought as she crawled around the desk towards the door, *but this time he's not alone.* Suddenly she was reliving her worst nightmare in which she was back in the ship, and the alien was coming towards her as he had that day. In her dream, she throws the knife and it strikes the alien in the throat. But this time, instead of the alien screaming in pain, it laughs a deep guttural sound and as she watches it begins to cleave itself in half starting at the point where the knife had penetrated. Within seconds, two aliens stand before her. She throws a second knife and a third in rapid succession, both of them sinking deep into the chests of the two aliens. She watches in horror as the two multiply to four, as once again the knife wounds only prompt them to divide once more.

Pat shook her head so hard her ears rung. She was back in Homlin's office, the voices and footsteps drawing closer. She reached the door to his office and cracked it open. The voices were coming from the hallway, and she could almost make out what they were saying.

Pat sighed with relief as she recognized some of the words and realized it was only a pair of watchmen coming down the hall — dangerous in their own right, but at least human. She continued to listen and watch from Homlin's office as the two guards passed by. One of them stopped long enough to check to be sure the outer door was still locked. *Thank goodness I pulled it shut*, Pat thought as she watched the doorknob being jiggled.

As the voices faded down the hall, she glanced at her watch. 12:30. Only thirty more minutes, and now that she knew there were night watchmen afoot, it complicated things. She would have to be much more careful as she left. Still, she had a couple more minutes. What other secrets could she uncover? She left Homlin's office, tiptoeing down the hall in the opposite direction of the night watchmen, looking for any other doors that might be secured with a digital lock. With only a few minutes remaining, she found one. Quickly she tripped the lock with the decoding device and entered.

She found herself in a much larger room this time. The light of her flashlight shone around the walls, checking for windows. As she suspected, it was an inside room with no windows. She started to flip the light switch on, but at the last minute thought better of it. For some reason, the thought of being in a well-lit room threatened her. She'd try to examine the room with the flashlight. If that didn't work, she'd consider the overhead lights.

She noticed the room's temperature was much cooler than it had been in the hall. It felt like she'd stepped into a very large cooler. She shined her light along the walls again. She estimated the room to be at least thirty feet by forty. Spaced every three or four feet was a row of stainless steel cabinets that went from one end of the room to the other. She walked over to the closest one. The cabinet stood about four feet in height and had a clear Plexiglas top. Pat estimated the top to be at least three inches thick. She shined the light down through the glass.

Her breath caught in her throat as she almost dropped the flashlight. Larvae. Although she'd only heard about them from Allan, she instantly recognized them. Hundreds of them. She strolled down the aisle shining her light first on one side and then the other. On both sides, hundreds upon hundreds of sausage-shaped, grayish-white larvae, stacked in rows, their small blunt ends pointing towards the ceiling.

As Pat stood there staring at the grotesque display before her, her mind raced. Suddenly, all the pieces were coming together. She felt like she'd been studying a picture that looked like some abstract piece of art only to suddenly realize that it was a close up photograph of a cow or some other simple object taken from a strange perspective.

Homlin had not found the knife or the alien. Homlin was the alien, and here before her were hundreds, maybe thousands, of other aliens just waiting to develop into whatever form needed, just like the larvae Allan had found had done.

Pat thought back to the letters from the FDA. FreeForm. The larvae. Homlin was on the verge of getting approval to ship these alien seeds across the country to other research labs. If Homlin convinced the FDA to allow him to do that, all would be lost. Within weeks, thousands of larvae across the country would start transforming, and her worst nightmare would come true.

Pat ran back to the door. She must get some pictures of the larvae. Maybe they would help her convince the FDA not to approve Homlin's request. She switched on the overhead lights, feeling completely exposed. She ran back to the closest set of cabinets and snapped a half-dozen pictures. Back at the door again, she snapped the rest of the roll of film showing the size of the room. Then she switched the lights off again, throwing the room into darkness just as she heard the pair of night watchmen approaching. *Had they seen the light shining under the doorway?* Pat wondered as she crouched in the dark, waiting for her eyes to adapt once more. Had she pushed her luck too far?

ALLAN PULLED THE HANDLE on the car door and was startled at the rifle-report sound the latch made in the silence. He counted to ten, listening intently for any indication that someone might have heard him. When everything remained quiet, he stepped out of the car and crept towards the clump of bushes where Pat had disappeared less than an hour before. The heavy underbrush continued for about fifteen or twenty yards before clearing to reveal the security fence of Biogentrix.

Allan kept himself hidden behind the last line of shrubbery as he studied the fence line for any signs of trouble. *Too quiet. No lights, no movement, no sound. Nothing. Including, no Pat. Well, here goes nothing,* he thought as he half crawled and half walked towards the fence. He'd only taken the first step or two when he caught his left foot on some invisible obstacle, and in the same moment, felt a sudden push from the rear.

He fell to the ground and tried to roll with the fall but found his attacker pressing heavily on his back. He tried to roll onto his stomach, but his assailant successfully pinned his left arm behind him and caught his right arm over his head in a half-nelson. He was completely immobilized. They had him which meant they must also have Pat and had simply been waiting in ambush for him. If they had them both, the jig was up. He wondered if he'd have the chance to explain to Pat why he had disobeyed her orders before they both were killed. It didn't really matter. He didn't know what he could say to her.

"What are you doing out here?" A strangely familiar voice asked from above him. "I thought I told you to go for help if I wasn't back within an hour." Pat released her half-nelson but gave his left arm a final twist before letting go of it.

"Ouch. Easy there, partner," Allan whispered as he pushed himself up to his hands and knees and followed Pat into the bushes. Neither of them spoke until they were both back in the car.

"You've got some explaining to do," Pat said between clenched teeth. "I'm not accustomed to having my partner ignore me."

"So fire me," Allan replied, suddenly angry now that he knew Pat was out of danger. "I was worried. I just wanted to see if I could find you before I left to go fetch the cops. Did you find out anything?" He asked, hoping she'd take the bait and change the subject.

"I'll say I did," Pat replied. "Let's get out of here. I'll explain once we're back at your place. I'll need to call the airport too."

"The airport?" Allan didn't like the sound of that.

"Yep. We've got to get to Washington, D.C."

"What about Dawn? Why Washington? What did you find . . .?"

"We'll call my office when we get a chance," Pat said as she leaned over and turned the keys in the starter for him. "You drive and I'll explain everything to you on the way."

Allan started the car and made a full circle to head back in the direction they'd come. Once they reached the main road, Pat let out a heavy sigh. "You were right about one thing," she said. "Homlin has TJ." She told him about the pictures she'd seen on his desk.

They drove for a few minutes with neither one speaking. Finally, Allan said, "I'm sorry I didn't follow orders. I was worried sick about you. I guess I panicked. I promise it won't happen again."

Pat placed her hand on his where it rested on the gear shift knob. "I understand, Allan, and I forgive you this time, but it can't happen again. From here on out, every step could be a matter of life or death and not just ours, but possibly thousands, even millions of others. The stakes are too high to let our emotions get in the way of sound judgment."

Allan nodded, but even as he did so, he realized he had one other clandestine mission to complete before taking off for D.C., and this one would have to be without Pat. He needed to see his son one last time.

Who Am I - Really
Sunday Evening, Dec. 5

Allan glanced down at the luminescent dial of his watch. 11:07 p.m. Bo promised to meet him here around eleven. *I'll give him until 11:15 before I freak out*, Allan thought. A moment later he heard a light tapping on the roof of his car. Bo had arrived.

Allan made sure the cab's overhead light was turned off before opening the door and climbing out. While they were a long way from the Homlin's home, there was no telling what kind of surveillance he may have had installed. Better safe than sorry. He climbed out of the car. Even though his eyes had adjusted to the dark, he couldn't really see his friend until he felt a hand on his shoulder. He jumped despite himself.

"Sorry, Doc. Wasn't trying to sneak up on you," Bo said, but his chuckle suggested otherwise.

"That's okay. Not your fault. I'm just particularly jumpy tonight," Allan replied after he caught his breath. "I'm not used to this clandestine business."

"What's up?" Bo said, then added, "Oh, that's right. You can't really tell me."

"That's right. I'm sorry to be so secretive, but the less you know about it, the better, just in case we get caught. I sure do appreciate you being willing to help me."

"Happy to do it. Like I said on the phone, I used to work at the reserve back when the Smileys owned it. Nice place, but even back then it was kind of spooky."

"Well, how do we proceed?" Allan was anxious to get on with it before he chickened out.

"We'll go in over there. There's a rip in the fence that Convoy showed me a while back. We'll take it slow and easy through the woods and circle around to the back of the main house. There's an old entranceway into the basement that almost no one knows about. It's pretty well hidden. If it's still there, it'll be pretty easy to gain access to the interior. You're pretty much on your own from there except..." Bo pulled a sheet of paper out of his coat pocket. "This is a diagram of the floor plan as best I remember it. The first floor is on this side, and the upstairs is on the back. It's probably not exact but should be pretty close." He handed the paper to Allan.

Allan took a quick look at it before folding it back up and sticking it in his pocket. "Thanks again, Bo. I'm not sure how I'll ever repay you..."

"Don't worry about it, Doc. What are friends for if they can't occasionally help another friend break into someone's home? Let's get going."

THE TWO MEN STARED down at the clump of overgrown shrubs that, according to Bo, hid the entranceway to the basement of Homlin's home. "Trust me, Doc, it's there. It's even more grown up than when I worked here, so there's no way anyone could have discovered it. Let me see the map."

Allan pulled out the map Bo had drawn for him. Bo shined a small penlight on it. "Once you're in, there should be a set of stairs, right about here, that go up to the first floor, just outside the kitchen area. Your best bet to get to the upstairs would be the backstairs here." He traced the route with his index finger. "After that, you're on your own." He handed the map back to Allan.

"I can't thank you enough for helping me out..."

Bo raised a hand. "Don't sweat it." He handed the penlight to Allan and then turned to leave, then stopped. "Just remember, if you're caught, you did this all on your own."

"Sure thing," Allan replied, but Bo had already disappeared into the darkness.

Bo was right. The cellar door was exactly where he said it would be. It took Allan a couple minutes to clear away the brush so he could open the door, stopping frequently to listen to be sure no one heard him. He breathed a sigh of relief when he finally had the area cleared enough to try lifting the door, and after a moment of hesitation, it opened with a squeaking on its rusty hinges that felt loud enough to be heard back at his clinic. He froze, waiting and listening. After a minute, he lifted the door a few more inches and waited again. Finally, he had the door open enough to slip through. As he did so, he switched on the penlight. *Just like me to stage a breaking and entering in the middle of the night and forget to bring a decent light*, he thought as he made he way down the rickety stairs, brushing spider webs away from his face as he did so. Luckily, the light Bo had left for him gave off a high intensity beam that made it easy to find his way.

As he entered the basement he looked around until he found the stairs Bo had pointed out to him. So far so good. The light cast creepy shadows around him, made even creepier by the thick growth of spider webs. Was that the scurrying of roaches, he heard, or something larger? He decided it was best not to investigate. He really didn't want to know what he might be sharing the basement with, so he stumbled his way straight to the stairs and straight up, pausing at the top to listen.

All's quiet on the western front, he thought, wondering where such weird memories came from and why they had to suddenly appear in moments of stress. He placed his hand on the doorknob, then paused to say a short prayer before attempting to turn it. *Please, God, let it be unlocked*. It was.

He pushed the door open a couple inches and peered out into the darkened hallway. When he didn't see anyone, he pushed the door open enough to slip through. *At least I had enough sense to wear tennis shoes*, he thought as he crept down the hall towards the kitchen...at least where the kitchen was on his map, but he never reached the kitchen to find out. He came to the rear stairs first. *How am I ever going to find TJ?* He wondered as he took one step at a time. Homlin's home was large. He'd heard that there were at least six bedrooms, most if not all of them upstairs. That meant that it was likely that Homlin and his goon squad had their own bedrooms. *It'd be just my luck to end up dropping in on Homlin.* He'd wondered about this before, and each time, he'd finally concluded that he'd just have to cross that bridge when he came to it. *And now I'm at that bridge,* he thought as he reached the top of the stairs.

He was just about to step out into the hallway when something stopped him — a feeling that he was no longer alone. He switched off the light. A moment later he heard a shuffling of feet that verified his suspicion, followed a moment later by a voice.

"Did you check on the kid?" Someone asked.

"Yeah, that's where I just came from," another voice responded. "What else would I be doing down there? Don't understand why Homlin insisted on putting the squirt so far away from the rest of us. Just makes that much more work for me."

"He said he wanted the boy to have a good view from the front of the house. I don't have the foggiest idea why," the other voice replied. "At least the kid seems okay with the arrangements. At least you don't have to get up every three hours to feed him his gruel."

Allan stayed hidden in the stairwell, a tightening sensation building in his chest that was at least partially relieved when he remembered to breathe. *Gruel every three hours? What was that about?* At least he had a better idea where he'd find TJ. He waited until well after the lights in the hallway had been cut off and the sound of a house shutting down for the night diminished to only the creaking of old wooden joints. He switched on the penlight but kept the lighted end partially covered. He wanted his eyes adjusted to the dark as much as possible and just enough light to navigate without tripping over anything. He felt strangely safe in the stairwell, especially when compared to stepping out into the hallway, where just a few minutes before, two of Homlin's goons had stood. *But TJ isn't coming to me here,* he thought as he squared his shoulders and snuck a look down the hall.

He stepped back to take a final look at Bo's map. The floor plan was simple. The hallway split the upstairs in half with rooms running off of either side. According to the goons, TJ should be in one of the bedrooms closest to the front of the house. *At least I have a fifty-fifty chance of getting the right one,* he thought as he stepped back out into the hallway and slowly made his way past the other rooms. He kept his eyes focused on the outlines of a window he could just make out at the far end. When he was finally standing in front of the window looking out over a moonless view of the reserve, he allowed himself to take another deep breath. *One last bridge,* he thought. *But how do I decide which room to try?* The old eenie-meenie-miney-moe approach seemed just a little too unscientific for such an important decision, but was there any other way?

He decided to try using his senses first. He stepped over to the door to his right first, and gently placed his ear against it. Closing his eyes, he listened for any sound that might alert him to the bedroom being occupied by a small boy. After about thirty seconds he stepped across the hall and repeated the same thing on the left-hand door. Nothing on either one. But wait a minute. There had been something different about the two doors — not a sound difference but a very slight odor difference. The right-hand door had smelled just like you'd expect an old, musty house to smell, but at the left-hand door Allan thought he picked up a slightly pungent, almost soured smell. As he checked the two doors again, he remembered what one of the goons had said about feeding the kid gruel every three hours. Could this be the smell of the alien gruel?

Realizing it was the best information he had to go on, he returned to the second door, and gently turned the knob. He kept the penlight on and partially covered with his hands to minimize the lighting. Closing the door behind him, he turned and looked around the room. As he did so, he heard a slight click of the table lamp turning on. There before him, leaning over in the bed was an older boy than he'd expected — older yes, but very definitely TJ, just as Todd had looked at five or six.

With just a moment of hesitation, Allan smiled his most benevolent smile developed over years of giving pet owners bad news about their beloved pets. "Hello son."

"Daddy?" TJ replied, blinking his eyes as they adjusted to the sudden light. "Is that you?"

"It's me," Allan replied, taking a step towards the bed but stopping when he noticed the look on TJ's face change from confused to frightened. *Wow, has he grown,* Allan thought. *He looks years older. I bet he's old enough to start school.* "Shh, it's okay, son. I'm not going to hurt you. I just needed to talk with you, but we must be quiet. Okay?"

"But what are you doing here?" TJ asked as his gaze flitted around the room like a wild animal looking for a way to escape.

What am I doing here? Allan had been asking himself a similar question since he'd gotten the idea to come. What did he hope to accomplish after all? He stared at the boy who, despite growing substantially since he'd last seen him, still looked remarkably like Todd. Suddenly, he knew the answer.

"I've come to take you home," he replied.

"But I am home," TJ replied.

The simple statement sent a shiver through Allan. He decided to try another tactic.

"Are they treating you okay? It appears they're feeding you well."

"Yeah, I guess, but it's mostly that yucky gruel stuff. It's supposed to help me grow faster."

"Well, it sure seems to be working. I hardly recognized you."

There was a long pause during which the two of them stared at each other. Finally, Allan asked, "Are you happy here?"

TJ shrugged. "It's alright, I guess."

"You called me 'Daddy' when you first saw me. Do you know what it means?"

TJ shrugged again. "Yeah, it means...daddy...I mean, like I'm part of you, but you're not really my daddy, are you?"

Allan thought about how to answer that. "Well, not exactly, but I was there when you were born, so in some ways you could say I'm your dad." *More than Homlin,* he almost said, but then decided against it.

"But I don't really have a daddy, do I?" TJ asked, staring intently at him.

It was Allan's turn to shrug. "Well, no, I guess not — least not as far as I know, but I was raising you as my son. Doesn't that count for anything?"

TJ smiled just a little at that. "How's Kendra?" he asked.

"Okay, but she misses you. I told her you went back to my brother."

There was another long pause.

"Who am I?" TJ finally asked, "And where do I belong? I mean, I'm not really your son, though I look like he did, and I feel kinda like you're my...daddy, I guess. But then I have this...this feeling that I'm supposed to be here...with Dr. Homlin, and he tells me I'm one of them, and that feels right and not so right too."

The pained, confused look on TJ's face made Allan's heart ache. Maybe his coming here was a bad idea after all. What right did he have to put this young boy through such a difficult decision?

"I do know one thing," TJ continued. "I like your food a lot more. I miss my Cheerios."

Allan laughed, and a moment later, TJ joined him. After the laughter died down, he decided to try again.

"Come home with me, son, and you can have all the Cheerios you want. Kendra misses you...I miss you. Won't you come home with me?"

TJ seemed to consider it for several seconds before replying. "I think I better stay here, at least for a while. Maybe I can come visit you later, if that would be okay with you."

That's sure as hell never going to happen, Allan thought. *Homlin would never let his new recruit out of his sight, I may as well let TJ have some hope to hold onto.*

Allan realized he'd said his piece. What more could he say to convince TJ to come with him, especially when he wasn't sure it was what was best for the boy?

"Yeah, maybe you can do that," he finally replied.

TJ nodded. "Yeah, I'll come visit you someday soon."

"Well, okay. Guess I'll just have to send that case of Cheerios back to the store."

TJ eyes twinkled for a minute, then realized it was a joke. "Yeah, or give it to Kendra. She seemed to like them pretty well herself."

"I better be going," Allan said. "Don't want to overstay my welcome." He turned towards the door.

"You might want to go out the window, Daddy," TJ said. "It's a pretty easy climb down, and it would save you going back by the others' bedrooms. I don't think they'd be too excited to see you here."

AS ALLAN LEANED AGAINST his car, he glanced at the luminescent dial of his watch — almost one a.m. His exhaustion from two late nights was made worse by a feeling of hopelessness and defeat. *Time to face the facts, like Pat said. My son is dead...has been dead for years. Whoever or whatever I was just talking with is not my son.* When would those facts finally land as the truth? He didn't know, but he felt like tonight had been an important step in the right direction. Or was he simply fooling himself again.

Part Four

A Game of Cat and Mouse, but which One is the Cat?

Lost in Charlotte
Monday Morning, Dec. 6

D awn pulled the cord that drew the heavy curtain away from the window and stared out from the 22nd floor onto the early morning skyline of Charlotte, N.C. Even though she knew by usual city standards, Charlotte was considered just a medium size, to her the city looked huge. It had grown considerably since her last visit to the Queen City, some fifteen years earlier when her high school class had taken a field trip to Discovery Place.

Dawn turned her attention back to Pat's plush apartment, shaking her head for the tenth time since leaving Waynesboro. Who would have ever thought when she took the job with quiet Dr. Pritchard that one day she would end up in a swanky uptown apartment in Charlotte masquerading as a private eye so that her boss and the real P.I. could run off and do...do what? That part, well, she wasn't sure what they were doing.

Oh well, all in a day's work as a receptionist. Dawn strolled into the kitchen to fix herself a cup of coffee. It took her five minutes to find the coffee, but she finally located it on the door of the freezer along with a wide selection of herbal teas.

In a few minutes, she had her customary coffee and dry toast. She took both, along with the Sunday edition of the Charlotte Observer, and walked over to the most massive and most comfortable sofa on which she'd ever sat.

You know, I could get used to this style of living, she thought a few moments later as she sipped on her coffee, the paper pleasantly strewn around her. She glanced at her watch. 8:05. She was to meet Allison, one of Pat's assistants, at Pat's office at 9:30. It was mostly to keep the masquerade up, but at the same time, there were several small items which Pat had requested Dawn pick up while she was in Charlotte.

I'd best be getting myself ready to go, Dawn thought as she pushed herself off the sofa and walked back to the kitchen to freshen her coffee. Since she wasn't sure how far away she was from the office, she didn't want to be late and keep Allison waiting. As she strolled past the picture window again, she paused for a moment.

Somewhere down there on the street was a gray sedan. Inside were two men. Those men had followed her all the way from Waynesboro. Men up to no good. She didn't know what exactly they were up to, but she knew from the little that Pat and Dr. Pritchard had told her that the men were not the kind you'd want to meet in some dark alley. Or for that matter on some deserted road late at night.

Dawn found herself shivering just thinking about them. So, best not to give them too much thought. *Just do my job and keep my eyes and ears open*, Dawn told herself. *I'll be just fine as long as I do my job and stay awake.*

She walked into the bathroom, disrobing as she went. She'd been waiting to take a bath in the room since she'd first laid eyes on it yesterday, particularly when she found bubble bath in the cabinet under the sink. The next thirty minutes would be worth all the worry and concern. Just to be able to soak in a tub in such a gorgeous room. Yes, she could get used to living this way.

ALEX LEANED AGAINST the Plexiglas sides of the phone booth, waiting to make a connection. He hated this. Tailing this dame was demeaning. He had other men for such trivial matters. Yeah, sure they were short handed and yeah, maybe the dame was important to keep an eye on, but Homlin needed him elsewhere. Except it had been Homlin who had sent him on this wild chase. Okay, he would follow orders, but he didn't have to like it.

"Come on. Answer the damn phone," Alex said into the receiver, as the phone continued to ring at the other end.

Finally, someone picked up, and Alex curtly reprimanded him for taking so long. "Patch me into Homlin wherever he is. This is important. And be prompt about it. I don't know how much time I have."

Within a couple of moments, the connection was remade, this time with Homlin.

"Good morning, Alex. How is the Queen City?" Homlin's pleasant tone caught Alex by surprise. Everything must be going well in D.C. *That's where I should be,* Alex thought. *I should be up there where the real action is, instead of following this dumb broad.*

"Everything is fine here," Alex answered somewhat sullenly. "It's all in control. In fact, I see no reason that Julian can't take care of this part on his own..."

"No, no. You must stay with Julian. I need to know at every moment where Ms. Vogt is. I am counting on you. I know you'd rather be here, but believe me, I need you there. Where is she right now?"

"She's in her apartment. She's been there since she arrived early yesterday evening," Alex replied with a sigh. It had been worth a try, and he intended to keep trying until he got his way. "How is everything in D.C.?"

"It's all going splendidly," Homlin replied. "Right according to our plans. It won't be long now. Just a couple more days. That's why it's vital that you keep an eye on Vogt. She is the only factor that could foul up the works. As long as she's behaving herself, we'll be fine."

"Well then, we've got nothing to worry about. I'll keep you posted." He hung up the phone. *When this is over, I'm going to settle up with our little Ms. Vogt in fine fashion. Homlin promised her to me. It's the one thing that makes this all worthwhile.*

———— ※※※ ————

"ALLISON, YOU'VE BEEN most helpful. I appreciate you having all these items ready to go," Dawn said as she placed the top back on the box. "I can understand why Pat has you run things while she's away."

"Oh, no bother at all. Pat pays me to do this. I think it's great you're willing to help her out. I imagine it must feel pretty funny driving around in a strange city dressed up as somebody else."

Dawn laughed. "Well, I must admit it wasn't exactly how I planned to spend my weekend, but to tell you the truth, it's a lot more exciting than what I did have planned."

She glanced at her watch. "I better be getting on back to the apartment. Dr. Pritchard said he would probably give me a call this morning to be sure everything was going okay."

"Well, I hope you enjoy your stay in Charlotte. Do you know how long you'll be staying?"

"Not really. Until Dr. Pritchard tells me to hightail it back to Waynes-boro, I will stay here. I've already told Marva, our technician, that I might not be coming in on Monday. Bless her heart, she won't know what to do if she has to open up by herself. Luckily, this is a slower time of the year for us. I'm sure she'll manage."

Dawn picked up the box and headed for the door. "Thanks again. I'll be sure to let Pat know how much help you were."

"Glad to do it," Allison said as she opened the door for her.

After Dawn left, Allison returned to her desk to finish some typing she'd promised to one of the other investigators. It was ten minutes before she glanced over to the other desk and her eyes fell on the city map Dawn had laid there when she'd first come in.

Allison walked over and picked it up. A direct path connecting the office with Pat's apartment was clearly highlighted in red.

"Oh, my goodness, she won't be able to go back that way," Allison said out loud as she studied the map. Charlotte's maze of one-way streets and constant construction had thwarted many a newcomer in recent years. It looked like Dawn was about to become one of them.

"DAMN!" DAWN POUNDED on the steering wheel as she found her way stopped for the third time by new construction. In the last five minutes, she had gone from confused to hopelessly lost. She'd pulled over twice to look for her map and had finally decided she'd left it back at the office. She would have gladly retraced her steps to recover it, but the maze of one-way streets had prevented such a simple solution.

Meanwhile, she glanced in the rearview mirror to find the gray sedan continuing to follow her. *Great. This has got to look just great*, she thought. What to do? She had to get back to the apartment. Dr. Pritchard would be calling her any minute, and there was no telling what he would do if she weren't there to take her call.

She passed a stopped Charlotte Police car. She considered stopping to ask for directions but decided against it. It might raise even more questions for the two men following her. They might panic if they saw her talking to a cop. No telling what they might do.

The answer to her problem suddenly came to her as she spied a pay phone just past the police car. She'd call Allison. In a quick phone call, she could get directions out of this and let Allison know what to tell Dr. Pritchard if he called. It made sense. She pulled over, forcing herself not to look in the rearview mirror. She stepped out of the car as nonchalantly as possible and prayed the men following her wouldn't do anything stupid.

"SOMETHING IS FUCKING wrong here," Alex shouted to Julian. "This dumb broad hasn't the foggiest idea where she's going. Pull in behind her but don't be too obvious."

Julian did as he was told and pulled in behind a parked patrol car.

"Oh great!" Alex said as he noticed where they were parked. "She's making a fucking phone call. What the hell is going on?"

"Maybe she's calling for directions," Julian replied.

"But why in the world would she need to do that? She's from this damn city. Unless? Oh, shit. I've got a funny feeling something is really screwed up here." He sat there for a few moments, considering his options. He had to find out for sure who they were following but how without tipping their hand?

His eyes focused on the patrol car in front of them. The officer sat in the driver's seat, his head down as though he was either writing something or taking a nap on the job. Alex suddenly had an idea.

"Stay here and be ready for anything. I'll be right back." He stepped out of the car and headed towards the patrolman.

DAWN KEPT HER BACK to the gray sedan she knew must be behind her, afraid that if she faced them, she'd give herself away with the distressed look on her face. The phone rang for the sixth time. Oh god, she's already left. What was she to do now? The phone's seventh ring was cut short by Allison's voice.

"Vogt Investigations, this is Allison."

"Oh Allison, am I ever relieved to hear your voice! This is Dawn. I've done a foolish thing."

ALLAN'S EYES FLUTTERED open. He continued to lie on his back as his eyes focused on the unfamiliar ceiling and surroundings. Where was he? He glanced next to him and was pleased to find someone familiar. Pat was still asleep beside him. It all came back to him, as the memory of the last twenty-four hours cleared the cobwebs from his mind. This was the Marriott hotel at the Greensboro airport. They'd driven up during the early morning hours, after finding out there was a mid-morning flight to Washington. They'd checked in for a couple of hours of much-needed sleep. Had they overslept?

Allan suddenly shot up in bed and squinted his eyes to make out the digital display of the alarm clock. Only 9:00 a.m. The flight didn't leave until 11:00. They still had plenty of time. He lay back down, relieved. Pat stirred beside him. Two hours before their flight. Let's see, what could they do to entertain themselves before their flight left? He thought he had a good idea.

He turned over and faced the still sleeping Pat. He gently ran his fingers over the curve of her shoulder. Such soft skin. Such a beautiful face. Pat stirred, and her eyes fluttered open. Allan watched as her eyes focused and went from a confused look to one of recognition. Pat smiled and pulled him towards her. It was a most pleasant way to wake up in the morning.

REASSURED BY THE DIRECTIONS she had received from Allison and by the instructions she had given her regarding Dr. Pritchard, Dawn returned to Pat's Cherokee much more relaxed. She sat in the driver's seat for another moment, reviewing the notes she'd taken on Allison's directions. After making sure she knew which turns to make, she leaned forward to start the car.

A shadow fell across the steering wheel, startling her. Dawn looked up to find a young policeman smiling at her through the window. Dawn forced herself to smile back. *What in the world have I done now?* She asked herself. Did she run a light in her confusion or make an illegal turn? She didn't think so, but couldn't be sure.

"Yes, officer?" She politely asked as she rolled down the window.

The officer continued to smile as his eyes flickered from her to the insides of the car and back to her. *He's taking in everything about me,* Dawn thought. *I wonder if he thinks I've stolen the car. What if he asks for the registration? Pat never told me where she kept it.*

"I just saw you sitting here, and I was wondering if I could help you? This part of downtown can be difficult to navigate even without the construction detours," the officer said as he leaned forward.

He's really quite cute, Dawn thought, then almost burst out laughing at herself. *Now, now. Let's not go trying to pick up some young guy that's probably half your age.* Despite herself, she couldn't help but return a pleasant smile.

"No, officer. I'm fine — now. I just called for the directions I needed, but I thank you for asking. I'll just be on my way if that's okay with you."

"Sure, lady. Enjoy your stay in Charlotte," the officer said as he tipped his cap to her.

"Oh, I will officer. It's been a long time since I've been here. It certainly has grown, but I won't let that keep me from enjoying it. Good day." Dawn rolled up the window. Her hand fumbled for the key. She started the car, then in her excitement, ground the starter a second time.

She glanced in the rearview mirror and watched the officer return to his patrol car. A couple of spaces behind, she noticed the gray sedan. *Well, nothing seems any worse for wear*, she thought as she pulled out from the parking space and turned left at the first light, just as Allison had told her.

ALEX WATCHED THE CHEROKEE turn the corner before making his move. With a final glance to the partially nude body of the dead cop, he flung the door open and ran to his car.

"Quick, get behind her. Be sure she returns to the apartment," he yelled to Julian as he hopped into the passenger seat and took off the policeman's cap. "We're screwed. We're royally screwed."

"What's wrong?" Julian asked as he pulled out from behind the patrol car and started out after the Cherokee.

"The woman we're following isn't Pat Vogt. I don't know who she is, but she isn't Vogt. Homlin will shit when he hears this. When we get back to the apartment, I'll call in to find out what we should do next. Boy, are we screwed."

Flight Delay
Monday, Dec. 6

"She's what? Are you sure? What the hell happened?" Homlin swung his legs out of bed and grabbed the phone from the nightstand and started pacing. "Are you sure?" He repeated the question. "Just this morning you were saying..."

"I know what I said. Everything was fine — at least I thought so, but then she started acting strangely. She got lost coming back from the office to her apartment. That's when I grew suspicious." Alex filled Homlin in about how he had discovered the switch.

"Do you have any idea who the hell she is?" Homlin asked as he continued to pace. He was wide-awake now, even though he had dozed off after Alex's first call. He'd been up late the night before and had been enjoying sleeping late. He'd instructed the hotel to not disturb him except for long distance phone calls.

"I don't know for sure. She's wearing a black wig and all, but I think it may be someone who works for Pritchard. They could have made the switch in his office. That's all I can figure."

"Do you still have the police uniform?" Homlin asked. His mind was already thinking of what the most effective action was. This was a setback, no question about it. But it wouldn't stop him. It couldn't. He'd not be stopped by anything at this point.

"Yeah. I've still got it on," Alex replied, pulling at one of the sleeves. The shirt was a little too tight for his large frame.

"Good. I want you to keep an eye on our little Miss Whoever-she-is. Let her get settled in and comfortable then I want you to pay her a visit. This is all going to work out. Now pay close attention."

"WHAT DO YOU MEAN, THE flight has been canceled? You can't cancel the flight. We've got to get to Washington, D.C. We drove for hours in the middle of the night to get here for the flight." Pat's face was livid as she shouted into the phone. She listened for a few moments to the polite ticket agent on the other end. Finally, with a great deal of effort, she calmed herself enough to ask when the next flight out would be.

"There is another flight out today, isn't there?"

"Yes, Ms. Vogt. We already have you and your traveling companion booked on it. Its departure time is scheduled for 1:45 p.m. this afternoon. If you like, you may come to the ticket counter to pick up a voucher for breakfast."

"Oh, thank you so very much," Pat replied sarcastically as she slammed the phone back in the cradle.

"1:45 pm. Can you believe it?" She walked over to the bed and plopped down on her side.

"Well, I know it's exasperating, but does it really make any difference what time we get to D.C. as long as we're there by 8:00 on Monday morning?"

"No, I guess not," Pat answered with a sigh. "It's just that I'm afraid something will happen. We've got to be there tomorrow morning. Maybe we should go ahead and drive up there."

"Well, we could, but what's the point? There's just as much likelihood of something happening on the highway as in the air. Why not just relax and enjoy the little time we have." Allan reached over and started to rub Pat's back. "We'll get there in plenty of time, I promise."

Pat relaxed a little and leaned back against him. "Okay, you're right. I'll take it easy. But nothing else better happen, or I'll simply go ape-shit."

"Nothing else is going to happen. Just relax," Allan said as he rubbed her scalp and she nestled further into his arms.

DAWN POURED THE SOFT drink into the glass of ice then stepped back to review her work. A bowl of chili, a dish of potato chips, a soft drink, and a pickle. Anything else? She reached over the counter and pulled off a paper towel and then at the last minute placed a second pickle on the dish. There. Everything was ready for a leisurely afternoon in front of the television.

Yes, she was definitely getting used to this kind of living. She walked over to the sofa and placed the tray on the coffee table. She flicked the television on with the remote then scanned the stations to see what there was to watch. Mostly pre-game football shows. Boring. An old movie. Unfortunately, it was one she'd seen at least four times. A good movie, but not worth watching for a fifth time. She finally settled on a local news show. *May as well get caught up with what's happening in the big city*, she thought as she took the first mouth full of chili.

The show was drawing to a close when the newscaster was handed a special report. He studied it for a moment, frowned, then looked back to the camera.

"I'm afraid the Queen's City crime continues to escalate. Moments ago, the body of Officer Tim MacDonald was found in his patrol car. He was brutally strangled."

A photo of the unfortunate officer flashed on the screen. Dawn gasped as she recognized the young officer she'd met only a few hours ago. *How sad*, she thought. *He seemed like such a nice fella.* The report was short. Details were sketchy. As the news show ended, Dawn felt a hollow emptiness. The warm, cozy living room seemed suddenly chilled. She picked up the remote and switched through the channels looking for something to cheer her up. She picked a rerun of MASH but found she couldn't keep her mind on the story. She kept remembering the bright smile of the young man who had tried to help her — who was now lying on some cold slab in the city morgue.

She shivered despite the warmth of the room. She decided to see if she could find a blanket or quilt to wrap around her. Halfway to the bedroom, the doorbell rang. Who on earth would be calling on her? Well, no one of course. They'd be calling on Pat, but wouldn't everyone know that Pat was away on leave? Maybe not? Dawn walked over to the front door of the apartment and peered through the peephole. For the second time in less than an hour, she gasped at the face before her. It was the young officer. The one who had supposedly been killed.

She breathed a sigh of relief. It had been a mistake. They must have reported on the wrong officer. True, someone was lying down there in the morgue, but at least it wasn't her young man.

She unlocked the door and flung it open. "Am I ever glad to see you." The officer smiled with a confused twist to it. "According to the news report, you're supposed to be dead." Dawn stepped back to give him room to enter.

The officer's eyes darted around the room, taking in everything in one quick moment. Stepping into the room, he closed the door behind him. "Well, you know you can't believe everything you see on TV these days."

"WHAT DO YOU SAY AFTER I take a shower we go down and get our free breakfast?" Pat asked as her shoulder muscles finally began to relax under Allan's talented fingers.

"Sounds good to me. I think I'm going to be lazy for a little longer while you take a shower, then I want to call Dawn before we go out."

Pat stood up and walked into the bathroom. In a few minutes, Allan heard the sound of the shower water beating against the sides of the fiberglass tub. He closed his eyes and tried to relax his tense muscles. It was still a little hard for him to believe everything that had happened. What in the world was he doing here in Greensboro, anyway?

Why, I'm on the way to Washington, D.C. to stop a mad alien from taking over the world. He answered his own question. Were the two of them crazy? Had he simply gone off the deep end a few months ago from too much stress in the practice or from too much grief? Maybe they were just two nut cases like you read about in the paper all the time, living in their own world of delusion? Maybe Homlin was just an ordinary scientist trying to get his discovery accepted.

He could just see the D.C. paper now. "Attempted Assassination of Famous Scientist Thwarted." And the sub-heading, "Both Assassins Shot."

Well, if so, the die was cast. He wasn't going to stop now. It had all really happened, was still happening. Homlin was an alien, and he was out to overthrow the world. There was a plant a few hours from here filled with thousands of alien life forms waiting for distribution. It all had to be stopped.

Allan opened his eyes and reached for the phone as he heard Pat cut off the water in the other room. He read the instructions on how to get an outside line. In a few moments, he was dialing Pat's apartment number. He was surprised when, after the fourth ring, Pat's answering machine picked up. Where was Dawn? Wasn't she supposed to be at Pat's apartment all morning? She should be back from her trip to Pat's office.

He waited for the end of the message. "Hello, uh, Pat ..." He'd almost asked for Dawn, instead. "This is Dr. Pritchard. I'm sorry I missed you. When you get in, please call me at this number." He glanced at the number on the phone, but before he could give the number, he heard Dawn's voice.

"Hello, don't hang up. Wait just a minute." There was a pause on the other end. "Hello..."

"Dawn, is that you? This is Dr. Pritchard."

"Oh, I'm sorry. I must have dozed off on the sofa."

"Are you okay? You sound a little funny." Allan said, uncertain what he was picking up that sounded strange.

"No, everything is fine here. I'm just a little drowsy. It's been a lazy morning. Where are you?"

"Pat and I are at the Airport Marriott in Greensboro. We're getting ready to fly to Washington, D.C. for some important business. I'm calling to let you know we're fine and that we want you to stay in Charlotte for a couple more days. Is that okay?"

"Sure, no problem. I'm having fun. Do you want me to continue to pose as Pat?"

"Yes, including going into her office each day for at least a couple of hours. We want to be sure it looks like you're down there for business reasons."

"No problem. When will you be in Washington?"

Allan glanced down at the pad of paper where Pat had jotted down the time and gate number of the new flight. "We're scheduled to leave at 1:45. I don't know the arrival time. It's a new flight. Our original one was canceled."

"Well, don't worry about anything down here. I'm enjoying being a big city private eye."

"Just be careful, Dawn. The people that are following you are not to be taken for granted. I'm sorry I had to get you into this mess in the first place. I couldn't stand it if anything happened to you."

"Don't worry, Allan, nothing is going to happen. I'm a big girl. I can take care of myself. You go and do what you have to. Don't worry about me."

Allan continued to hold the phone against his ear, but he couldn't get any words out of his mouth. Something was wrong here. Something was terribly wrong, he just knew it. In the seven years, he'd known Dawn, she had never once, no matter what the circumstances, called him by his first name. It had become one of their common jokes. To Dawn, he would always be Dr. Pritchard. Who was he really talking to?

"Listen, I need you to do one more thing." He finally managed to get the words out. "Call Marva in the morning and tell her that Mrs. McGee's schnauzer can go home in the afternoon. Will you do that?"

"Sure, I'd be happy to."

There was no doubt about it. This wasn't Dawn with whom he was speaking. The real Dawn knew perfectly well that they had put Mrs. McGee's schnauzer to sleep on Thursday. It had been very upsetting to Dawn to have to hold the old dog. He had been one of their longest standing patients and one of Dawn's favorite. Mr. McGee had picked up the body that afternoon for a backyard burial.

Allan hung up the phone but continued to sit on the bed staring at the receiver. Something had happened in Charlotte. Dawn was in trouble. For all he knew, she might be dead by now. There appeared little doubt that their little switch had been discovered.

Damn, I've just told somebody other than Dawn what our plans are, he thought. *I've played right into their hand.*

Pat walked out of the bathroom, a towel wrapped around her slender form. With a second towel, she was drying her hair.

"Did you reach Dawn?" She asked as she walked over to the chest of drawers where they'd stacked their suitcases.

Allan didn't answer at once; his mind seemed unable to catch up with what had just happened. He finally wrestled his eyes away from the phone and stood up.

"Yes, no... I mean, I reached your apartment but whoever I talked to wasn't Dawn."

Pat stopped rubbing her hair in mid-stride. "What do you mean? Is something wrong?"

"It wasn't Dawn. It sounded like Dawn down to almost every detail—except one." He repeated the conversation he'd just had.

"Are you sure? Couldn't you have been mistaken? Maybe she was trying to make you feel more at ease or something."

"Dawn hasn't been able to call me by my first name in casual conversation in all the years we've known each other. It's been a standing joke with us. But, let's just say that she did — just this once. There's no way she wouldn't have known that Mrs. McGee wasn't going to pick up her dog. No way. I tell you, whoever I talked to wasn't Dawn, but they sure wanted me to think they were. They've gotten her. That's all there is to it, and what's worse I didn't know it until I had already told them where we were headed."

"Shit," Pat said as she sat on the bed and absentmindedly toweled her hair again. After a moment she said, "Well, let's see. This is what we'll have to do. We'll have to split up. You head down to Charlotte, and I'll head to Washington."

"But they know you're coming."

"Yeah, so what? Let them know. I'm still going. I have to go. They've got to be stopped, and you've got to go see if you can help Dawn. I feel awful for getting her caught up in this, I really do. I'll notify Allison that you're on the way and have her stake out my place. She's good, Allan. If anyone can get Dawn out of there alive, Allison can."

That is if she's still alive, Allan thought, but what was the point in saying the obvious.

Pat continued to sit on the bed for a few minutes as she continued to dry her head. Finally, she stood up and headed for the bathroom. "It's getting sticky, no question about it. We're going to have to dig deep to pull this one out. So, I guess that's just what we'll have to do."

HOMLIN PICKED UP THE phone on the second ring. Alex quickly explained his short conversation with Allan.

"So they've found out about the meeting, and they're coming to stop it," Homlin said with a chuckle. "Okay. We'll have to be on the lookout for them. Let's see." He paused for a moment. Alex waited patiently for his orders. "Here's what I want you to do. What time did you say their plane was leaving?"

"1:45," Alex answered.

"Great. I want you on that flight with them. It's our best chance to pick up the trail again. Who do you have down there with you?"

"Julian," Alex winced. He knew Homlin's opinion of Julian wasn't good. It was also an opinion that Alex shared. Julian was somewhat of a fuck-up, but surely he could watch one small, tied-up woman without blowing it.

"Okay. That's just the way it is, I guess. I'll see if we have someone at the lab that can drive down and be with him. Anyway, leave him there to look after our little imposter, and you find Vogt and Pritchard. Don't do anything but follow them. When they check into a hotel, you do the same and call me from there. Is that clear?"

"Very clear," Alex replied. Within a couple of hours, I'll be back on the trail of that bitch. *It's only a matter of time before Homlin gives me instructions to kill both of them.* "I'll call you from Washington."

Dawn's Dilemma
Monday, 12:28 pm Dec. 6

Allan pulled the Blazer to the curb and turned off the engine. He stepped out of the car, pulling the collar of his jacket up to help shelter himself from the wind. He walked down the street towards the address Pat had given him, leaning into the blustery wind. It was getting colder with each day. For the South, it was just the beginning of winter — Allan's least favorite season. Every year he thought it would be okay with him if fall simply continued until spring and then spring could simply continue until fall again. In a perfect world you only really needed two seasons. And in a perfect world, there weren't monsters or aliens or even bad guys who abducted gentle ladies like Dawn.

After walking a couple of blocks, he saw the sky blue sedan that Pat had described to him exactly where she said it would be. He walked towards it and climbed into the passenger seat and found himself staring at the large black hole of a large gun being held in the small hand of an attractive young woman.

"Are you Allan?" The woman asked, and without thinking, he almost said yes. Then he remembered what he was to say to the question.

"No, I'm Dr. Pritchard," he said, trying to force a smile without much success.

"Good." The woman lowered the revolver and stuck it back in her shoulder harness. "I'm Allison. Pat has told me so much about you, but she didn't tell me how cute you were."

This time Allan smiled more successfully. "It's a pleasure, Allison. I only wish it had been under different circumstances."

"You can say that again. I was so shocked to hear that Dawn had been kidnapped. It was only a few hours ago when I spoke to her on the phone. She was worried because she'd become lost."

"Oh boy! That must have been the giveaway. They must have suspected something right then."

"Pat didn't have much time to explain what was going on. She had to catch her flight. She told me you would fill me in on what I needed to know."

Allan nodded. Pat and he had sorted out how much they could tell Allison. Even though Pat trusted Allison completely, Pat still wasn't anxious to let anyone know what was going on, so they had decided on giving Allison a partial story.

"A gang of thugs was following Dawn thinking she was Pat. It was the only way we could get Pat clear of them so she could work on finding their ringleader. That's what she's doing in Washington. Unfortunately, they've discovered the switch."

"I'm only going to ask one question. Is this about the case Pat's been working on for ten years?"

It took Allan a second to understand Allison's question then he answered, "Yes, it is."

"Say no more. No one has ever understood what the case was about, but all of us have seen how consumed Pat has been with it. If there's anything I can do to help resolve it for her, I'll do it, no questions asked. So, let's get to work."

Allan smiled. For some reason, he wasn't surprised to find that Pat had a loyal staff. Still, it was refreshing.

"Okay, what's been happening in there?"

"Not much. I've seen one man leave and go down the street. I didn't follow him for fear they might slip Dawn out while I was gone. He came back with a bag of groceries. It would suggest to me that at least two people are holding her."

"Okay, good. Have you seen any sign of Dawn?"

"No, 'fraid not."

Allan pondered the situation for a moment. He'd had his mind on nothing else for the entire two hours of the trip. He still hadn't come up with a good plan for getting Dawn out safely. For that matter, he didn't know if she was still alive, but the fact that the thugs were still around and shopped for groceries gave him hope.

"Well, Allison, I'm far from an expert in matters of this kind. About as close to the criminal world as I've ever gotten was giving first aid to a stranger for a dog bite. I didn't find out until later that he'd received the bite while breaking into a house. He convinced me he came to a vet because he figured that was where people that had been bitten by an animal went. It sounded plausible to me. Anyway, I'm open to suggestions."

Allison nodded and pulled her key out of the ignition.

"After speaking with Pat, I called Frank and Cindy. They're a husband and wife team. They don't actually work for Pat, except for an occasional contract, but they're always willing to lend a hand. They are on the other side of the building, watching the back. In a situation like this, surprise is the only thing we have on our side. If I understood Pat correctly, the men inside aren't aware they gave themselves away to you. Is that correct?"

"Yes, I'd say so. I wasn't even sure until I had hung up and thought about it."

"So, I doubt they'll be suspecting us to show up on their doorstep suddenly. The fact that one of them went out for groceries would suggest this is true as well. About the only thing I know to do is to go in quickly and in force."

Allan thought about it for a moment. As he worked to come up with a plan, he stared out the window of the sedan. There wasn't much foot traffic on this blustery Sunday afternoon. Just an old fella in a worn out army jacket, his shoulders hunched over, hands dug deeply into the pockets of the jacket.

He reminds me of old Mr. Sorenson, Allan thought. Sorenson had been Allan's gruff yet soft landlord for three of his four years in vet school. In the three years, Allan could only remember a couple of occasions when he'd seen Sorenson without a similar army jacket. A thought suddenly came to Allan, and he leaped out of the car after the bum, unzipping his own down-lined ski jacket as he ran after him.

PAT LEANED OVER THE back seat and paid the taxi driver.

"Keep the change," she said without realizing she'd just tipped him almost half of the fare. Her mind was on other matters.

"Gee, thanks, lady." The cabby jumped out to open her door.

As Pat climbed out of the back seat, she had an almost irresistible urge to glance over her shoulder, but she resisted the temptation. It wasn't really necessary. She knew what she'd see, either the dark blue sedan or the black one. They'd become more careful with the tag, using two cars instead of one, but they had still been easy to spot by a professional who knew for what they were looking.

The cabbie ran around to the rear of his car and pulled Pat's suitcase out of the trunk.

"Would you like me to take it to your room?" The cabbie asked.

"No, that won't be necessary," Pat answered, seeing him for the first time and realizing she must have over-tipped him. "I believe they have someone here at the hotel who will take care of it. We better let them do their job."

The cabbie smiled and nodded then pulled a rumpled business card out of his shirt pocket. "Don't hesitate to call when you need to go somewhere and be sure to ask for Archie. If I'm on duty, I'll dump whoever I'm driving and come running."

"Thanks, I'll keep that in mind." Pat took the card and stuck it in her purse, wondering how much she must have tipped him to get such service.

One of the bellhops from the hotel came out and placed her bag on his dolly. Archie looked for a moment like he might take issue with the bellhop but then realized it was time to release his best customer of the week.

Pat walked through the revolving door of the hotel. Not until she was on the other side of the reflecting glass did she turn around and study the street. In a moment she found what she'd been looking for — the black sedan, parked on the other side of the street fifteen or twenty yards from the front entrance of the hotel. She wondered, as she walked over to the front desk to check in, whether the driver and occupant of the car were still inside or if they had already checked into her room ahead of her. She decided to request the largest bellboy on staff to take her bag up to her room. She was really too tired to take on two thugs on her own. All she really wanted to do right now was to take a hot soaking bubble bath. Could they please leave her alone long enough for that?

THE ARMY JACKET REEKED of body odor. Great for the image Allan was trying to convey but hard on his own senses. He pounded on the door again, ignoring the doorbell.

"Come on, Ms. Vogt, I know you're in there. I saw you drive up yesterday. If you don't open the door and give me my rent, I'm going to have to call the cops." Allan stepped back away from the door, being sure he didn't glance to either side where Allison, Frank, and Cindy stood, flattened against the wall waiting to rush in on Allan's signal.

Was Dawn still alive or was he risking his own life and the lives of three other people just to recover a cold, stiff corpse? What if there was more than one man inside and they couldn't get to all of them before one of them did something to Dawn?

Shut up, he told himself as he heard someone on the other side of the door slip the lock. His left hand twitched slightly, notifying the other three to be ready.

The door opened and there in front of him stood Pat, tugging on the rope belt of a white terry cloth bathrobe. Allan stood frozen to his spot out in the hallway, his mind racing. It couldn't be Pat, could it? He'd left her in Greensboro two hours away, waiting to fly to Washington. But here she stood just as clearly as could be. But it couldn't be.

The thoughts raced through his mind in a millisecond. It couldn't be. That was the bottom line. The person or thing standing before him had done a remarkable job of mimicry. *Just like one of them had done with copying TJ*, Allan thought as he lowered his head and right shoulder and dove through the doorway, catching the Pat look-a-like just below the solar plexus with his shoulder. It was a most satisfying yet confusing experience to see the shocked and frightened look on the Pat look-alike just before he knocked the breath out of her. The other three followed closely behind Allan. Allison joined him in subduing his target while Frank and Cindy ran towards the bedroom to find Dawn.

If Allan had been momentarily surprised by who he was attacking, Allison was thunderstruck when she realized they were overwhelming her boss of ten years. Still, much to her credit she didn't hesitate but planted a knockout punch to the left temple, sending the Pat look-a-like crumpling to the floor.

"Good work," Allan said as he stared down at the unconscious woman.

"Yeah but ... are you sure ... " Allison stuttered to a stop, unsure what to say.

"I'll explain it all to you later. Trust me, we're doing the right thing," Allan said as he ran towards the bedroom to see if he could help Frank and Cindy. Cindy and Dawn were sitting on the bed. Cindy was cleaning dry blood from Dawn's forehead while Frank finished untying the last bond from around one of Dawn's legs.

"She'll be okay," Cindy said as Allan rushed over to them. "She's pretty frightened, but there doesn't appear to be any serious injuries. I know of a doctor we can take her to that won't ask too many questions."

Allan felt the tears welling up in his eyes. He had never stopped to think how much Dawn meant to him—until now.

"Great work. It's obvious why Pat has been so successful as a private eye with a team of people like you." Allan sat down beside Dawn on the bed. She threw her arms around him and began to weep.

"It's all over, sweetie," Allan said. *At least for you, it's all over,* he thought. *I've got a couple more hands to play out.*

"Now listen closely. I don't have time to explain in detail right now. Just trust me when I say the person in the other room is not who she seems."

"Oh, I believe you," Allison said. "If I didn't, we'd all be out of a job."

"You've got to keep her or it under very tight surveillance for the next twenty-four hours. After that, we can decide what to do from there."

"How 'bout you? Where are you going?" Allison asked.

"There's some unfinished business that needs attending to in Washington. I noticed you have a phone in your car. If you take me to the airport, I can call from the car to see when the next flight to Washington is. Pat or I will call to let you know what to do with this one. We'll explain everything at that time. For right now, the less you know the better."

Allan gave Dawn a final hug then held her out at arm's length so he could look into her eyes. "I'm going to leave you here with Frank and Cindy. When Allison comes back, you go stay with her." He glanced questioningly at Allison who nodded.

"I don't want you driving home to Waynesboro just yet." He decided not to tell her that it might not be safe for her to go home. She'd been through enough for one day. "I may need to ask you a few questions later, and it'll be easier if I know where you are." *Not to mention, I'll worry less if I know where you are*, Allan thought.

He stood up but continued to hold Dawn's hand for a moment longer. He gazed down at her and gave her a reassuring smile. "It's going to be okay. I promise you. When this is all over, life in Waynesboro will be too boring for you."

"I can't think of anything I'd enjoy more than to be bored in Waynesboro," Dawn answered with a tired smile.

ALEX GLANCED AT HIS watch. 4:15 and still no sign of the vet. He picked up the portable phone and punched in Homlin's number. After a couple of rings, Homlin answered.

"Still no sign of the doc. Vogt checked into the Marque about an hour ago. I think it's the right time to snuff her before her boyfriend shows."

Homlin was silent at the other end. Alex waited patiently for his boss's orders. This was the moment he'd been waiting for, ever since Vogt had dug her heel into his foot and made him look foolish in Homlin's eyes. *It's time to pay for your mistakes, bitch*, he thought as he waited for Homlin's decision.

"Okay, fine. Wait for another hour for her to settle into her room. Then slip in and take care of her. Tell Lenny to stay outside and watch for Dr. Pritchard and to call up to her room if he shows up."

"You've got it, boss. I'll take care of her — real good care."

"Alex, I know you have your own plans for her. I don't even want to know what they are. Just be careful. Don't let your silly games jeopardize the operation. Is that clear?"

"Perfectly," Alex answered with a smile. *Silly games, maybe, but Vogt wouldn't think they were so silly. By the time I'm finished with her, she'll be begging for me to end it.*

Alex cut the connection and put the phone back in its case. He reached over and shook Harrison's shoulder. "Wake up. I need you to watch the hotel for a while. I'm going out."

"Where are you going?" Lenny asked as he pulled himself up by the steering wheel in front of him.

"I'm going clothes shopping. Ms. Vogt is going to have a surprise visitor in a little bit. Stay awake. I'm going to take the phone. If she comes out of the hotel, call me from the pay phone over there—immediately. I won't be gone long."

Lenny nodded and rolled down the window to get some fresh air.

"THAT'S THE FIRST FLIGHT you have out?" Allan asked for the second time. He covered the receiver with his hand and whispered to Allison. "Nothing before 5:45 this evening."

"I have an idea. Hang up."

Allan thanked the airline agent and hung up.

"Punch in this number 554-2233, and give me the phone," Allison said. Allan did as he was told and handed the phone to her.

"I'm calling a friend of mine, Steve Runyon. We use him from time to time. He has a small airplane leasing company. If he's in, we'll get you up to Washington in a couple of hours. If not, we'll just have to find another way." Allison smiled as the connection was made.

"Hello, Stevie. This is Allison. I know you hate to hear my voice on a quiet Sunday afternoon, but I've got a real problem. One of those life and death situations. I know you'll charge us an arm and a leg for me to say it, but it's really important we get someone up to Washington, D.C. this afternoon. Can you help us out?"

Allison listened for a few seconds and signaled Allan with a thumbs-up.

"That's great Steve. We're on the way to the airport now. How long before you can be there? Super. I owe you a dinner for this one."

She hung up the phone. "You're on your way."

PAT WALKED OUT OF THE bathroom, wrapping the thick terry cloth robe the hotel supplied around her still wet body. *My second bath of the day,* she noted to herself. *It seems like the closer I get to my alien, the dirtier I feel. I must be getting close. I feel like I need another shower already.* She strolled over to the phone and punched in the number to Allison's apartment. Allison picked up the phone before the second ring.

"Oh, it's so good to hear your voice," Allison said after Pat identified herself. "Everything is fine down here. Dawn is in my spare bedroom right now, napping. It was pretty scary for her, but she's no worse for wear. A couple of days of rest and she should be as good as new."

Pat breathed a sigh of relief. "Oh, I'm so glad. Take real good care of her, Allison. Allan thinks the world of her, and so do I. Speaking of Allan . . . "

"He's on his way to you at this very moment. We couldn't get a commercial flight that worked so we put him on one of Steve's specials. I hope you don't mind."

"Goodness, no. Good thinking," Pat replied. "What time should I expect him?"

"I don't know exactly. Allan sent me on my way before they took off. He wanted me to get back to be with Dawn. I'd guess somewhere between five and six though."

Pat looked at the digital clock beside the bed. 4:05 pm. She had an hour or two of free time. "Let me give you my number. You should be able to reach me here until tomorrow morning. Allan knows which hotel I'm staying at, but he may call you to find out which room. More than likely, he'll just call me or come on over. I think I'm going to lie down for a while but don't hesitate to call if you need me for anything." She gave Allison the numbers.

"Will do," Allison replied. "Oh, Pat. There's one more thing. I know you can't discuss this case with me right now, but I've gotten the idea that something big is about to happen. Just be real careful. We all need you to come home safely. Okay?"

Pat chuckled. "Will do, sweetie, give everyone my love." She hung up the phone.

Yes, it was all coming to a head. After ten years of searching for him, she finally had her alien cornered in her old stomping ground of Washington, D.C. — where the search had begun. 'Her alien.' Funny, how long had she thought of him like that. Years. And now it was almost over. Either she'd have finally tracked him down and stopped him, or he would have finally won out. His long years of staying in hiding, scheming quietly to overthrow human civilization. It had been a difficult ten years for both of them. Both struggling for the survival of their respective races.

Pat pulled the covers back on the double bed and climbed under them. It felt good to lie down between the clean sheets and let her tense muscles relax. Somewhere in Washington, Homlin waited as well — waited for the final moment when he could safely disseminate his race across the country and then the world.

He knows I'm out here and that I intend to stop him. He'll be out to stop me first. It really is coming down to who stops who. Their first meeting had been a draw. She'd survived his assault, but he'd also managed to escape. There would be no draw on this next meeting. It was time to end the ten-year game of cat and mouse.

She found herself smiling as she drifted off to sleep. *Funny*, she thought, *I've never figured out which one of us is the cat and which the mouse. I prefer being the cat this go around.*

Kink in D. C.
Monday Evening, Dec. 6

The harsh noise of the jangling phone sliced its way through Pat's sleep until she found herself sitting upright in bed with the receiver against her ear.

"Yes, who is it?" She asked with her eyes still closed. Where was she? Not in her own bedroom, that much was certain, but it had been so long since she had slept at home, she wasn't surprised by that. But where was she?

"Hello, Ms. Vogt. I'm sorry to disturb you, but there is a gentleman down here by the name of Dr. Allan Pritchard. He is asking for your room number."

Allan...room number...it all washed over her and started to make sense. She was in D.C. at the Marque. She leaned over to the nightstand and twisted the digital clock around so she could read it. 5:15. She'd been asleep for a little over an hour. It felt like she'd been asleep for days.

She swung her legs over the edge of the bed. "That's fine. Send him on up. I'm expecting him." She told the voice at the other end of the phone. She hung up the phone and walked into the bathroom to wash her face.

5:15, she thought, *He made good time getting up here.* She threw a clean bath cloth in the sink and ran cold water over it. It would be excellent to be back in Allan's arms. Maybe they'd order dinner through room service and just stay in the rest of the evening. Stay in and cuddle, maybe make love. Who knows, it might be the last chance they'd get for quite a while.

"Room 444. Take the elevators over there to the fourth floor and turn left. Ms. Vogt is expecting you." The desk clerk demeanor had altered since the phone call.

Alex smiled. "Thank you," he replied as he turned towards the line of elevators. *She's expecting me, huh? Won't she be surprised?*

As he stood waiting for the elevator, he gazed at himself in the wall of mirrors between the elevator doors. *Not bad*, he thought. He'd only seen

Pritchard a couple of times, but he had made it a point to notice every detail. He suspected having the vet's physical attributes down, as well as having as many of his behavioral characteristics as possible, would be useful one day. Today was the day. He even thought he'd done a good job of picking out his wardrobe. It was unlikely he had matched what Pritchard had been wearing when he'd last been with Vogt, but it was close enough that he doubted she would notice. If so, he was prepared to explain how he'd had to change clothes while on the plane. The silly lady beside him had spilled her drink all over his other outfit.

The elevator chimed, and the door opened. With a final gaze, Alex stepped into the elevator and pressed the button for the fourth floor.

HOMLIN STARED OUT THE window at the city lights below. Although it was only dusk, already most of the lights were on. He looked up into the sky and saw the lights of a plane circling. He'd grown accustomed to the constant air traffic around D.C. Tonight, it seemed more noticeable, perhaps because on one of those flights might be one of the two humans that could thwart his plans — plans he'd been building on for almost ten years.

He now knew where Vogt was, and he expected to hear from Alex within the hour of her tragic accident. That would leave only Pritchard. It was strange, even though he didn't know where Pritchard was at the moment, he was less concerned with him than he was with Vogt. Pritchard would show up wherever Vogt was. Hopefully, by the time that happened, it would be just a matter of having Alex kill him as well. He'd rest easier once he knew both Vogt and Pritchard had been eliminated. There was no reason at this point in taking any other risks. Get rid of them once and for all. By this time next week, FreeForm would be in the labs across the country, and Earth's destiny would be decided.

Not that his job would be over. There'd still be the transition stage. He suspected the human race would put up some resistance. Then there would be the cleanup and the administration of the new order. No, in some ways his job was just beginning, but for Homlin the fun part, the really challenging part, would be over and done. Within a few weeks, life would become pretty routine. Not all at once. At first, it would be hectic and probably from time to time a little nerve-wracking but in a much different way.

Would he request another settlement? That was always the question he asked himself, but careful to not ask it too early, however. This one wasn't over yet. Vogt could still pull something fast, and even Pritchard could cause some trouble. Better wait and be sure this one was in the bag before looking towards the next planet.

PAT PULLED THE KNOT tight on her robe as she walked to the door. Peering through the peephole, she confirmed that it was Allan before opening the door and flinging herself into his arms.

"God, it's good to see you," Pat said as she pulled him into the room. "I didn't know I could miss someone so much in such a short time."

"I've missed you too," Allan replied, blushing a little from so much attention.

Pat threw her arms around his neck again. "I don't know why, but I've been horny all day. Maybe it's pent-up energy from what we are about to do."

Allan smiled. "Well, maybe we should see what we can do about it. I could hardly wait to get here myself. In fact . . . " He paused for a moment, the smile turning to a look of mischief. ". . . I was thinking on the plane that it might be fun if we went a little beyond our normal lovemaking."

Pat pulled back a little from him, a look of mock horror on her face. "Whatever did you have in mind, sir?"

"Well, the idea came to me while I was waiting to get on the plane. Everywhere I looked, all the men were wearing ties. I thought that strange for a Sunday afternoon, but then I started thinking about all the old ties I have in my closet. Well, one thing led to another, and I remembered this old x-rated movie I saw several years ago while I was in college. This guy used his old ties to tie this luscious blonde to his bed."

Allan reached into his coat and pulled out a paper bag. "I stopped on the way in at a second-hand store and made a minor purchase."

"You didn't!" Pat said as she grabbed the bag out of his hand and pulled out a handful of men's ties. "Silk. You don't go second class with your bondage, do you?"

"Well, I figure it might be a one time deal. Might as well go all out. What do you say? You interested in a little fun?"

Pat draped a couple of the ties around her neck and slid back into Allan's arms. "I don't know. I might be talked into it," she said as she gave him a long slow kiss.

The phone rang, interrupting the moment.

"Who could that be?" Allan asked as Pat walked over to pick it up.

"I don't know. Probably Dawn is checking to see that you got here all right."

Pat picked up the phone with a friendly, "Hello."

She listened to the familiar male voice on the other end of the phone. The identical voice that had just asked, "Who could that be?"

"I just got into the D.C. airport. I'm coming right to the hotel. I just wanted to hear your voice and be sure you were okay," Allan said on the other end of the phone.

What was going on here? Who was this on the phone? It couldn't be Allan. Allan was here in her room only a few feet away. Or was he? 5:15. It had been early, earlier than she'd expected him to be able to get to the hotel. She glanced at the clock radio. 5:40. Yes, it made more sense for him to be at the airport. Pat stifled a shudder that threatened to run the entire length of her body. Who was this man who wanted to tie her up? Allan was a fun loving guy, but the suggestion had been out of character for him.

"Hello. Are you okay?" The voice asked on the other end.

"Yes, everything is fine. Allan arrived just a few minutes ago. He's a little tired right now and can't talk. I'll tell him you called, Dawn," Pat replied.

There was a pause on the other end. "Pat, hang in there. I'll be right there."

"That's fine. I'll be sure to take real good care of him." She winked at Allan's impersonator. She hung up the phone and took a deep breath before turning back to her guest.

"Well, what are you doing with your clothes still on?" She asked with a laugh.

The man smiled as he reached down and unfastened his belt. "We're going to have a lot of fun."

Pat strolled over to him and ran her hand along his chest. "We sure are," she replied. "I have only one request."

"What's that?" Allan's look-a-like asked as he removed his shirt.

"Ladies first, I want to tie you up and make mad passionate love to you first. Then you can do the same with me. Fair?"

He hesitated for only a moment. "If you like. Sure. We can do it that way. Whatever you say."

Pat stroked his bare chest with her fingernails, noticing as she did the subtle differences in his physique. Would she have noticed without the phone call? It was hard to say. "I promise you an experience you won't soon forget."

ALLAN RAN THROUGH THE airport like a man possessed, expecting at any moment to be hailed by one of the airport authorities, but evidently berserk men dashing through the crowd was a common occurrence. He was fortunate to find an empty cab as soon as he exited the automatic doors leading to the outside.

As he slipped into the back seat, he tossed a fifty-dollar bill through the small hole in the Plexiglas partition separating him from the driver. "I'll match that with another one if you get me to the Marque in thirty minutes or less."

The black man grabbed the bill, glanced at it a moment to be sure it was real, glanced at the nut that had leaped into his cab and smiled, showing a mouthful of white teeth.

"It's impossible, man. It's at least a forty minute drive, but we'll sure as hell go for the record." He slammed the car into gear and tore a layer of rubber off his tires as he pulled away from the curb.

"I THOUGHT I'D DONATE your tie collection with a couple of pairs of nylon stockings," Pat said as she tossed a handful of them on the night table next to the bag of ties.

"You're really planning to tie me uptight, aren't you?"

"That's the idea, isn't it? What good is bondage if you know you can get right out of it?" Pat said with a little too much edge. She pushed him down on the bed. "Relax, this is going to be fun," she said more softly. "For the next little while, you are going to be my love slave. You'll have to do everything I tell you and let me do all the naughty things I've wanted to do with you."

"I think I can stand it," the man said. "Aren't you going to take your robe off? Fair is fair. If I'm going to be naked ..."

"Who's giving the orders here?" Pat said in a mocking voice. "Your turn will come in a little bit. Now, shut-up and behave yourself. I'm the master here." She pushed him all the way down on the bed until his head rested on the pillow, then straddled his chest with her long legs.

"Close your eyes. Pretend you've been drugged or something. Maybe you've had too much to drink and passed out. I want you to be completely helpless for the next couple of minutes."

The impostor obliged, shutting his eyes and relaxing his entire body. Pat picked up his right hand and quickly knotted a tie around his wrist, leaving plenty of fabric for the bedpost. She repeated the exercise with the other hand and both ankles. With his eyes still shut, she pulled each extremity out to the corner of the bed, stretching him out in spread-eagle fashion. When all four corners were firmly attached, she slid off the bed for a moment.

"No peeking," she said as his eyelids fluttered. "You're still out cold until I tell you otherwise." She then grabbed the handful of stockings and tied two of them together. She repeated this with a second pair. She then tied both sets around his neck and attached them to either side of the bedpost.

"That's tight," he said, although he kept his eyes closed.

It's supposed to be, you jerk, Pat thought but didn't say. "If it's too tight, I'll loosen it in a moment. I just want to be sure you have the full sensation of be-ing helpless. I've read that is what makes this kind of sex so stimulating."

He must be one of Homlin's goons, she figured. In which case, Allan was probably not the only shape into which it could transform. She wasn't sure she'd be able to keep him bound if he started changing shapes, but she had to try.

With the last knot finally tied, she stepped away from the bed to study her handiwork. The alien was stretched across the bed in a large X, the center of the X accentuated by his taunt manhood, which pointed to the ceiling. She had half a mind to tie it to one of the bedposts or better yet, cut it off and..." *Never mind*, she thought. *It's time to finish the job.*

"In a moment, I want you to wake up, not yet. In a moment. When you do, I want you to try to stretch, like you're really waking up and take a big yawn. Then you'll notice that you can't move and panic a little. Only then, do I want you to open your eyes. Got it?"

"Man, you're really getting into this."

You can say that again, Pat thought as she balled the last nylon in her hand.

"Okay, begin to stretch, yawn big, and then open your eyes."

The man did just as he was told and at the peak of his yawn, Pat jammed the stocking deep into his mouth. He immediately tried to cough it out and gagged. His eyes flew open, a look of stark panic on his face. He mumbled something unintelligible and began to struggle against his bonds, but quickly realized he was choking himself when he did.

"Who the fuck are you?" Pat asked as she slipped a tie around his mouth to hold the stocking in place. "Never mind. I know you can't answer me and it's not important.

"You're not taking my planet. That's all there is to it. We won't let you. Not if I have anything to say about it and obviously I still do."

The man glared at her with eyes filled with hate and fear. He mumbled something else, straining so hard against his ropes it looked like he might burst a blood vessel.

Then he suddenly stopped struggling and tried another strategy. As Pat watched, he began to change shapes, but Pat had been expecting it and was prepared. She threw a glass of cold water in his face to momentarily distract him.

"Oh no, you don't! I like you just the way you are."

He shook his head to clear the water out of his eyes, glared back at her for a second, and began the metamorphosis again.

Pat picked up the heavy lamp sitting on the nightstand with both hands. Lifting it over her head, she brought it down with a crushing blow on the left side of his skull.

"Lights out," she said as the light bulb blew and the alien sunk into deep unconsciousness.

Oliver's Discovery
Monday, Dec. 6

Lenny was just nodding off when the cab screeched up to the entrance of the Marque. Before the cab had come to a full stop, the back door flew open and out stepped Allan Pritchard.

"Oh shit," muttered Lenny as he grabbed the mobile phone and quickly dialed Homlin's number. Homlin answered on the second ring, but already Allan had ducked into the hotel. He quickly explained what had happened.

"Son-of-a..." Homlin started then stopped in mid-sentence. "Okay, listen closely. I can't afford to risk losing both of you. Alex will have to handle those two on his own. The worst that could happen is they get away from him and show up tomorrow, in which case we'll handle them along with the other two doctors. I'm sure Alex will have no trouble taking care of both of them. Get yourself back to your hotel and wait for my call."

Lenny broke the connection and set the phone down in the seat next to him. He started the car engine with a sigh of relief. Finally, he'd be able to go back and get a good night's sleep. He wondered if he should somehow try to warn Alex but then decided Homlin was right. It was too risky. Besides, Homlin was boss. If he said to go back to the hotel, who was he to question the orders? He pulled the car away from the curb. Alex might be angry for being left, but he wouldn't be able to say anything. It was Homlin's orders.

HOMLIN RESTED THE PHONE in its cradle. He hated being so short-handed. Would Alex be okay? It was a calculated risk. He had hoped to have Vogt and Pritchard out of the picture before tomorrow morning's meeting, but it might not be possible. *It's getting tight,* Homlin thought. At the very worst, Vogt and Pritchard might show up at the meeting and try to convince the panel members to reconsider. Homlin smiled as he pictured the scene. Well, let them come. He would make sure they received a warm welcome.

ALLAN WAS SURPRISED to find Pat's door partially ajar, kept open by the metal bar used for additional security at night. He tried peering through the crack and listening for voices but could see and hear nothing. He finally pushed the door open an inch at a time.

"Come on in, honey. Everything is under control."

Pat's calm words were the most reassuring sound he thought he'd ever heard. He pushed the door all the way open and walked in. His eyes fell immediately on the naked figure spread eagle on the bed. At first glance, it looked like his twin, but on closer inspection, he noticed that the figure was different, less sharp and distorted.

"He tried to change shape, probably to his true form, but I changed his mind for him." Pat walked out of the bathroom and straight into Allan's arms. She threw her arms around his neck and kissed him passionately. "I'm so glad to see you. I don't think I've ever been so frightened. Not since that night on the spaceship, anyway. Sit down while I finish packing. We're getting out of here."

As she packed, Pat related what had happened since the phone call. Allan sat in the chair next to the bed, glancing first to Pat and then to the form lying tied to the bed. His anger bubbled as Pat told her story. By the time she finished, he was filled with emotion — hate for the alien that had impersonated him, pride and awe for the woman he loved.

"You're something else," he said when she finished the story. He shook his head. "You really are some kind of woman. I would never have had the nerve to try what you did. What if he had caught on?"

"Not very likely; his hormones were running so rampant I think he would have done just about anything I asked him if it meant getting a chance to me. I just managed to use what was driving him to my advantage." She closed the suitcase she'd been tossing clothes in and snapped it shut.

"Now what?" Allan asked.

"Well, we've gotta get out of here, that's for sure. No telling how many others of these monsters are around."

"What about him?" Allan said nodding towards the bed.

"I've got an old friend in town. We used to work together at B.I.U.F.O. I'd like for the two of them to meet. I gave him a call just before you arrived. He wasn't home, but I left a message on his machine. If I know my friend, he won't be able to resist. We're not waiting around to find out. Where are your bags?" Pat asked as she picked hers up off the bed.

Allan's face flushed. "Back at the airport. They never crossed my mind once I heard your voice on the phone."

"Well, that pretty much answers where we're going from here. Keep your eyes open on the way out. There's a very real chance we might be followed." Pat walked over to the nightstand next to the bed and laid a folded piece of paper on it.

"What's that?" Allan asked.

"A note introducing my friend to Romeo here. I don't want him to be unprepared." Pat glanced at her watch.

"All we have to do is hang low for another fourteen hours and be sure we're at that meeting tomorrow morning. I still haven't figured out exactly what we're going to do to unmask Homlin but one way or the other, we're going to stop him at that meeting tomorrow. I don't care if I have to take an Uzi with me and mow the whole lot of them down."

"You're kidding, of course." Allan shut the door to the room, being sure to leave the metal bar in place.

"I'm dead serious," Pat replied.

———✠╫\\╘╫———

OLIVER CUT OFF THE answering machine and rewound the tape, erasing the message as he did so.

"Any messages?" His wife, Ellen, asked as she came into the room, her hands still full with packages from their shopping trip. Sunday afternoons had always been her favorite time to shop for the family. Oliver hated it but obliged her. She had to put up with a lot more from him. It was the least he could do.

"No, nothing," Oliver answered, distracted by the flurry of thoughts and memories the brief message had stirred up. "I need to go out for a while."

"Well, okay, but I was hoping to have dinner a little early tonight. The kids are coming over later."

"Start without me." Oliver pulled his jacket back on. "I may be a while."

The familiar look of concern appeared on his wife's face. "Where are you going?"

He walked over to where she was standing and hugged her. "I've got some unfinished business that needs my attention. An old friend needs me. I'll explain later."

Oliver walked into his office. He pulled his keys out of his pocket and unlocked the bottom drawer of his desk. He pulled it open and removed the revolver. It had been years since he'd fired it, but he had made a point of cleaning it on a regular basis. He had never known why. Now, he knew. It was a strange weapon to take on a deer hunt, but then, it was a most unusual deer he was hunting.

OLIVER FOUND THE ROOM exactly as it had been described in the message. The door propped open with the security bolt and a lone naked figure tied securely to the bed. A bizarre scene for most people, but Oliver took it all in stride. In the twenty years he'd been with B.I.U.F.O., he'd adapted to going with the flow, no matter how strange.

Oliver walked over to the still form and checked its pulse. Still alive. He breathed a sigh of relief. At least he wasn't walking in on a murder case. He sat down in the chair next to the bed. Now what? He glanced around the room, and his eyes fell on the note on the bed stand. He suddenly felt as though he was on a treasure hunt, each message giving him another clue without any clear answer for what he was looking.

He recognized the neat handwriting despite the ten years it had been since he'd last seen it. He read the note through three times. Ten years. She'd been on the hunt all this time. It was hard to believe. Why had Pat dragged him back into it after all these years? Who was this unconscious person tied so securely to the bed? The note had been emphatic about one thing. The naked man was extremely dangerous and should be kept securely bound no matter what. Oliver decided to heed Pat's warning. He sat back in the chair and waited for the man to come to. Despite the long day, his nerves were too much on edge for him to worry about falling asleep. He patted the revolver nestled in its shoulder holster. Strange, it felt like a long lost friend coming home.

It felt good to relax after the many hours of shopping. He bet they'd walked five miles through the three different malls they'd visited. Next time he would stay in the car. He could usually persuade Ellen to let him do that about every third trip. As he settled in to wait, his tired muscles began to unknot. It was good to sit down. Very good indeed.

Oliver's eyelids slowly fell to half-mast then three quarter. Within five minutes he was asleep.

OLIVER AWOKE WITH A start. His unfocused eyes fell on the thrashing form in front of him. *What the hell?* He squinted his eyes and pressed his fists into them to clear his vision. It wasn't possible what he was seeing. The bound man was changing shapes in front of his eyes. He struggled against his ropes, tossing his head from side to side despite the tight nylons encircling his neck. His thrashing shook the bed.

Oliver squeezed out of the chair and backed away from the bed, reaching for the .45 as he did so. What was happening? He must be having a nightmare. What was happening in front of him was impossible. But even as he had the thoughts, he knew he was not asleep. His mind flashed back to a night over ten years ago — the glowing ship, the wounded deer, the explosion, and the cover-up. He knew what he was witnessing was all connected. It had not gone away. Although it had been successfully covered up by the agency and the bureaucracy, it had continued to fester like a malignant abscess. An abscess that was now coming to a head.

The half-man, half-beast noticed for the first time he was not alone in the room. His hate-filled eyes met Oliver's for a brief moment. The two locked gazes; time stopped. If looks could kill, Oliver would have exploded on the spot. Instead, he came to an immediate decision. Nothing so vile and hateful should live. Not on this planet. Not here on earth. Not if he could help it. He could.

Oliver raised the .45 and took aim. The form continued to alter in front of him as he gazed down the barrel. It had lost all resemblance to a man by the time Oliver squeezed the trigger four times. All four slugs struck the struggling form in the chest. Bluish-Red blood flowed from each wound and down onto the white sheets. The alien continued to struggle for another minute or two as its life forces ebbed.

Only when the last throes were complete did Oliver pick up the phone. He waited for the front desk to answer.

"I want to report a murder," he said calmly into the receiver. "Please send security to room 444 and call the police." Not waiting for a reply, he placed the receiver back in its cradle. He stared at the still form. Thank God it hadn't changed back into the human form. That would have been difficult to explain. He had enough explaining to do as it was.

FDA Confrontation
Monday 6:00 a.m., Dec. 6

Homlin hung up the phone. Everything back at Biogentrix was all set. A line of twenty trucks, each filled with insulated shipping crates housing anywhere from six to twelve individual FreeForm larvae, sat inside the grounds of the lab waiting for the signal to roll. Once the papers were signed, the trucks would be free to deliver their cargo. Some of them would hit the road carrying their packages across the country. About half of them would travel to various shipping and postal agencies including the Federal Government Postal Service.

Within forty-eight hours, FreeForm would be thoroughly circulating through the arteries of the country. The FreeForm would be irretrievable, and there'd be no turning back, no stopping the infiltration. It would take another four to six weeks for the FreeForm larvae to begin to be nursed along by the hundreds of research facilities, but it would be impossible to stop the process. Researchers were too unpredictable, too difficult to stop once they had a new toy like FreeForm with which to play. Even if the Federal agencies realized what was happening and tried to stop it, the dissemination would be too far along to stop the development of thousands of the larvae. Homlin had seen it often before, on other planets. The next few hours were the critical juncture. How long it took for FreeForm to overcome the planet might vary by several weeks, but the outcome was inevitable.

Time to shower and get dressed. Today was a big day for his people. His ten years on this planet had all been leading up to this day. He intended to enjoy every minute of it. As he turned the water on, he wondered if Vogt and Pritchard would dare to show up at the meeting. His bets were on them doing just that. He would be disappointed if they didn't try some last ditch effort. *Let them come*, Homlin thought, lathering himself with soap. This time he was prepared for Vogt. He wouldn't underestimate her again.

The trucks will roll despite all of Vogt's efforts and most important of all, Vogt and Pritchard will have played their best card without winning the hand. And he would make sure it was the last card of the last hand they would ever play against him again.

MONDAY 7:30 AM

Pat slipped into the passenger seat of the rental car next to Allan. The warm interior of the car felt good, but still, she found she couldn't stop shivering.

"There's no way to get the Uzi or any other type of firearm in there," she said as she closed the door. "There are security stations at every door with metal detectors. At least this means we'll be on even terms. No guns for us and none for Homlin. I'll settle for those odds."

"It also means we'll have to depend on our evidence to stop him," Allan pointed out.

"He's not getting the okay to go ahead with his plans. He's just not. Evidence or no evidence, we've got to stop him right here, right now." Pat's determination came through clenched teeth.

As she finished speaking, a black Lincoln Continental pulled up to the curb thirty yards in front of them and out stepped Dr. Fredrick Homlin dressed in a black wool coat and carrying a matching briefcase.

"My, doesn't he look dapper this morning," Pat said with crystals of sarcasm in her voice. "No one would ever suspect, would they?"

"Looks just like hundreds of other professional people coming to work on Monday after a pleasant weekend with the family," Allan agreed as he cut the car engine off. "Shall we follow him?"

"Give him just a few seconds to get ahead," Pat replied. "I wonder where his entourage is? I don't like that he's by himself."

"The odds are more in our favor if it comes down to anything physical," Allan pointed out.

"True," Pat said, but she was unconvinced. "Where do you think his bodyguards could be?" Pat asked, a worried look knitting her brow. "Well, let's just consider maybe luck is starting to shine on us," she said after a moment. "Let's go stop an alien."

Before getting out of the car, she slid the machine gun under the front seat and removed her revolver. She suddenly felt naked and defenseless without it. She reminded herself that Homlin would be without any firearms as well. *But not defenseless*, her mind reminded her. He could quickly transform himself into a brutal killing machine. He would be more than capable of killing her, Allan, and no telling how many others if need be. Their best chance would be to jump him before he had the opportunity to change. It was going to be an interesting morning.

As Homlin disappeared inside the federal building, Allan and Pat strolled behind him towards the same doors. As they entered the building, Pat suddenly worried the security guards would stop them from following Homlin if they didn't have proper papers giving them entry but was relieved to find that no such surveillance was taking place. The checkpoint seemed only to keep weapons outside.

Homlin continued through the security station, unaware or unconcerned with whether he was being followed. *He's too damn cocky*, Pat thought. *No bodyguards, not the least bit concerned about being followed. He must know Allan and I are somewhere around. He should care. He should be sneaking around or be surrounded by his gorillas.* Pat's alarm system which had been finely honed over the last ten or fifteen years blared.

Nothing she could do about it. There was nothing else to do but follow him to the meeting room. Maybe he had sent his gorillas on ahead, or maybe they were at this very moment closing in on Allan and her. Despite herself, Pat glanced behind her at dozens of indifferent faces, governmental executives coming to work on Monday morning, bored, dead, unenthusiastic about their jobs, but no signs of anyone threatening the two of them.

"What are you looking for?" Allan whispered as they walked through the security check.

"I don't know. I don't have a good feeling about this. He's too confident, too assured. He should be nervous. Where the hell are the rest of his people?" Pat whispered back.

"I'd tell you to calm down except I notice I can't get my knees to stop knocking myself."

"Oh hell. Did you remember to bring the photos?"

Allan held up the briefcase. "Everything is in here."

Pat breathed a little easier. Allan's calm demeanor worked. She noticed the tension ease a little. Then she had a sudden thought. *What if Homlin's meeting wasn't on the first floor?* How would they be able to follow him? She couldn't imagine stepping in the same elevator with him. They could lose him and not find him for hours. She then noticed a directory between the elevator doors they were approaching. FDA offices were on the fourth floor. The letters she'd photocopied had been on FDA letterhead.

She watched as Homlin stepped into one of the waiting elevators.

"Now what do we do?" Allan asked as Homlin's elevator door closed.

"We take a risk and go to the fourth floor," Pat said as she pointed to the directory. "And pray all the FDA offices are on the same floor."

THEY FILED INTO THE crowded elevator and requested the fourth floor. They stopped at every floor on the way up. As they stepped out on the fourth floor, Pat glanced down the hall in both directions. At first, she didn't see Homlin and her breath caught in her throat. Then a man in a gray suit stepped to one side, and Homlin was strolling down the hall. He stopped halfway down and entered one of the offices to the right.

"Bingo." Pat pointed in the direction Homlin had disappeared. "We'll wait out here for a few minutes and see who else enters. There's no hurry now that we know where he is."

Allan nodded.

In the next ten minutes, five other men exited from the elevator, strolled down the hall, and entered the same office into which Homlin had disappeared. Five more minutes went by. Pat glanced at her watch. 8:00 a.m. on the dot.

"Should we go in?" Allan asked as the hallways began to clear.

"No, we'll wait for the meeting to get underway a bit. I want Homlin to think he's home free before we pay our visit."

"I wish I had a cigarette," Allan said.

"Silly, you don't smoke."

"It seems like a good time to take it up."

Allan sat down on a cushioned bench stationed between the elevator doors under another directory.

Pat continued to pace up and down the hallway, too nervous to sit. She continued to glance at her watch. Finally, at 8:10 she walked over to where Allan was sitting.

"I don't think anyone else is going to arrive for the meeting. They should be underway by now. I don't want them signing whatever they're planning to sign while we wait outside. Let's go see what we can stir up."

With a heavy sigh, Allan stood up and grasped the handle of the brief-case. "I'm with you all the way." He gave her a reassuring smile.

"Thanks, it makes a lot of difference," Pat replied. They turned and walked down the hall.

All eyes turned to the door as Pat and Allan stepped into the meeting room.

"I'm sorry, but this is a private..." One of the men seated at the long table across from Homlin started to say.

"I know what the meeting is," Pat interrupted, walking straight towards Homlin. "I have evidence to file against this 'man.'" The note of sarcasm on the last word was unmistakable.

"Why, if it isn't Ms. Vogt and her trained vet," Homlin said as he stood up, a twisted smile of unconcern on his face. "Do come in and join us. You say you have something to contribute to this discussion?"

"We most certainly do." Allan stepped between Pat and Homlin. He glared at Homlin for several seconds before breaking eye contact and turning his attention to the five men sitting on the other side of the table.

"This man must not be allowed to transport anything from Biogentrix," Allan said as he opened his briefcase and pulled a file folder from it. "We have evidence here which proves that he is an enemy of this country. For that matter, he is a threat to all humankind. We must not play into his hands by allowing him to spread his seeds across this country."

"What on earth are you talking about?" One of the other men asked as he picked up the folder and began leafing through it.

"The material you have in your hands is a compilation of reports uncovering the most diabolical plot to overthrow this and every other government in the world," Pat spoke up. "I have been following this 'man' for the past ten years. He tried to kill me on the interstellar ship which brought him to this world.

"Some of those papers are the few official reports that were not destroyed by B.I.U.F.O. when the landing site of an alien spaceship was investigated. I was on the investigation team. I was the only one who saw the alien that was on the ship. This being," she said pointing to Homlin, "is attempting to get permission to disseminate the larval form of his race across this country."

"This is the most preposterous story I have ever heard." A second man spoke up as he grabbed some of the papers out of the folder and began leafing through it.

Homlin stood calmly studying Pat and Allan, shaking his head.

"Gentlemen, be calm. I'm afraid this poor lady has indeed been following me for many years ever since she was released from B.I.U.F.O. for being mentally incompetent. For some reason, I've never quite understood why she picked me out of nowhere to be a major player in her little fantasy. For the most part, I've humored her. Occasionally when it has gotten out of hand, I've had to have one of my employees take action.

"It's unfortunate that she is so unstable. She seems to have found a second mental case to keep her company. Perhaps, Dr. Harrison, if you would be so kind as to call security so we could proceed with our meeting."

"I'd be happy to," Dr. Harrison said as he picked up the phone.

"Not so damn fast," Pat yelled. At the same moment, Allan lunged across the table and knocked the phone out of Harrison's hand. "Look at the damn papers. It's all there. This is not a man, and FreeForm is not what you think it is. I know it sounds crazy, but there is at least enough evidence there for you to open an investigation. You can't possibly ignore..."

Two of the other council members pulled Allan away from Harrison. Harrison picked the phone up off the floor. "Send security to room 422 immediately. It's an emergency."

Pat started around the table where the two men were still struggling to keep Allan away from Harrison but found her way blocked by Homlin and one of the other council members. The odds were not looking good. No one had even bothered to look at their evidence. Her story was simply too far-fetched. True or not, it was just too much for anyone to take seriously. What good would it be to try to overpower the committee? It certainly wouldn't persuade them to consider her story. Homlin obviously had them eating out of his hands.

Pat stopped a few feet away from Homlin and the other man. Her mind raced. What were the chances of strangling Homlin on the spot? No chance. Homlin looked to be a pretty even match, to begin with, and she doubted the other five men would stand around and watch someone be murdered.

She was still staring at Homlin when she heard the door behind her open. It seemed security in this building was damn quick. Pat turned towards the door as a large man in a rumpled suit entered the room, followed by four men in military uniforms. Each of the four men carried revolvers pointed towards the ceiling but in readiness to pull down in a deadly aim at any instant.

"Hold everything right there," the man in the rumpled suit shouted. The two men who had been struggling with Allan froze, then relaxed their grip on him. Allan yanked himself away from them.

"Oliver! It's so good to see you again," Pat said. "Thanks for bringing the cavalry."

"No problem, Pat. It's the least I owed you after all these years," Oliver replied. "Which one is the alien?"

"Well, that one for sure." Pat pointed to Homlin. "And I wouldn't be surprised if we didn't have a few more in here."

"What?" Allan and Oliver asked at the same time.

"It suddenly dawned on me during the excitement where Homlin's bodyguards were." Pat turned and met Allan's puzzled look. "What better way to assure the meeting would be a success than having the voters completely on your side."

"Oliver, I strongly suggest you take the entire committee under custody. I imagine it won't be too hard to figure out who is and who isn't human."

"With pleasure, men, place everyone except the lady under arrest."

"Oh, Oliver, not that one there," Pat said, pointing to Allan. "He's with me." She winked in Allan's direction then started towards him.

As Pat walked by Homlin, there was a sudden blur of motion as Homlin yanked Pat in front of him, shielding himself from the aim of the marksmen with her body. He grabbed her with his left arm around her shoulders. As he brought his right hand to her throat, the hand melted into an animal-like paw with six razor-sharp claws, each one pressed against the tender flesh of Pat's throat.

"No one move or I will have no choice but to kill this lovely specimen," Homlin shouted as he backed himself against the wall, pulling Pat with him. He slithered his way along the wall in the direction of the door. "Put your weapons down, now!"

Oliver nodded to his men who did as they were instructed.

"You can't possibly get out of here," Oliver said as he took a step in Homlin's direction.

"Don't be so sure," Homlin replied. "Now, kick one of those revolvers over here. Nice and easy. I warn you. I'll rip her throat out if anyone makes a stupid move."

Oliver did as he was told. Homlin continued to pull Pat toward the door, stopping a foot or two from the gun lying on the floor.

"Easy, everyone," Homlin said as Allan took a step towards him. Homlin stooped down and picked up the revolver. When he had it in his left hand, he stuck it into Pat's ribs just below her left breast but continued to hold her against his body with the sharp claws of his other hand.

"Now everyone back away from the door and lie face down on the floor." Everyone complied except four of the five committee members who remained standing.

When everyone was finally on the floor, Homlin took the last couple of steps to the door. He stared at each of the men as though contemplating whether to chance shooting them in the back of the head.

Homlin looked at the four men who were still standing. "You're on your own. Your last assignment from me is to be sure I'm not followed for several minutes. Is that clear?"

The four men nodded. Before anyone else could move, Homlin slipped out the door with Pat and was gone.

The instant the door closed there was a mad dash by everyone to get to the remaining three guns. The four 'men' who had clearly been identified as Homlin's men dove for the weapons as did the uniformed men. No one was as fast as Oliver who stopped the blur of action by firing a shot from his own revolver he pulled from his shoulder holster.

"Back off there, or I'll blow you away!" He shouted at the top of his lungs. The four conspirators stopped in their tracks and stared at him. For two or three seconds, Harrison, who stood in front of the other three, studied Oliver.

"You heard what Homlin said," Harrison shouted as he lunged toward Oliver, followed closely by the other three.

Oliver fired point blank into the charging Harrison. The slug caught him full in the chest, but still, the big man charged. Oliver fired two more rounds. One hit Harrison in the left shoulder; the other removed most of Harrison's skull on the left side.

The momentum carried Harrison's dead body crashing into Oliver. What followed was a massive free-for-all between Oliver and his men and the three remaining aliens. As the aliens fought, they began to transform into hunter/survivors making the contest's outcome much less predictable.

Allan did not stay to find out the outcome of the battle. Instead, he dashed out the door after Homlin and Pat. As he ran down the hallway, he prayed he would see the two further down the corridor running towards the elevator, but they were nowhere to be seen. Where could they have gone? How could Homlin have disappeared so fast?

Allan ran to the elevators and stared at the number display above each door. None of the four elevators were even close to the fourth floor. The stairs. They must have taken the stairs. Allan rushed toward the stairway door. He flung the door open and rushed through.

As the door began to close, he heard a muffled cry behind him, but before he could turn to investigate, he felt the searing pain of a blow to his skull and found himself dropping into the dark pit of unconsciousness.

Hunting Homlin
Monday 10:00 a.m., Dec. 6

The pain threatened to lift the dome of his skull from the rest of his head. As Allan struggled to regain consciousness, it ebbed and flowed with the pounding of his heart. The first sign he was winning the battle was the pain returning. The second was the muffled sound of men talking.

"I think he's coming around, Oliver," Allan heard through the mud puddle of his mind. He tried shaking his head and immediately regretted it as the jackhammering pain increased in volume and frequency.

"Get me some cold water," he heard after an interminable time, then a little later, felt the chill of a wet compress being applied to his forehead. After several more minutes, he forced his eyes open. The light sent shards of pain deep into his skull, but he refused to submit to the black ebb that called to him. He kept his eyes open.

"Where am I?" He finally asked. A face, faintly familiar but he couldn't remember from where came into blurry view.

"Take it easy. He slugged you pretty hard."

"Who?" Allan asked, still uncertain what was going on.

"Homlin, of course," the man answered.

Homlin. Oh yeah. It all flashed back to him now. He'd been chasing after Homlin. The door to the stairs, the muffled sound, then nothing. Allan tried to sit up, but the pain was too great.

"Not so quick. You're lucky to be alive. It certainly wasn't because Homlin pulled his punch."

"I believe it," Allan replied with a moan. "Did you catch him?"

"No. Not yet. Somehow, he managed to escape the building. We haven't figured out how. There is an all-points bulletin out for him, though. He won't get very far."

The FreeForm! What had happened with the pending shipment? Through dry lips, Allan asked the question.

"Oh, don't worry. We've confiscated everything at Homlin's lab and game reserve. It's all under government lock-up. If Homlin is stupid enough to show up at either place, we'll nab him."

Allan tried sitting up once more. This time, despite the pain, he was successful. He found he was lying on the long table in the conference room.

"We found you in the stairwell. I had a couple of my men carry you in here. You've been out almost two hours."

Two hours! Two hours and they still hadn't found Pat and Homlin. He had to look for her. There was no telling what Homlin would do to her. Allan gently swung his legs over the side of the table then fought a wave of vertigo. He felt like someone had piled ten hangovers on him all at once. He shut his eyes for a moment and waited for vertigo and nausea to pass. When it finally did, he lifted his head and looked at the man.

"Who the hell are you, anyway?"

"Oliver Sykes. I was Pat's superior when she was with B.I.U.F.O. I helped to cover up the story."

Allan nodded. Pat had spoken about Oliver during one of their late-night conversations lying in front of the wood stove. It seemed like it had been years ago but was only a few weeks.

A uniformed man — Allan thought it was one of the men that had burst into the meeting but he couldn't be sure-handed Oliver a note.

Oliver read the note, then crumpled it and tossed it in the vicinity of the trash can.

"What did it say?" Allan asked.

"The D.C. police have just had a report of a car stolen from the parking lot across the street. It could have been taken by Homlin."

Oh, hell, Allan thought. Homlin's got a car. How in the hell would they ever find him? He struggled to his feet. Oliver grabbed his arm to steady him. He shrugged it off.

"Where do you think you're going?" Oliver asked.

"To find Homlin before he kills Pat." Allan stumbled unsteadily towards the door.

"Do you think you can find him?"

"I'll find him. I've got to," Allan replied without turning around.

"Wait up. I'll go with you," Oliver said. "We can take my car. I've got a CB radio. We can stay in touch with the police search."

"Fine with me." Allan continued down the hall towards the elevators.

As the two men waited for the elevator, Allan glanced over at the larger man. "You wouldn't happen to have a couple of aspirins, would you?"

Oliver smiled. "Not on me, but I think there's a bottle in my glove compartment. I might even have a flask of whiskey to wash them down with."

"Sounds like the right combination to me," Allan replied.

THE TRUNK SMELLED OF old rags, rubber, and gas fumes. On top of which it was cold and damp, but worst of all it was pitch black and tiny. Pat fought the urge to scream. She had tried that for at least thirty minutes with no results except to worsen her headache, the result of her trying to keep the trunk lid from shutting.

Despite her winter coat, she was chilled to the bone. Her hands and feet were numb, and her muscles ached from the close confinement. She wasn't even sure into what kind of car she had been stuffed. Not much more than a subcompact, if the trunk space was any indication. The gas and exhaust fumes added to her headache and discomfort.

How long had she been locked inside the trunk? She could only guess since she was unable to see her watch dial or anything else for that matter. *It's a fine mess I've gotten myself into this time*, she thought as she struggled to pull her coat tighter around her.

I completely blew it. I had the chance to stop Homlin, once and for all, and I failed. Well, maybe not entirely. Oliver had come through—finally. Or had he? Who knew?

She'd heard gunshots as Homlin dragged her down the hall, but who had done the shooting? Had the shipment been stopped or not? That was the real question. And not knowing the answer to it contributed more to her headache than the fumes or the bump on the head.

They'd been traveling for quite a while without stopping. Pat figured she'd been in the trunk for at least a couple hours. Except for the sound of the rear tires on the road and an occasional car passing, no sound penetrated through the trunk. No doubt they had left the city, but heading in what direction? Where was Homlin taking her and more importantly what did he have in mind once they arrived? None of the possible answers her mind came up with for that last question appealed to her.

Yes indeed, she'd gotten herself into a fine mess this time.

AS OLIVER AND ALLAN opened their respective doors to Oliver's sedan, they stopped and stared at each other over the roof.

"Where do you think we should go?" Allan finally asked the question that was on both of their minds.

Oliver laughed and shook his head. "Damn if I know. Where do you go to look for an escaped alien on the run?"

"Well, there's got to be something we can do. We can't just sit around here. Think of something." The words jangled in Allan's head, tormenting his headache that much more.

"I've got an idea. Let's go," Oliver said as he climbed behind the wheel and started the engine.

"Where are we going?" Allan asked, climbing in beside him.

"Sooner or later, hopefully, sooner, someone is going to spot the baby blue Toyota Homlin stole. When they do, we want to be ready to get to it real fast. I've got an old friend, James Stepp. These days he flies a traffic 'copter for one of the local TV stations. He'll be more than happy to take us wherever we need to go."

"Now you're talking," Allan said. For the first time since being knocked unconscious, his head felt like it might one day stop pumping pain down to his toes. Maybe no day real soon, but . . .

Monday 1:45 pm

"Allan, wake up." A firm hand shook his shoulder. Allan turned his head to one side. He opened his eyes to find himself staring at the ice pack he'd been using to relieve his headache. He had shut his eyes for only a minute, he felt certain, but when he went to put the ice back on his head, all that was left was a bag of cool water.

"What's happening?" He asked as he tossed the used-up ice pack back on the bed.

"They've found the Toyota," Oliver replied.

"All right. Now we're getting somewhere."

"Abandoned. Neither Homlin nor Pat were anywhere around it," Oliver finished.

"Shit, you've got to be kidding. Are you sure?"

"No question about it. The report just came in from the Pulaski, Virginia police." Oliver sat down on the bed beside Allan.

"Pulaski, Virginia? Where's that?"

"Western part of the state a couple of hours north of the North Carolina border."

The two men stared at each other for several seconds. "Are you thinking what I'm thinking?" Allan finally asked.

"Don't know, but I'm thinking the bastard is returning to his old stomping grounds," Oliver replied.

"You don't think he'd be stupid enough to try to get back into Biogentrix, do you?" Allan picked up the spent ice pack and tossed it from one hand to the other.

"No. He must know we've got both places staked out." "Well, do you think we can get James to fly us that far?"

"Sure, no problem. While you were resting, James called his TV station and told him a little of the story. Don't worry; I didn't tell him what Homlin is. I just said we were looking for a kidnapper. He told his station he has a chance at an exclusive. They've given him carte blanche to fly us anywhere we want. We're checking for any other reports of stolen vehicles in the area. It won't take us long to pick Homlin's trail up again. Let's go."

Allan tossed the ice pack to Oliver. "Do you think I could get a refill on this before we go?"

MONDAY 1:05 PM

The trunk of the Mazda was a little larger and didn't smell quite as bad as the last car, but it was still far from being a comfortable way to travel. Homlin had given Pat no chance to escape on the change. Being stuck in the trunk for four or five hours had left her at a distinct disadvantage. When they'd finally stopped, Homlin had left her in the trunk for quite a while. After a while, Pat began to wonder if he'd abandoned her with the car, but about the time she'd decided that had happened, she heard Homlin unlocking the trunk. She tried to be ready to jump at the first chance, but her stiff body had refused to cooperate at the critical moment.

As Homlin unlocked the trunk, Pat tried pushing the trunk lid open with all her might in the hope of catching him off guard. Unfortunately, the stiff muscles of her legs had made the attempt appear in slow motion. Besides, Homlin had been ready and had been standing several feet away from the car by the time Pat managed to crawl out of the trunk. Although he had both hands in his pockets, he left little doubt in Pat's mind that one of his hands was pointing a gun straight at her.

They were in a small town Pat didn't recognize, in what looked to be the only public parking lot in town. Homlin had already scouted around before letting Pat out of the trunk and had found a Mazda with the keys left in it. Pat glanced over at the small building where the attendant should have been, but there was no one inside.

"He's taking a little nap," Homlin said with a short nod in the direction Pat was looking. "He looked awfully beat when I drove up. Of course, not as beat as he is now."

"Get in," Homlin said as he unlocked the trunk of their new car. "Your carriage awaits."

"I'm not getting in another damn trunk," Pat said, crossing her arms in front of her.

"Have it your own way," Homlin replied. "Would you prefer I kill you here in broad daylight or simply knock the shit out of you and toss you in the trunk?"

"Neither," Pat replied, deciding to change tactics. "Just let me sit up front with you. I promise I won't try anything stupid."

"You already have, but it won't work. Now get in. This is the last time I'm going to ask so nicely." Homlin nodded toward the open trunk.

"I'm going to get you for this," Pat muttered under her breath as she climbed into the trunk. "You just wait and see if I don't."

"You've been a worthy opponent, Ms. Vogt. Perseverance and a never-say-die attitude are your strong suits. Unfortunately, you don't realize the game is over. Now, I suggest you lower your head a trifle more this time unless you want another bump on your head."

Pat did as she was told and a few seconds later found herself in total darkness again, in a little larger and less smelly trunk but still completely powerless. The feeling was becoming impossible to bear. She had to do something, but not just anything. She would probably only get one chance, and she had to make it count. But how would she know when the one chance was here?

Well, I have my instincts, she told herself. *I've been operating on skill, training, and instincts for the last ten years with this animal. Why should it be any different now?* But she wouldn't just wait for the right moment. She'd do whatever she could to create the moment, and when it came, she'd be sure to be ready.

Like right now. What can I do right now to prepare myself for that moment? She pondered the question for a few minutes. She needed something to balance the sides. Homlin was stronger than she was. And he had a gun. She did not. On top of which he could change into many different forms, including the killing machine that had almost taken her life on their first meeting.

Okay, how to balance the scale? She needed a weapon. Something? But what? The manufacturers of automobiles hadn't yet offered automatic rifles as optional equipment. What could she possibly hope to find in the trunk of a late model Mazda?

No sooner had she asked the question that she had the answer. Every car came with a spare tire (not much of a weapon there), a jack (a little better but too bulky), and ... a tire iron! That was it. A tire iron or lug wrench, whatever they were called. Every car came with one. Most of them lay in some dark recess of the trunk and was never needed. Well, one was needed now.

Pat began to rummage in the dark with her hands, checking every corner, every crack, every irregularity. She finally found a little compartment built into the side of the trunk. She pulled the plastic cover off and pulled out a small packet of tools. She opened the tool case and found two unexpected prizes—Phillip's head and flathead screwdrivers. Weapons!

She dug her hands back into the hidden compartment. The only thing left was the jack, tightly bolted to the floor of the compartment. Damn. Had the owner of the car lost the lug wrench? Surely not. It was a relatively new car. It was doubtful the owner had ever had a flat tire. Keep looking. The lug wrench must be around here somewhere.

Pat stopped her search for a moment. Where would you put a lug wrench if not with the jack and the other tools? With the spare tire, of course. She felt around with her feet and hands, but there was no tire. Impossible. There had to be a spare. Where did they put the spare in these tiny Japanese cars? They certainly didn't bolt them to the outside like with her jeep. No, they hid them, like they hid the tool kit and jack.

She continued to fish around in the dark looking for another hidden compartment. It would have to be a larger compartment. One large enough to hide a spare tire. Underneath her. It had to be on the floor of the trunk. Of course. She felt along the edge of the trunk until she found a hold to pull the floor covering away. It came away easily. A good sign.

Pat pressed herself against the back of the rear seat, pulling the covering towards her. She then shoved it under her body so she could get to the false bottom. She found the small space increasingly claustrophobic as she fought to move the flooring out of the way. Finally, she had it off to the side enough to reach down and feel ... the tire. Victory!

But no, not victory at all. She wasn't looking for the tire. It was the lug wrench she needed. Was it down there or not? She felt all around the tire but could feel nothing like a long iron rod. She finally determined that the tire was securely bolted to the floor of the car. The bolt ran through the center of the tire and was held in place with a large wing nut. It took her several minutes before she was able to loosen the nut. She was sweating now. Her activity had at least taken the chill off, although her feet were still like blocks of ice. Finally, she was able to remove the wing nut completely. The tire was smaller than she expected, then she remembered hearing someone in her office complain about the toy tires they were putting in new cars these days. Although it was small, it was heavy. She struggled to get her hands underneath the tire. She was pressed so hard against the back seat that she found it increasingly hard to breathe. *Calm, I must stay calm.*

She relaxed for a moment and caught her breath. *Please, have the lug wrench be under there*, she prayed to herself. After a moment, she began lifting the tire again, using one arm to lever the tire up while searching with the other hand. Her left hand finally felt what she'd been looking for. It was a long L shaped iron rod, slightly larger at the short end of the L. The tip of the long end was pointed like a large flat-headed screwdriver. Perfect.

The scales were beginning to balance. It took her a few minutes to get the wrench out from under the tire, but it finally came. She hugged her newly found prize against her chest. For the first time in several hours, she knew she had a chance to live through this ordeal. A small chance, but very definitely a chance. It was enough. It was all she ever expected out of life. A small chance. She began to put the tire and floorboard back in place.

MONDAY 2:05 PM

In his younger days, Allan had thought flying in a helicopter would be a lot of fun, but as the WXYY traffic 'copter lifted off the ground with the three men inside, Allan couldn't grasp why he'd ever had such a silly thought.

Although James had assured them several times that it was safe to have all three of them in the 'copter, as Allan felt his right side pressed against the outer glass, he doubted the man's judgment. Oliver was a large man and took up more than his share of the seat, leaving less than a foot and a half for Allan to wedge into. It was going to be a long flight and far from fun.

"How long before we get to Pulaski?" He yelled to be heard over the sound of the blades above them.

"Hard to say for sure. Depends a little on the weather and the winds. I'd guess two to two-and-a-half hours," James replied as he steered hard left to miss some high tension wires, then added, "Maybe three. But don't worry, this baby has an auxiliary fuel tank so we won't be running out of fuel. I've learned my lesson about trying to fly on fumes."

Allan groaned. It was going to be a *very* long ride.

Pack Animal
Monday 3:25 pm, Dec. 6

Homlin glanced over at the passenger seat beside him. His eyes fell on the folder of papers the car salesman had given to him. He smiled. Buying the car instead of stealing another one had probably earned him at least a couple of hours, maybe more. On top of which, the misdirection clue he'd left behind in the other car would at least keep his pursuer guessing, if not taking them off the track completely.

Yes, he was rather proud of himself, even for fooling his passenger. It hadn't been necessary, really. Just an added touch but it had been fun. Vogt had never noticed the Mazda dealership right across the street from the parking lot. As far as she knew, they were in another stolen car, which would leave her thinking her chances of being rescued were better than they really were. At some point, that useful tidbit of information might be used against her.

Homlin turned the radio back on and checked a half-dozen stations. Still no mention of any manhunt for him. Good. The idiots were still keeping it quiet, which would make Homlin's travels much easier.

Admittedly, he'd taken a big loss this morning at the meeting. A big step back, but the game wasn't over yet. Not by a long shot. They may have stopped his shipment of the FreeForm, but they hadn't stopped him or his people. Nor would they. He'd learned a lot about these humans. He had underestimated them for the last time. It was time to start playing dirty — time to start making up his own rules. He still had enough financial stability to quickly re-establish himself elsewhere. He'd been sure to have a backup just in case of disaster.

It was one of the cardinal rules of planet migration. Always have a contingency plan. Well, he did. He needed only to reclaim a couple small items before disappearing into the fabric of another society. Once he pulled his finances out of the half-dozen banks, he'd change his identity. South America

219

would do nicely. He'd find another way to disseminate the seeds of his people. Already he had a new plan brewing.

All he needed was the crystal and the cocoon. He glanced at the digital clock on the dash. And in a couple of hours, he'd have them. He reached down on the floorboard and picked up the bag of goodies he'd bought from the store next to the car lot. He chuckled to himself. A final little joke on Ms. Vogt before killing her. Just a little humiliating joke to pay her back for her meddling. It would be the perfect trick. Even the fool, Pritchard, would have to get the punch line and the message behind it.

MONDAY 4:15 PM

Oliver turned his head in Allan's direction and cupped his hands around his mouth so he wouldn't have to shout so loud. "James says we're coming up on Pulaski in the next few minutes."

Allan nodded and smiled weakly. The last two hours of the throbbing sound of the 'copter's blades had continually fueled his headache, which had continued full blast. On top of which he felt like if he didn't get on the ground pretty soon, he was going to be airsick.

He leaned over and put his face close to Oliver's ear. "Any word about another stolen car?"

Oliver frowned and shook his head. "No word. It doesn't make any sense. The police are checking other forms of transportation to see if they can pick up their trail. They did find an interesting item in the car that Homlin may have left behind."

Allan was about to ask him what they'd found when James tapped Oliver on the shoulder and pointed towards the ground at the small town of Pulaski, Virginia. They flew over the city looking for a place to land. As they flew over, Allan imagined that Waynesboro probably looked very similar from the air. Small, old, yet neatly kept only a few miles from the Interstate.

They managed to find an empty lot only a hundred yards or so from the parking lot where the Toyota had been abandoned. James landed in the center of the lot and pointed the way to Oliver and Allan. Allan was grateful to finally be able to open the door and climb out although even as he did so, he suspected it would only be a few minutes before he was climbing back inside.

The two men jogged over to the parking lot where a police car and a Virginia Highway Patrol car sat next to each other. Oliver strolled up to the three officers who were leaning against the cars. He quickly flashed something from his wallet, which Allan couldn't make out and suspected that neither could the officers.

"What have you got for us, boys?" Oliver's voice suddenly had the slight hint of a twang. Allan smiled at the subtle change.

"Not much, I'm afraid," the Highway Patrol Officer spoke first. "Artie here discovered the car a couple of hours ago. By the time I arrived, he'd also found the attendant lying unconscious in the little booth over there. They've already taken him to the hospital. At last report, he hadn't regained consciousness yet. We did find this wedged down in the front seat." He handed Oliver a wrinkled map.

"You mind if I use your hood?" Oliver asked as he opened the map.

"Be my guest," the officer replied.

Oliver spread the map out on the hood, and the five men gathered around to study it.

Oliver followed the pen line that had been sketched on the map. It started in Washington, D.C. and continued down Interstate 81 passing next to Pulaski and ending in Knoxville, Tennessee.

"What do you think?" Oliver finally asked no one in particular.

"From what I remember hearing Pat say about Biogentrix Labs, they're supposed to have a small subsidiary unit just outside Knoxville," Allan said.

"That must be where the son-of-a-bitch is headed," one of the officers responded.

"I'm not so sure," Allan replied.

Oliver turned and looked at him. "You're not? Where do you think he's headed?"

"Back to Waynesboro," Allan said simply.

"Even with this?" Oliver pointed to the map.

"Even with that," Allan replied. "First of all, we don't know for sure Homlin drew the line on the map, although I suspect he did. It could have been in the car all along. Maybe it shows the travel plans of the actual owner's trip to Washington, D.C."

"Well yeah, it's possible but . . ."

"But it's likely Homlin drew it. As I said, I suspect he did. I think he drew it and left it behind deliberately to throw us off."

Oliver pondered what Allan had said and began to nod his head. "That would be possible, no doubt about it. But why return to Waynesboro?"

Allan frowned and wrinkled his brow. His head hurt so much it was difficult to think straight. Why did he feel Homlin was returning to his old stomping grounds? He'd thought it from the moment he'd first awakened and discovered Homlin had escaped. But he couldn't answer why.

Then it came to him. "There's something Pat told me when we first started working on this case together. She said every time she would get frustrated tracking a dead end, she would return to the Waynesboro area. Eventually, she'd pick his trail up. There's something special about the area. I don't know what. Maybe it's an alien thing — always returning to the original landing spot. I just think there's something there Homlin is returning to. I wish I could tell you what it is."

Oliver looked down at the thin line on the map. After a few minutes, he looked up into Allan's eyes. "It's been a long time since I was in those mountains. I'd just as soon never go back there myself, but for some reason, I can't explain either, I think you're right. We'll go on to Waynesboro. I'll radio the Knoxville Authorities to stake out the Biogentrix lab."

"I suppose we have to get back in the damn 'copter." The throbbing in Allan's head seemed to increase just by the thought.

"It's the fastest way." Oliver folded the map up and handed it to one of the officers.

"I know. I know." And to think, as a boy, he'd thought such a trip would be fun.

MONDAY 3:53 PM

Homlin pulled up on the emergency brake and threw the stick shift in neutral. They were at the end of the line. At least, as far as they'd be able to go in the car—the rest of the trek would have to be made on foot. He turned off the engine and climbed out of the car. He stood next to it a minute and stretched his tired muscles. It had been a long day, and it was far from over. The walk would do him good. He needed to stretch his muscles out after a long time behind the wheel.

He strolled over to the other side of the car and opened the passenger's door. He removed the bags from the floorboard, including the special "gift" he'd purchased for Vogt. He set the bag on the roof of the car and opened the much larger bag. From it he pulled out a knapsack and half a dozen containers of freeze-dried food. He doubted he'd need it, but it was good to have a contingency plan in case he had to remain in the woods longer than he expected.

It was just about time to let his traveling companion out of the trunk. He needed to find only one small item. He walked around the woods for a few moments, enjoying himself. It was great to be back out here. He much preferred the great outdoors over nasty city life. He continued to stroll around, not straying too far from the car until he found what he'd been looking for — a good stout staff made of maple. He held it in both hands and felt the weight and diameter. It would do nicely.

He returned to the car carrying the walking stick with him. He took Vogt's bag from the roof of the car and placed it on the ground near the rear of the car along with the knapsack. He removed the car keys from his pocket and inserted one of them into the trunk lock. Holding the walking stick in one hand, he unlocked the trunk with the other then quickly stepped back and to one side.

The trunk lid did not spring up as it had the first time. Instead, it lifted a few inches and then remained closed. *Was Vogt sleeping?* Homlin wondered. Then it occurred to him that she could have suffocated. He hadn't thought about that. He certainly hoped that wasn't the case. It would ruin his surprise. He was about to lever the lid up with his walking stick when the lid began to rise on its own. Not actually on its own, but with Vogt's help.

"That's a good little girl. For a moment, I thought you were sleeping on the job. Now, step out very slowly."

The spring in the trunk lid allowed the lid to open entirely without Pat holding on to it. Despite the reduced light of dusk, she had to blink her eyes to adjust to the relative brightness of the outside.

"Can't you give me a hand? My legs are so stiff, I'm afraid I won't be able to get out on my own."

Homlin laughed. "You do play such an innocent little victim sometimes. Go ahead and fall down. Why should it bother me? Just get out now and do it very slowly."

Pat glared at Homlin for several seconds before finally deciding to give in. She decided the easiest way to get out was to climb out backward. That way if she did fall she'd at least have something to cushion her. She turned around and placed one foot on the bumper of the car. She held on to the car to steady herself as her two feet finally made it to the ground.

"Perfect, just perfect," Homlin said, and as Pat turned around to see what he meant, he brought the end of the walking stick down hard against her skull.

MONDAY 4:35 PM

Allan tried resting his head against the Plexiglas door of the chopper but quickly removed it when he found it only made the pulsing pain from the vibrating worse. It wasn't fair; his headache made thinking increasingly difficult, but it didn't seem to have the least effect on his worrying. If anything, his ability to worry seemed heightened by his discomfort. Life just wasn't fair.

What if they were wrong? What if Homlin wasn't on his way back to Waynesboro but was actually driving down Interstate 81 towards Knoxville? If they were wrong, it was quite likely the mistake would cost Pat her life — if she was still alive.

Allan had spent most of the day rationalizing that Homlin wouldn't dare kill Pat until he was sure he had escaped and no longer needed a hostage. How long would it be? Again, no way of telling, but it couldn't be very long. The longer Homlin was free, the more likely he would consider Pat unnecessary cargo. They had to find them quickly.

He leaned over to Oliver and shouted in his ear, "Tell me again, how far to the Waynesboro area?"

"We're guessing about an hour to an hour and a half. The landing area may be a little closer. It's north, northwest of the town," Oliver replied. "Try not to worry, we'll find them before . . ." There was no point in finishing the sentence.

MONDAY 4:32 PM

The floor of the trunk felt harder and more irregular, Pat thought as she struggled to wake up. As she regained consciousness, she realized she was no longer in the trunk and she'd not been sleeping. As she turned her head and became suddenly dizzy from the pain, she remembered turning just in time to see Homlin lowering the boom on her.

You bastard. I'll get you for this. You better believe it. Paybacks are hell. She started to push herself to a sitting position and found her hands snugly tied together in front of her with leather straps. She rolled around until she was in a position to push herself up. As she did so, she noticed Homlin leaning against the car, the trunk lid still open. What was he was holding in his hand? It looked like a rope or . . .

"That's a good doggie. Welcome back. You weren't out too long. Are you ready for our walk?" As Homlin spoke he tugged on the leather cord in his hand and Pat felt a strangling sensation around her neck as she was thrown off balance. Her hands instinctively went up to her neck. She wasn't quick enough to get them under her, so she landed hard on her face in the dirt.

"It'll take a little getting used to, but I'm sure you're at least as smart as the Golden Retriever you used to keep," Homlin said as he pulled on the leash a second time.

"Cut it out, you bastard." Pat tried shouting but could only get a hoarse whisper out. Her hands pulled at the metal choke collar cutting off her wind.

"Keep your hands away from it," Homlin shouted as he knocked her hands away from the collar with his stick.

Pat laid on the ground for several seconds trying to catch her breath and figure out what to do. As her mind finally began to clear, it became apparent

Homlin had been busy while she'd been unconscious. Not only had he tied her hands securely together in front of her with the leather thongs, but her feet were also bound so she could only take short steps. To top it off, she was wearing a knapsack with at least thirty pounds of supplies.

I'm a damn pack animal! How dare he, that son-of-a-bitch. He's going to die for this. If there had ever been any doubts in her mind that she'd kill him one day, they'd been thoroughly washed away.

Then she had a terrible thought. Had he found the lug wrench and screwdrivers tucked away in her coat pockets? If so, all was lost. She may as well hang herself with the choke collar for whatever defense she'd be able to muster. But as she lay there quietly getting her bearings, she was reasonably sure she could feel the heavy iron weight pressing against her right side.

He hadn't bothered to frisk her. There had been no reason for him to do so. She still had a chance.

"Let's go, pup. We've got a fair walk ahead of us." Homlin pulled on the leash for the third time. Pat experienced the momentary panic again as her wind was cut off, then Homlin let up on the leash, and the chain relaxed.

"You be a good little dog, and I'll let you live at least for a little longer." Homlin slammed the trunk lid down. "You give me any grief, and I won't hesitate to shoot you on the spot. Is that clear?"

"Yes, it's very clear," Pat said.

"No talking!" Homlin shouted and jerked the leash with both hands, dragging Pat off her feet before she'd fully stood upright. "You are now my pet dog. You're no longer a human being. Dogs bark, they don't talk. You have anything to say, you bark. One for yes and two for no. Do you understand?"

Pat lay on her side choking and gasping for air. She caught her wind enough to cough. After which she could taste the blood she'd spit up. She almost answered Homlin with a yes but stopped just in time. She decided it was best not to say anything.

"Do you understand?" Homlin jerked the leash again.

When Pat could finally breathe again, she managed an anguished "woof."

MONDAY 5:28 PM

The sun played with the crest of the mountain. In the last ten minutes, it seemed to dip with increasing speed. Once it dipped below the mountain, the sky would darken almost as though God had turned the lights out. The search, difficult already, would become nearly impossible.

Allan leaned over to Oliver's ear again. "We must be near the site. We've got to find them, at least some sign of where they are before the sun sets."

Oliver nodded and shouted back, "It's been ten years. I'm dealing with old memories but memories that I've dreamed about almost every night. The area is looking more familiar. We'll find them. We'll find them."

The last sentences sounded more like a mantra to Allan, but he decided it was as good a mantra as any to recite. He started repeating it to himself.

Suddenly Oliver turned away from Allan and leaned towards James, shouting something Allan couldn't make out. James changed course slightly and followed an old logging trail below them. They flew over the trail for another ten minutes as it slowly narrowed below them. Finally, the trail surrendered to the thick growth on either side of it. It just ended, but right at the point where it petered out sat a white Mazda partially hidden by the brush.

Oliver and Allan pointed to it at the same time, then turned to each other and shouted in each other's face. "We've found them, we've found them!"

James came around for another pass, a little lower this time. As they did so, they realized the automobile had been abandoned.

"This was as far as they could go by car," Oliver shouted. "They can't be too far from here."

"Yeah, but in which direction?" Allan shouted back.

"Over the crest, I think. It seems like it's on the other side of the mountain where the crash site was."

Allan realized they hadn't actually found them after all, but they were closer, much closer. *Please, Lord*, he prayed silently, *keep her alive just a little longer*.

MONDAY 5:13 PM

Homlin had kept a hard steady pace straight up the mountain. He would jerk on the leash whenever Pat fell behind, which was often since Pat's legs were still stiff from the long confinement, and she was additionally hampered by the heavy backpack.

"Come on, mush, my fine pack animal. You should be out in front of me pulling me up the hill instead of hanging back slowing my progress," Homlin said after one particularly brutal jerk on the leash that threw Pat into another coughing fit.

"Perhaps you would like to leave me here for your return trip. I promise not to go anywhere," Pat finally managed to say.

"Oh my dear Ms. Vogt, if I leave you here, I assure you, I'll leave you so you won't be able to go anywhere. Is this where you wish to die?"

Pat considered the question for a moment before answering. Was this the place to take a stand? Go for the bastard's throat? *No,* her inner voice answered. *Find out where he is going. There is something on the other side of the mountain he needs. Let him find it first then kill him.*

Pat shook her head. "No, I'm ready to go on."

They continued their journey up the mountain. Pat breathed a sigh of relief when they finally reached the crest, but it was short-lived. Going down the other side proved to be even worse. Homlin picked up his pace, almost running down the other side, yanking Pat off her feet half a dozen times.

The choker chain cut into the soft skin of Pat's neck, making each jerk from the leash that much more painful. *If I live through this, I'll start a campaign to prohibit the use of these collars on any animal,* Pat thought as she struggled to keep up.

Homlin suddenly stopped in his tracks much too quickly for Pat who continued by him, coming to a sudden stop of her own when the leash pulled her off her feet.

"Wait just a minute. I need to get my bearings. I think we're getting close." Homlin looked around for a moment before heading off to the right, downhill again, but at an oblique angle.

In a few minutes, he pulled up again a few yards from the mouth of a narrow cave. "We're here," he said simply.

Pat crouched down on all fours to catch her breath and to relieve the tension on the choker.

"Yes, catch your breath, by all means." Homlin looked down at her with a sneer on his face. "Catch your breath for those last few words you'd like to say."

Pat raised her head proudly in the air and glared at him. "You really are a bastard. It's going to be a pleasure killing you."

Homlin roared with laughter. "My dear Ms. Vogt, you really are a gem. Here you are at my complete mercy. I have the stick, the gun, and the controlling end of the leash, and you throw idle threats at me. Really, you've been most entertaining."

"But I mustn't dawdle. I have more important matters to attend to besides standing here talking with you. So, if you will excuse me for a moment, I need to fetch something from the cave. And, since I doubt I can trust you to simply sit here and behave yourself—not after what you've just said—I must restrict your movement for a few minutes."

Homlin looked around for a moment, then finding what he was looking for, he jerked Pat to her feet. He walked over to a nearby tree with its lowest branch about nine or ten feet above the ground. He threw his end of the leash over the limb, keeping his eye on Pat the whole time.

He then stepped on the other side of the tree and pulled the leash taut, forcing Pat to follow. He continued to pull the leash until Pat was directly under the tree limb, standing on her tiptoes, holding onto the leash with both hands to keep from being hung. Satisfied with her position, Homlin tied his end of the leash to another nearby tree.

"I shouldn't be too long," Homlin said as he stepped back to examine his handiwork. "When I return we'll end this little ten-year feud we've been having. I promise not to end it too quickly for you." With that, he turned and disappeared into the cave.

MONDAY 5:41 PM

The light was a little better on the other side of the crest, but even so, it was difficult to make out much detail through the trees. Finding two people down there, particularly when one of them didn't want to be found, wasn't going to be an easy task.

Allan was so absorbed in the search, he hadn't noticed James and Oliver talking until Oliver leaned over to him and touched his shoulder.

"You aren't going to want to hear this, but James has just pointed out to me that we only have enough fuel for another twenty or thirty minutes. Even then we might not make it back to where we can refuel."

Hell, what else could go wrong. They couldn't come this close and turn around without finding Pat. They just couldn't. Allan nodded and leaned toward Oliver.

"Tell James we can't turn back. We must keep looking no matter what. Isn't there somewhere around here we can land if we need to?"

Oliver considered the question for a moment then nodded. "There was an open area near where the ship landed, but that was ten years ago. It could be grown up with trees by now."

"We'll have to take a chance. We aren't turning back," Allan shouted back.

Oliver nodded and turned to James to relay the message. The two men shouted back and forth for a couple of minutes, but finally, James nodded agreement. Oliver turned back to Allan and gave him the thumbs-up sign. The three men turned their attention back to the forest below.

MONDAY 5:51 PM

Pat estimated Homlin had been gone less than five minutes and already her arms felt like they were about to pull out of their shoulder sockets. She couldn't hang like this much longer. She considered trying to reach one of the screwdrivers in her coat pocket but ruled it out. Trying to cut through an inch thick piece of leather with a flathead screwdriver didn't seem to make much sense.

I've got to think of something fast, she told herself. The "Vogt luck" was running out.

If she could just get herself up to the limb and over it, she'd be set. She tried pulling herself up hand over hand on the leash, but she didn't have enough strength left in her arms. Then she had an idea. What if she shimmied up the tree? She glanced over at the cave. Still no sign of Homlin.

Well, here goes nothing, she thought as she pulled herself as close to the tree as possible, then pulled herself up with the leash and hooked her legs around the diameter of the tree trunk. She dug her shoes into the rough bark of the tree and pushed herself up towards the limb. For the first time, she felt the choke chain relax its grip around her neck, and she knew she had a chance. She didn't need to climb over the limb. She only needed to get far enough up to slip the choker from around her neck.

The realization gave her a spurt of adrenaline, and she pushed herself another two inches with her legs. The choker was completely relaxed now, but its diameter was still too small to fit over her head. She pulled herself another couple of inches with one hand, then another and another.

As she did so, she thought she heard a deep roar from deep within the bowels of the earth. Homlin! He was coming back. She must hurry. If she was going to live, she must get free before he returned. In fact, if humankind was to survive, she had to get free now!

She squinted her eyes shut, took a deep breath, and let out a blood-curdling scream. She knew it might bring Homlin running, but it was what was necessary to manage the final inches. Still screaming, she held herself steady with her right hand and reached down with her left and slipped the chain noose from around her neck and head. As the chain slipped away, the strength in her right hand finally gave out as did her legs. She fell to the ground.

She lay there for a moment, sobbing and gasping for air. She was free. Free from the choker and free at least for the moment, but for how long? As she looked up towards the cave, she realized her freedom was short lived. From the mouth of the cave strolled a half-man-half-beast. Homlin stood at the mouth and roared his own blood-chilling scream.

He'd partially changed into the cat-like alien form that Pat had first come across a decade before, yet at the same time, he still resembled the human Homlin. He had torn most of his clothes off or perhaps they'd shredded from the bulging of the body within them.

Homlin threw his head back and roared again, then he stared at Pat, his eyes glowing in the semi-darkness of the evening.

"I couldn't decide whether it would be more fun to kill you in the human form or my true self, so I decided to compromise. Do you approve?"

Pat pushed herself onto all fours with her tired arms. "Come on you ugly bastard. I don't care what form you're in. I'm going to beat the shit out of you."

"For each idle threat, I'm going to make your death last that much longer and be more painful than you could possibly imagine," Homlin said through slurred lips. As he continued to change into his alien self, speaking became more difficult.

Pat stood up, yet stayed in a crouched stance. She began to circle around Homlin, trying to get on higher ground. As she did so, she pulled the two screwdrivers out of her pockets but kept them hidden in the palms of her hands. She knew she'd get only one shot at Homlin. It had to be her best.

The cat-like Homlin closed the distance between them, apparently un-perturbed by Pat's strategy to get above him. As he came closer, Pat noticed for the first time the crystal hanging from the chain around his neck. So that had been what he'd come here for. It made sense now. Whatever the crystal was, it was integral to his mission. Therefore, it was a weak point as well.

"I want you to notice that I plan to kill you with my bare hands," Homlin said as he circled closer to her. "No stick or gun. It would take the fun out of it for me."

"Now look who's giving idle threats. You're not going to kill me, you over-grown house cat. But you're going to wish you'd kept your weapons when I get through with you." Pat taunted him as she backed up the hill a few feet in an attempt to widen the distance between them.

Is he going to lunge for me? She wondered. She must wait for just the right moment. If he lunged at her, she might be able to stab him with one of the screwdrivers. Unless she hit a vital spot, it wouldn't be enough to kill him, but it might give her the advantage she needed.

They circled around each other until, without warning, Homlin made his move. He was lightning quick and was on top of Pat before she knew it. Reaching out with his right hand, he slapped her off her feet, his claws ripping through the thick fabric of her coat and digging deep gouges in her left side. As Pat rolled, she felt the warm, wet sensation on her side, followed closely by intense pain.

Homlin stood a few feet from her and roared with delight. Pat scrambled to her feet, the movement intensifying the pain. Homlin attacked and again was beside her before she could move out of the way. This time he kicked her feet out from under her with a sweeping motion of one leg. Pat hit the ground hard, the breath knocked out of her. Towering above her, Homlin threw his head back and howled in victory, extending his arms to the sky, his claws fully extended ready for the kill.

As he stood over her, his face raised to the heavens from which he had come, a blinding flash of light, followed a millisecond later by a thunderous noise, gave Pat one last chance.

While Homlin was momentarily frozen in confusion, Pat jammed the two screwdrivers deep into his crotch. Bluish red blood spurted on Pat's face and down her blouse. Without hesitating, she pulled both screwdrivers out and plunged them in again.

Homlin's high pitch scream echoed down the mountain and back again. He fell to one side trying to escape his tormentor, but Pat was relentless. As he rolled down the mountain, she chased after him. She dug the screwdrivers in again, this time in his back, then lost her grip on them as his turning body twisted them out of her hand. She reached into her coat pocket and pulled out the lug wrench. Holding it in both hands by the long end, she brought the shorter end crashing down, aiming at Homlin's head.

At the last second, he twisted to one side, the blow landing on the curve between his neck and shoulder, the bar catching on the chain around his neck. Pat jerked back ripping the chain off his neck, sending the crystal flying off into the bushes. Homlin jerked his head around trying to keep his eyes on his precious crystal. It was all the diversion Pat needed.

Without hesitating, Pat struck again with the tire iron and felt the satisfying sensation of bone-crushing beneath the blow, and a renewed cry of pain erupted from Homlin. Still Pat persisted. She struck again and again. Once more on the head, the third blow landing to the left side of his neck.

She couldn't stop herself now. She was no more than an animal herself — an animal fighting not just for its life but for the life of its species. As Homlin rolled against a large boulder and stopped, Pat leaped onto the rock above him and with a final powerful thrust, she jabbed the pointed end of the tire iron through his chest.

It took a couple of minutes before the breathing stopped and his blood began to clot. Pat continued to sit on Homlin's chest until she was absolutely sure he was dead. Then with a final blow of her fist, she stood up.

"I told you I was going to kick your ass." She took three steps towards the cave before passing out.

Safe at Last
Monday 6:03 pm, Dec. 6

"**B**ack there! Take it back around. Did you see it?" Allan screamed in Oliver's ear.

"I'm not sure. I think I saw something," Oliver replied as he tapped James on the shoulder and instructed the pilot to take them around again.

Allan's heart felt like it was going to beat its way out of his chest. It had to be them, although it had been difficult to tell. It had been something too grotesque to imagine. He was afraid to think what it might be. They'd been moving so fast the figure had been in the spotlight for only an instant.

As they circled around, Allan noticed the spotlight highlighted a small opening with only a few scrub pines that might cause a problem with the helicopter. He pointed it out to Oliver.

"Ask James if he thinks he could land this bird down there?"

Oliver gazed out the window at the small patch where Allan was pointing and frowned. He started to say something then thought better of it. Instead, he leaned over to James and asked the question. After a moment, James changed the course of the helicopter sufficiently to get a better look at the clearing. After studying it for a moment, he nodded to Oliver and gave him a thumbs-up.

"Land it then," Allan said. "We'll find them on foot."

The landing was the most hazardous part of the entire trip. To Allan, it looked like James had miscalculated. There was no way they'd have enough room to land without shearing off the blades of the helicopter. Fortunately, James was a competent pilot and managed to land with only a few feet to spare on all sides.

As the bird touched down, Allan's feet hit the hard-packed ground running with Oliver close behind. Each of them carried a large flashlight, the narrow beams cutting through the night.

What if we miss them? Allan thought. *What if what I saw turned out be a wild animal?* But even as he thought it, he knew better. It had to be what they were looking for. The real question was whether they'd find Pat before it was too late.

He slowed down as they neared the area. *Better be a little quiet. No reason to give themselves away to Homlin if they could help it.* As he slowed to a fast walk, Oliver caught up with him. They both turned off their flashlights and took the final thirty yards in the dark.

In the near darkness, they pushed their way through the final layer of underbrush. They could just make out a slit in the side of the mountain. Allan stopped on the edge of the clearing and waited for his eyes to adjust a little further. He could hear Oliver's raspy breathing beside him.

As his eyes adjusted to the reduced light, he spied two dark lumps lying on the ground, one only a few yards from the cave opening, the other further away. His breath caught in his throat. He could just make out the closer figure. It was Pat.

Allan decided to risk turning his flashlight on. Oliver did the same a couple of seconds later. The two men strolled into the clearing. Allan stooped down to Pat's still form.

"Please God let her be okay...be okay...be okay," Allan repeated over and over as he felt for a pulse. Not until he felt one did he dare take a breath. Meanwhile, Oliver shined his light on the two of them.

"Is she all right?" He asked.

"I think so. She's breathing at least," Allan replied as he began to check her more closely. He got only as far as her neck.

"Oh my God, she's been strangled. Her neck looks like someone tried to hang her." A moment later his hand felt the wet, sticky side of her coat. Allan felt a wave of nausea despite his years as a vet. After all, this was the woman he loved.

"Son-of-a-bitch," Allan muttered through clenched teeth. "She's lost a lot of blood."

Remembering the second form, Oliver picked up Allan's flashlight where he had laid it and shined it in the direction of the other shadow. "I think that's Homlin over there."

"Go check. I'm okay here," Allan replied. Oliver laid the still lit flashlight on the ground for Allan and walked over to take a closer look.

Still holding Pat in his arms, Allan began to clean her wounds and to wipe away the dirt and grime from her face. The process began to revive her. Her long lashes fluttered for a couple of seconds before her eyes opened.

Slowly, as her gaze focused on Allan's face, she smiled and in a weak voice said, "We make quite a team, don't we? We finally got him."

At the sound of her voice, tears welled up in Allan's eyes and cascaded down his cheeks. He kissed her gently on the lips. Continuing to hold her firmly, he rocked her back and forth—and wept. This time, they were tears of joy.

A few minutes later, Oliver returned to his side. "Yep, it's Homlin, or at least what's left of him." He turned to Pat. "Remind me to never get on your bad side."

Pat shrugged, then winced in pain.

"Oliver, help me get her back to the chopper, will you? She's pretty banged up herself."

"Sure thing," Oliver replied. They helped Pat up and started walking back the way they came, each of them on either side of her. They'd made it about twenty yards when Pat stopped. "Damn. I hate to ask this, and I know it's crazy, but could you go fetch the tire iron I used on Homlin? I'd like to keep it, a sort of memento of the day I kicked an alien's ass."

"Sure," Allan replied. "I'll go get it. Oliver, help her back to the helicopter. I'll meet you there." He turned and retraced his steps.

He found the bloody wrench lying not far from Homlin's cooling body. He stared down at the half-man, half-beast, shaking his head. It has been an interesting last few months. He was ready for some normalcy for a change.

He turned back in the direction of the helicopter, but stopped again after taking a few steps, a cold shiver running up and down his back by the sound of a soft rustling behind him. Homlin was dead, right? He slowly turned back in the direction of the cave where he thought he'd heard the sound. He shined his flashlight at the mouth of the cave. At first, he didn't see anything out of the ordinary. Then slowly, he noticed movement from deep within the cave. As the form moved into the beam of light, Allan heard a familiar sound that threatened to stop his heart.

"Daddy..."

Bonus Content of FreeForm Reborn

Book 2 of the Saga of the Dandelion Expansion Series

Pick Up Your Copy Today!

Available at your favorite online store

amazonkindle

Or grab your **free** copy at:
http://www.wbradfordswift.com/fform

Chapter One

"Daddy," the young boy said, a look of confusion mixed with fear etched on his face as he stood at the mouth of the cave from which he'd just exited. Allan stared at him for a moment frozen in place.

"TJ?"

What in the world is he doing here? Allan wondered as he glanced around at the barren mountain landscape and the black abyss of the cave entrance.

Not your son. He heard Pat's voice reverberate through his mind and another part argue with her.

Yes, yes, it is my son. He looks just like Todd.

But you told me Todd was killed the same house fire that took your wife years ago.

I know, but...but...but. Allan had no answer to that statement, for it was true. Allan shook himself back to the present and studied the boy in front of him.

Even though it had only been a day since he'd last seen the boy he would have sworn TJ had grown at least another inch. *Probably my imagination,* Allan thought. *I know he's growing fast, but not that fast...right?* TJ looked to be between five and six years of age in appearance even though Allan knew his actual chronological age to be less than a year; more like six months. The FreeForm larva from which the boy had developed had amazing properties that Allan was still learning about.

"Daddy," TJ repeated, his voice wavering, a perplexed look on his young face. "She killed him. Why were they fighting?"

Allan glanced from TJ to the bloody half-man, half-catlike creature lying on the ground; all that remained of Homlin, the alien being that had started this whole mess; the alien being that had been instrumental in bringing FreeForm to the world and therefore indirectly TJ.

"He was a bad...man," Allan said, not quite knowing how to finish the sentence. "He hurt her and would have hurt a lot of other people as well."

"Does that make me bad as well?" TJ asked.

"No, of course not," Allan replied. "Why would you even think such a thing?"

"Well, I'm part him, aren't I? That's what he said."

Allan noticed the boy shiver then tilt his head to one side. Allan wasn't sure if TJ's shivering was from the frigid temperature that was continuing to drop as night approached or from the question he had just asked.

Allan glanced at the large black wound on the side of the mountain once more and wondered for a moment what lay inside. This was a stark, isolated part of the North Carolina mountains; inhospitable, to say the least, and made even more so by the plunging temperatures and the slate gray sky that promised snow. Allan put down the tire iron Pat had asked him to retrieve and took off his jacket, offering it to the boy.

"Here, put this on. You're freezing."

TJ took the navy blue jacket and wrapped it around his shoulders. Clutching it in front of him, the windbreaker reached down to his ankles.

Allan reached out to him and started to pick him up, but TJ pulled away.

"Easy there. I'm not going to hurt you. We just need to get out of here before the snow comes."

"Home? Can we go home? See Kendra? Have Cheerios?"

"That's right," Allan said with a chuckle. "We're going home." Allan bent down to retrieve the tire iron before picking up his son. He strolled towards the helicopter where an injured Pat and an anxious Oliver waited.

Chapter Two

In the deep recesses of the cave twenty or thirty yards from where Allan held the boy, a small ellipsoid-shaped globe the size of a large, slightly flattened grapefruit pulsated with a bluish purple glow. The anguished screams and waves of pain of the Primary had awakened the AI contained within it moments before. A high pitch whine reverberated from it throughout the cave and beyond, pricking the ears of several wild animals in the vicinity.

The violent attack on the Primary, known on the home planet as Sluneg, had caused the beta version of the Fail Safe Protocol to be initiated. The AI who referred to itself as Aeo struggled to manage the emergency and recover the consciousness of the Primary now known on this greenish-blue orb as Homlin. Unfortunately, the subject was in the final stages of dying, and nothing could be done to reverse the process. In use for the first time, the fail-safe mode had been designed for less intrusive, less violent, and less rapid cessation of the body that housed the Primary. In short, Homlin's consciousness was strung out all over the place and dissipating rapidly. Aeo struggled to pull all the pieces together and back into the cocoon for safe keeping.

Okay, I can do this, Aeo thought as it began the download process. *It's all out there. I just need to pull it together.* But the brain was dying rapidly, and the electrical signals that contained the information grew weaker by the second. Aeo finally had to admit that it would be unable to retrieve every part of the primary subject. It would have to make do with what it could retrieve and fill in the gaps later.

In the meantime, it scanned the cave and took inventory of the FreeForm available and was satisfied to find Homlin had stocked several in the pupal stage in the cave. *At least I'll be able to reconstruct another body for the Primary.* The Primary's mission could still be fulfilled. Aeo set to work to pick up the pieces of a mission that had gone bad.

ALLAN PUSHED THE DOOR to Pat's hospital room open and stuck his head in. Glancing around, he was surprised to find her room looked more like a guest room you'd see in your favorite aunt's home. Then he remembered reading in the Waynesboro's *Chronicle* that someone had willed a sizable amount of money to the institution expressly to rehab the rooms to be less sterile and more hospitable. That had been money well spent, Allan thought as he noted the small flowered wallpaper that matched well with the bouquets of flowers that set on the chest of drawer and window seal.

Pat lay in bed with her head turned towards a window that looked out on the snow-covered courtyard. The snow had been falling for over eight hours. All details of the courtyard were utterly obscured, resembling mounds of cotton. Already the weather forecast it might be the worst storm to hit the southeast in over twenty years with accumulations up to two feet. Even in Pat's four-wheel drive Cherokee, it had taken Allan close to a half hour to drive the ten miles from his home to the hospital, a drive that usually took no more than fifteen minutes. Travel was hampered in large part because of the Southern drivers without four-wheel drive who didn't have a clue how to maneuver in such conditions.

He noticed Pat had turned her head away from the window and was smiling weakly at him. He stood there smiling back as relief washed over him. Only then did he realize how afraid he had been of losing her.

"Are you just going to stand there gawking, or are you going to come over here and give me a kiss?" As she raised one hand to beckon him over, he noticed the attached I.V. drip. Her neck was bandaged from where the choker collar had cut into it. While she was still pale and weak, she looked better than when he'd last seen her in the helicopter the previous night. By the time he'd arrived at the helicopter, Pat had been securely strapped in by James, the pilot, and Oliver. Allan hadn't been able to tell if Pat had fallen asleep or had passed out, and he'd been too scared to ask. James and Oliver had stared at TJ with equally perplexed looks.

"What the hell happened?" Oliver asked. "Who's that?"

"I'll explain later," Allan promised, though he didn't have a clue what he'd tell them. "We've got to get her to a hospital."

Allan walked over to Pat's bed. His small bouquet of flowers looked puny next to the larger arrangements, but it had been the best he could do, considering the conditions outside where things continued deteriorating by the minute.

"Oh, they're lovely," Pat said as Allan bent over and kissed her. *Her color is better than last night*, he noted to himself, but her face was still missing its ordinarily vibrant color. He could only imagine the hell she'd been through over the past twenty-four hours. Thankfully, it was finally over. Now they'd be able to get on with creating a life together without the concerns of an alien invasion.

Then again, there was TJ. How was he going to break the news to her about him? As far as he could tell, she'd been out of it last night and unaware of TJ's presence in the chopper. Maybe it would be better to wait until she was stronger, but even as he had the thought, he knew it was his way to put off an awkward conversation. So after a few minutes of pleasantries, he decided to broach the subject.

He started to sit in the straight back chair next to her bed, but Pat insisted he sit on the edge of the bed so she could see him better as well as hold his hand.

"What do you remember about the flight back to Waynesboro last night?" Allan finally asked.

"Not much, I'm afraid. Really nothing about the flight. The first thing I remember was waking up here sometime in the middle of the night with one of the nurses checking my vitals. I could just make out the snow falling, and then I fell back into La-La land."

"I see," Allan said. "Well, I have some...some good news." At least, he considered it good news, and he hoped she would as well.

"Oh, good. I could use some good news right about now. What is it?"

"We found TJ last night. Actually, he found me. Isn't that great?" Allan held his breath as he studied Pat's face for a reaction.

Pat sat there. Her hand that had been gently rubbing his stopped suddenly. She stared at him, a startled look growing on her face.

"What?" she finally asked. "What did you say?"

"TJ. You know. He ran away a few days ago, and now he's back." He decided, given Pat's reaction, it might not help his case to let her know TJ had walked out of the cave where Pat and Homlin had fought to the death.

"And this is good news how?" Pat asked.

"He's alive," Allan answered, feeling the hackles on his neck rise. "My son is alive and well."

Pat slowly removed her hand from his and placed both of hers on her lap as she turned and stared out the window for close to a minute. Finally, she turned back to him.

"You've got to be kidding, Allan. He's not your son. He's not even human. He's as much an alien as the one I killed on that mountainside last night. We've got to let someone know about him."

Allan didn't know what to say in rebuttal, so he didn't say anything at first, but continued to stare at the woman he loved. How could he talk to her about TJ and how he felt when he wasn't sure himself? Part of him knew the boy wasn't his son, Todd, even though TJ was the spitting image of his son at that age. But Todd had come from his wife's womb in a conventional pregnancy like everyone else on Earth...everyone but TJ. He had come from a late night C-section Allan had performed at his veterinary clinic back in March. At the time, he'd removed several larval looking fetuses from a stray dog that had taken up at the Parkers. Not knowing what to do with the strange creatures, he'd taken them to his home to observe. All the larvae had died in just a few days; all except the one that had slowly changed from looking like a premature puppy to his son. It had all happened by accident at first, and Allan had kept the larvae in the den. After all the other larvae had died, Allan had relocated the lone survivor to his son's old bedroom, surrounded by baby pictures of Todd. Over a few days, the larva went from resembling a puppy to looking like a small human baby. Allan had planned to contact someone in the government about what he had found, but he just couldn't bring himself to do it. He had to see what the larva was turning into.

And in the process, Allan had grown to love the boy he now called TJ. However, he also loved the woman lying in the hospital bed in front of him. Pat had almost been killed for a second time by an alien that had secretly been trying to take over the world, and who had been the source of those larvae that Allan had removed from the Parker family's stray dog.

Allan rose from the side of the bed and walked over to the window where he stared out at the falling snow. He'd always found snowstorms peaceful and calming, even severe ones like this that would wreak havoc on the area for several days. It seemed like a blanket of snow made everything less noisy, as though it absorbed much of the extraneous noises of life.

He'd probably been standing at the window for a good five minutes or more when he heard someone behind him clear their throat and a nurse say, "Visiting hours are over in five minutes, Dr Pritchard."

He turned around and tried to smile back at her. "Thank you."

After the nurse left, Allan walked back to Pat's bed. He reached out with one hand and took hers. Finally, he said, "Can we agree not to do anything about this for at least a couple days? Let's get you back on your feet and home. Then we'll sit down and decide the best course of action. Okay?"

He could hear the pleading tone in that last word and hated himself for it but was relieved when he felt Pat squeeze his hand and nod before replying, "Where is he now?"

"Oh, he's at my house. Kendra came over last night before the storm became too bad. She's looking after him."

"I see," Pat said. "And what are you going to tell her? Are you going to keep lying to her as well?"

Once again Allan didn't know how to answer the question, so he just shrugged. "We'll have to sort that out as well."

A Message from Orrin Jason Bradford (a.k.a. W. Bradford Swift)

As an Indie Author I know just how important readers are. Without people who enjoy reading, authors are pretty useless. Oh, I know I enjoy the thrill of writing the *next great American novel,* but that's really not enough. I need readers like you who enjoy reading my stories. So, thank you. I sincerely appreciate your taking the time to read *FreeForm*.

Perhaps you would enjoy some of my other books and stories. If you'd like to stay up to date on new book releases, special discounts, and my occasional giveaways, you can also join my **OJB's Amazingly Awesome Readers Group**. Just go to my author's website and blog: www.wbradfordswift.com

There's one last thing you could do if you would be so kind. Go to your favorite online bookstore and leave an honest review of *FreeForm*. Honest reviews are really important to help other readers like you know which books to try next. And thanks for being an amazingly awesome reader.

Orrin Jason Bradford (aka W. Bradford Swift)

Acknowledgments

Writing a book is a labor of love for me as well as being a wonderful way to express my life purpose. It's also something that I could not do alone, so I want to thank some of the people who have contributed to this project. My sincerest thanks go to my lovely and patient wife, Ann Swift, who probably wishes she'd read the small print in our marriage contract that states she'd have to read everything I wrote, often multiple of times.

Thanks also to Victor Habbick who designed a cover that had me stretch to make the inside worthy of the outside. Many thanks go to Tracy Cartwright, my editor, and Cynthia Wisehart, my writing buddy who continues to inspire me to keep writing. Last but not least, thank you Mrs. Crabtree for feeling sorry for my mom who I was driving crazy from being so bored. You cared enough about both us to introduce me to the world of books so many years ago.

Porpoise Publishing

Flat Rock, NC 28731
www.lifeonpurpose.com
Library of Congress Cataloging-in-Publication Data
ISBN: 1-930328389
Electronic: 9781930328372
FreeForm/ W. Bradford Swift.
1. Science Fiction 2. Speculative Fiction 3. Technology

Cover design by Victor Habbick ~ www.victorhabbickvisions.co.uk/
Typeset in Book Palatino
Printed in USA
First Edition

Did you love *FreeForm*? Then you should read *Babble* by Orrin Jason Bradford!

One young boy is the key to the universe.

In this supernatural thriller, a young boy is discovered to be the link between the human race and the farthest reaches of the universe. For Bobbie Cagle, the normal difficulties of growing up are overshadowed by his unique condition, being misdiagnosed as autistic. Caught between his loving mother and those who would use him for their own purposes, Bobbie stands at the center of the universe and forces the human race to the edge of their own evolutionary line.

The Lord said, "If as one people speaking the same language they have begun to do this, then nothing they plan to do will be impossible for them. -Genesis 11:6

Upon the Towers of Babel, the people of the Earth scattered, and silence fell. Now, on the brink of a new age, the human race leaps forward into the evolutionary void and changes the course of human history forever.

For young Bobbie Cagle, the normal difficulties of growing up are overshadowed by his unique condition. Placed on the spectrum, Bobbie's inability to communicate normally is misdiagnosed for years as Autism and masks the great part in human history that he is destined to play. Unknowingly able to receive transmissions from the farthest reaches of the universe, young Bobbie's life is forever changed when his unique ability is discovered. Coveted by those who would use him for their own purpose, Bobbie and his mother flee their home out of desperation and fear. In the course of their escape, the truth behind Bobbie's gift and the effects it may have on the planet begin to the reveal themselves, all the while the future of the human race hangs in the balance.

Find out what fate has in store for the human race and grab your copy of *Babble* today!

Read more at www.wbradfordswift.com.

About the Author

Orrin Jason Bradford is the pen name W. Bradford Swift uses for his adult fiction to distinguish it from his nonfiction and young adult novels. An avid reader from childhood, he continues to read and study science fiction and fantasy. As a young man, he promised one day to write his own fiction in gratitude to the many authors who kept him entertained and more or less sane over the years.

Swift is best known for his visionary fiction and nonfiction that "entertain while also enlightening and encouraging the reader to expand their sense of what is possible, and then applying that expanded awareness to their life." He is a graduate of Clarion West in Seattle, WA – a residential workshop for writers of science fiction and fantasy. He lives in the "paradise found" of the Blue Ridge Mountains of North Carolina with his wife, Ann, their daughter, Amber and a menagerie of four-legged family members.

His other speculative fiction includes the six-book mega-series, **Saga of the Dandelion Expansion** which includes the FreeForm trilogy and the Kindred trilogy, *Babble, Fantastic Fables of Foster Flat*, and others.

Read more at www.wbradfordswift.com.

About the Publisher

Porpoise Publishing is the imprint of indie author W. Bradford Swift who also writes under the pen name of Orrin Jason Bradford. It is best known for publishing visionary fiction--stories that entertain while also inspiring readers to imagine greater possibilities for their lives.